ANNE SIBLEY O'BRIEN

IN THE
SHADOW
OF THE
SUN

ARTHUR A. LEVINE BOOKS
AN IMPRINT OF SCHOLASTIC INC.

All rights reserved. Published by Arthur A. Levine Books, an imprint of Scholastic Inc., *Publishers since 1920*. SCHOLASTIC and the LANTERN LOGO are trademarks and/or registered trademarks of Scholastic Inc.

The publisher does not have any control over and does not assume any responsibility for author or third-party websites or their content.

Library of Congress Cataloging-in-Publication Data

Names: O'Brien, Anne Sibley, author.
Title: In the shadow of the sun / by Anne Sibley O'Brien.
Description: First edition. | New York, NY : Arthur A. Levine Books, an imprint of Scholastic Inc., 2017. | Summary: Twelve-year-old Mia is on a five-day tour of North Korea with her older brother, Simon, and their father, Mark, an food aide worker, but she is scared because her father keeps sneaking off at night, and terrified that her brother's sullen, rebellious behavior (which has absolutely nothing to do with the Koreans) is going to get them in trouble—and things get much worse when she is pulled into a deadly political game that seeks to expose North Korean atrocities, and her father is arrested.
Identifiers: LCCN 2016032888 | ISBN 9780545905749 (hardcover : alk. paper)
Subjects: LCSH: Brothers and sisters—Juvenile fiction. | Father and child—Juvenile fiction. | Tourists—Korea(North)—Juvenile fiction. | Secrecy—Juvenile fiction. | Conspiracies—Korea (North)—Juvenile fiction. | Korea (North)—Politics and government—2011—Juvenile fiction. | Korea (North)—Social conditions—21st century—Juvenile fiction. | CYAC: Brothers and sisters—Fiction. | Father and child—Fiction. | Secrets—Fiction. | Conspiracies—Fiction. | Korea (North)—Fiction.
Classification: LCC PZ7.O1267 In 2017 | DDC 813.54 [Fic] —dc23 LC record available at https://lccn.loc.gov/2016032888

10 9 8 7 6 5 4 3 2 1   17 18 19 20 21

Printed in the U.S.A.   23
First edition, July 2017

Book design by Carol Ly

Photos ©: cover barbed wire: chronicler101/iStockphoto; cover texture: STILLFX/Shutterstock, Inc.; x: Katherine Welles/Shutterstock, Inc.; xi top: Goddard_Photography/iStockphoto; xi bottom: Viktoria Gaman/Shutterstock, Inc.; xii top: btrenkel/iStockphoto; xii bottom: Reuters/Alamy Images; xiii: Attila Jandi/Shutterstock, Inc.; xiv: Ng Han Guan/AP Images.

Map by Jim McMahon

**FOR THE PEOPLE OF
NORTH KOREA**

A NOTE ON THE KOREAN ALPHABET, ROMANIZATION, AND PRONUNCIATION

Both North and South Korea use hangul, which means "Korean letters," a highly accessible phonetic system created in the fifteenth century for spoken Korean. Hangul is sometimes referred to as the most perfect alphabet in the world, with twenty-four letters you can see on the facing page.

These letters are combined into blocks of syllables to form words, so, for example, Mia's Korean name, Han Sung-mi, would be written as: 한성미. Korean vowel sounds are soft, as in Spanish, where *a* (ㅏ) = *ah*, as in *father*; *u* (ㅓ) = *uh* as in *sun*; *oo* (ㅜ) = long *u*, as in *woo*; and *i* (ㅣ) = *ee*, as in *prima*.

Representing those sounds consistently in English, however, poses a number of challenges. For instance, South and North Korea currently use two different romanization systems. (North Korean spellings of *Pyongyang*, *Kim Il-sung*, and *Kim Jong-un*, if written using the current South Korean system, would become *Pyeongyang*, *Kim Il-seong*, and *Kim Jeong-eun*.) And because the sounds of English vowels can change by the word (consider the *a* sounds in *father*, *fame*, and *fat*), there's no immediately recognizable, accurate, and wholly consistent way to render the pronunciation of Korean in English spelling.

For the purposes of this novel, then, I have chosen to reproduce Korean words and phrases with the spelling that most closely represents the actual pronunciation, to make it easy and consistent for young readers, many of whom won't speak Korean. (This spelling usually resembles how it would be written using the North Korean romanization system.) For ease of deciphering, I've used hyphens between the syllables of an individual word or phrase, and between the two syllables of a given name. Korean words and phrases appear in italics only when they are spoken by someone for whom Korean is a foreign language.

KOREAN ALPHABET

VOWELS

ㅏ	ㅑ	ㅓ	ㅕ	ㅗ
a	*ya*	*ŏ*	*yŏ*	*o*

ㅛ	ㅜ	ㅠ	ㅡ	ㅣ
yo	*u*	*yu*	*ŭ*	*i*

CONSONANTS

ㄱ	ㄴ	ㄷ	ㄹ	ㅁ	ㅂ	ㅅ
k, g	*n*	*t, d*	*r, l*	*m*	*p, b*	*s, sh*

ㅇ	ㅈ	ㅊ	ㅋ	ㅌ	ㅍ	ㅎ
ng	*ch, j*	*ch'*	*k'*	*t'*	*p'*	*h*

NORTH KOREA!

In this guide, you'll find some basic information about the Democratic People's Republic of Korea (DPRK) and a list of guidelines to help ensure that your journey will be safe and rewarding. The DPRK is known as the most isolated country on earth, and tourists are allowed into the country only on state-approved visits directed by official North Korean guides. Please follow all rules, as the consequences for disobedience can be severe.

NORTH KOREAN HISTORY:
INDEPENDENCE & INVASION

✶ ✶ ✶

1392-1905

- The peninsula is ruled for 500 years by the Chosun Dynasty, isolated by geography and interacting primarily with its neighbors, China and Japan.
- In the 1800s, ships begin to arrive from the West. The kingdom of Chosun is gradually forced to open its ports to traders, missionaries, and diplomats.

1905-1945

- Japan seizes Korea as a protectorate, then colonizes the peninsula by force.
- Many Koreans fight for independence throughout this period.

1945

- At the end of World War II, Japan is forced to surrender territory it seized, including Korea. Without consulting Korean citizens, the United States and the Soviet Union agree on what was meant to be a temporary solution: a "joint occupation," dividing the peninsula along the 38th parallel.
- The US installs Rhee Syngman to lead the newly formed Republic of Korea (ROK) in the south. The Soviet Union chooses **Kim Il-sung**, an anti-Japanese guerrilla fighter, to head the Democratic People's Republic of Korea (DPRK) in the north.

1950s

- The Korean War breaks out on June 25, 1950, when 75,000 North Korean troops cross the 38th parallel, intent on reunifying Korea by force. North Korea claims that the US and South Korea invaded the north.
- US and United Nations forces fight alongside the South Korean army. The Soviet Union and later China send troops to support North Korea. The US drops more bombs on North Korea than it did on either Germany or Japan in World War II.
- Huge numbers of refugees flee south.
- After terrible losses, the conflict for control of the peninsula ends in an armistice in 1953. The Korean War has never officially ended, as a peace treaty has never been signed.
- The division of Korea becomes permanent, with a heavily guarded border between the two countries known as the Demilitarized Zone (DMZ). Families are separated, with members trapped on both sides, unable to reunite.
- Both new nations struggle to rebuild in the aftermath of war.

1960s

- Thanks to aid from China and the Soviet Union, North Korea's postwar standard of living improves faster than South Korea's.

1970s

- North Korea's growth slows dramatically. Meanwhile, South Korea's economy takes off with aid from the US and Japan.

1980s

- As North Korea continues to stagnate, South Korea's economy booms as it prepares for the 1988 Summer Olympics, on its way to becoming one of the world's industrial superpowers.

1990s

- During a devastating famine in the north, as many as one to three million North Koreans die of starvation. Causes include the collapse of the Soviet Union, the end of Soviet aid, lack of fuel, economic mismanagement, international sanctions, isolation, droughts, and floods.
- Partly as a response to South Korea's growing economic power, North Korea begins to develop a nuclear bomb.
- In 1994, the DPRK is shocked by the sudden death of President **Kim Il-sung**, the "Great Leader." After three years of mourning, his son, **Kim Jong-il**, the "Dear Leader," officially takes power.

2000s & 2010s

- Economic conditions improve, but famines recur.
- The threat of nuclear weapons development keeps North Korea in the news worldwide.
- At the death of **Kim Jong-il** in 2011, leadership passes to his son, **Kim Jong-un**, the "Grand Marshall," aged twenty-eight.

NORTH KOREA TODAY:
CONTRASTS & CONTRADICTIONS

✷ ✷ ✷

The DPRK, a nation of 25 million people, describes itself as a social-ist paradise, where the state claims to provide for all the needs of the people: housing, education, jobs, clothing, and food. In reality, everything is controlled by a king-like Supreme Leader and a group of advisors. The smallest sign of criticism or rebellion against the Leader is punished. Citizens are taught that the US is an arch-enemy, ready to make war on the DPRK and controlling South Korean politics.

Framed portraits of **Kim Il-sung** and **Kim Jong-il** are found in every building, office, subway car, and family home. Monitors check to make sure that they are cleaned regularly, with a special cloth reserved for this purpose.

Every adult citizen is required to wear a badge with a portrait of the Great Leader, the Dear Leader, or the national flag pinned over their heart. Foreigners are not allowed to wear these badges.

The capitol of Pyongyang is an international city with sky-scrapers, amusement parks, and glittering tourist hotels. Some residents are members of the elite classes and enjoy a lifestyle of relative ease and plenty, with children attending fine schools and colleges. Many North Koreans have approved mobile phones that use a domestic cellular network, but they can't access international networks or browse the Internet.

Several hundred foreign diplomats, aid workers, investors, businessmen, teachers, and students live in Pyongyang, and approximately 5,000 foreigners visit per year, mostly on state-controlled tours through the capital and to approved sites in other parts of the country.

Outside of Pyongyang, especially in the northeast corner of the country, life is often far more challenging. Food shortages and hunger are prevalent. The children's welfare organization UNICEF estimates that 45 percent of children are affected by malnutrition, which can lead to stunted growth. The breakdown of the food distribution system in the 1990s and resulting famines taught many people they had to rely on themselves in order to survive. There are now many independent vendors and markets, often outside of government control. The average North Korean now survives by offering goods or services for sale.

Every day people try to escape over the Yalu/Amnok and Tumen rivers between North Korea and China. Some 200,000 escapees are said to be in hiding in China, at least 30,000 have fled to South Korea, and others have sought refuge in countries around the world, including more than 200 in the United States.

Citizens who are considered disloyal — especially those who are not wealthy or connected enough to bribe someone — can be sent, without fair trial, to one of three types of brutal camps, sometimes with their entire families: labor training centers, for manual labor and many hours of political indoctrination, for six months to several years; reeducation camps, where inmates perform forced labor for years, with the possibility of release; and "total control zone" prison camps, where inmates perform slave labor and from which no one is released. Though the North Korean government denies they exist, it's estimated that as many as 150,000 people are held in four massive total control zone camps.

Both North and South Koreans think of their own nation as the rightful government of the peninsula, and many on both sides — as well as Koreans all over the world — long for the reunification of Korea.

WHAT TO DO AND WHAT NOT TO DO ON YOUR NORTH KOREAN TOUR

✯ ✯ ✯

1. Stay with your group. Do not go anywhere outside of the hotel without a guide, especially late at night.
2. Obey all instructions from your guides and other officials.
3. Only take photographs when given permission. If you don't follow directions, photographs could be deleted or your camera seized.
4. Until 2013, all cell phones of international travelers were confiscated at the airport. Recently, tourists have been allowed to keep their cell phones and, with an added SIM card, to text and make international calls, but this can change at any time.
5. The DPRK prefers that foreigners use euros, dollars, Japanese yen, or Chinese yuan for currency.
6. Though there are continuing rumors of electronic surveillance in tourist hotel rooms, these reports have not been confirmed.
7. Don't bring up or argue politics. Even casual conversation that is deemed inappropriate could result in negative consequences for you and your guides. In severe cases, foreign travelers have been expelled or even arrested.
8. Show respect for North Korea's leaders, policies, ideology, and customs.

We are guests here, and compliance with these conditions is the price of being one of the tiny number of foreigners allowed to travel within the DPRK.

ENJOY YOUR TRIP!

CHAPTER 1

OCTOBER 1

The scraping of a door jolted Mia from sleep.

Click. The door of the next room closed. Dad and Simon's room.

She reached for her watch and pressed the button to light it. 12:21 a.m.

Mia slipped from her bed to the door, cracking it open without a sound. It took a second for her eyes to adjust to the corridor's dim light. A dark form crept along, halfway down the hotel hallway. She squinted, trying to focus. It looked like . . . Dad?

She started to call out, then caught herself. Her father was moving funny, a little hunched over. He was sneaking down the corridor like he didn't want anyone to see or hear him. It was Dad, wasn't it? Yes, there was his old brown corduroy jacket as he passed under a lamp. He disappeared through the door that led to the stairway.

The *stairs*? Their rooms were on the fifteenth floor.

She stepped back, pulled her door closed, and leaned

against it, tugging on her lip. Her skin had that prickly feeling — *here comes trouble.*

It didn't make any sense for Dad to sneak around the hotel in the middle of the night. They were here on vacation. Dad was just showing them the country where he sometimes worked. But even if he'd been on a work trip, she couldn't imagine that would involve prowling around the hotel at 12:21 a.m.

She could knock on their door and try to wake up Simon. No, that was hopeless. He was taking sleeping pills to get over jet lag. If she did manage to wake him up, he'd just yell at her, then turn over and go back to sleep. She wished Mom were here, sharing the room with Mia as planned.

Maybe Dad was just going down to the lobby for a drink. If she followed, she could sit with him and talk like they did at home sometimes, just the two of them in the dark.

She grabbed a sweatshirt from her open suitcase, yanked it on over her pajamas, and wedged her feet into her sneakers. Grabbing her room key from the bedside table, she eased the door open again, slipped through, and carefully, carefully, let it close behind her.

She looked both ways down the hotel corridor before darting to the elevator. . . . But Dad had used the stairs. If he was trying to be quiet, she wouldn't be helping by activating the lights, sounds, and movement of the elevator.

She opened the stairway door and slipped inside. A dark tunnel plummeted down, down, down, with only occasional pinpricks of light. Clearly, the hotel did not expect their guests to creep down the stairs before dawn. Mia grabbed hold of the railing so she wouldn't miss a step in the gloom.

Maybe Dad was just going to take a walk. He was having a harder time with jet lag than Simon and Mia — because he was older, he said — even though they'd stopped in Beijing for three nights on the way, and even though he took trips like this all the time. He might have gone to get some fresh air.

But he couldn't just walk out of the hotel; that was one of the things on the tour company's *What Not to Do* list. She kept coming back to how Dad had looked. As if he didn't want anybody to know he was in the hall.

Nighttime activities that had to be hidden seemed even more dangerous.

She started down again. She hadn't thought to count the floors when she began; had she passed by four landings or five? She realized now that she had no way of knowing if Dad had just gone to another floor, to someone else's room.

She stopped again. Maybe she should just turn around and go back to her room. But she didn't know what floor she was on, so she couldn't count her way back up to the fifteenth. They must have been marked with numbers somewhere, but it was really hard to see in the dark.

This was all a terrible idea. She never did stuff like this, jumping in without a plan. Her brother was the one who acted first, thought later. Mia was careful. And right now, here, stuck in a dark stairwell in a strange hotel in a foreign country, she couldn't think of a better plan than being wherever Dad was. She might as well find him.

It seemed as if she had been moving endlessly downward when she noticed she could see a little better. The light was gradually increasing in the stairwell. The door on the landing below her had a glowing window. It must be the lobby.

Mia stood on tiptoes to peer through the glass in the door. All the glittery chandeliers were turned off. The wide room was lit by only a few lamps attached to pillars. The part she could see looked deserted.

She pushed open the heavy door and slipped through, stepping into the shadow of a pillar to scan the area. Down a far corridor, lights and faint music came from the hotel bar. But no one was in sight in the open lobby area, except a clerk behind the reception desk, who was bent over some work, not looking in her direction.

Okay, Mia, now what? She'd gotten all the way down here, but she didn't actually have a plan. Except to be where Dad was. To make herself feel safer. And — somehow — to keep him safe. That seemed kind of ridiculous now.

To her left, a huge framed painting hung on the wall. Kim Il-sung, standing with his son, Kim Jong-il, on top of a mountain. The first two dictators of North Korea, both dead now. Though most of the lobby was darkened, a spotlight was directed on the painting, illuminating the faces of the two men. They were smiling, but here in the hotel lobby in the middle of the night, it felt to Mia as if they were watching her.

Mia shivered. The idea of being watched made her want to crawl into a hole. And if people were observing her, then if what Dad was doing was secret, she might actually put him in danger. But she couldn't stand the idea of going back to her room without finding him. She pressed herself against the pillar, paralyzed with indecision, for long minutes.

Then she heard a door opening. Mia swiveled around the side of the pillar in time to see two figures moving through a side door leading into the lobby. As they passed near one of the lamps, she saw it was her father, with a Korean man. Dad had been outside! But he was safe for now, and the two men were coming in her direction. She had to disappear, fast. She lurched for the door to the stairwell and fled upward. She took the stairs two by two, remembering to count floors this time, until she had to stop to catch her breath.

A door closed below her. She kept moving again, as fast as she could pull herself up, step after step after step. Fifth floor, seventh floor, tenth floor. She was dragging now, but she had to beat her father back to their rooms. That other man could still be with him. Or Dad might be alone, but she didn't want him to know that she'd followed him when it seemed clear he hadn't wanted to be seen.

Gasping, thighs burning, she finally reached the fifteenth floor. She yanked open the door with what felt like her last strength and jogged down the corridor to her room.

Once inside, she slid the door closed, quietly, quietly, and leaned against it, panting. She'd done it. Now she just had to stand here until she could breathe again, and wait for Dad's door to close.

Mia reached over automatically to flip the wall switch. Everything was weirdly vintage in her room, like a set from one of those '70s sitcom reruns Mom liked to watch. But instead of Brady Bunch innocent, it all looked kind of sinister. Especially in the middle of the night with Dad acting strange.

She thought of the portraits in the lobby, her feeling of being watched. Could there be cameras behind the pictures? Perhaps there were cameras in the rooms too. The tour group pamphlet had mentioned it as a rumor. She sat heavily on the edge of the bed, trying to look as if it was just jet lag that had woken her to leave her room for a stroll. She kicked off her sneakers and collapsed back on the bedspread, pulling the chain holding her locket out from under her sweatshirt, rubbing the pendant between her thumb and finger. With her other hand she picked up her guidebook. But none of what she needed now would be found in its maps and instructions.

She tossed the book next to her on the bed and picked up her phone, which was useless. Dad said they could survive without their phone connections for five days — one more reason Simon was mad. But even if she could text Alicia and Jess, they were on the other side of the planet, where it was still yesterday.

Ages later, there was another scrape. She sat up, straining to hear. Definitely Dad and Simon's door. Then the reassuring click. So Dad — *It had to be Dad, didn't it?* — was safe. For now.

But they were still in North Korea, and she had no idea what was going on with her father, or her brother, or this crazy country. She switched off the lamp and burrowed under the covers.

CHO SOO-YUN

✦ ✦ ✦

Soo-yun woke in the predawn, happy, thinking of the fish. Squatting on the concrete floor of the apartment bathroom, she bent over the metal basin to scrub her face until her skin tingled and glowed, as if she were scouring herself clean of faults and failings as well.

Glancing at her reflection in the mirror, she combed and arranged the waves of her permed hair, feeling as always the pang of her not-quite-prettiness, her insufficient offering. It had been a miracle — of course, only by the grace of the Dear Leader, Kim Jong-il — that she'd been selected for the training program as a guide for foreign tourists. The Dear Leader had recommended prioritizing language skills in addition to appearance, so her excellence in English studies had balanced out her too-big teeth and too-weak chin. It still stung a bit, that she wasn't as pleasing to look at as the other young women in her program, as if she were a slightly stunted flower in an otherwise beautiful bouquet. She longed to shine, to reflect the light of the Great Leader, the Sun.

In the tiny kitchen, she moved with quiet efficiency, granting her mother and brother a few more moments of sleep as she prepared their breakfast. She scooped a careful measure of corn-rice from the Public Distribution sack into a small pot. She rinsed the grains under running water, drained them, laid her hand on top and let the water fill to cover it, then set the pot to boil on a burner. She turned to the side dishes with extra pleasure, thinking of the fish and how it would make the meal special.

Returning home the previous evening as the market was closing, she'd seen an old woman seated behind a plastic bucket with two small fish swimming in it. A bit of fortune: they would be fresh. And another bit of luck: She had a few bills, from the neighbors whose children she tutored in English.

The old woman had kindly cut off the heads, scaled, and gutted the fish on the spot. Climbing the dark stairwell to their apartment — once again the elevator was broken — Soo-yun had decided to save the fish for the morning. Salted, they'd last overnight. A treat for her mother and brother, and a way to celebrate her own new opportunity.

She rinsed the fish now and began to prepare it, sautéing it in a bit of oil before adding green onions and garlic. The oil in the jar was low, she noticed, and as the monthly rationed supplies were now coming once every two months, there wouldn't be more until the first of next month. She'd have to be vigilant; she was the only wage-earner in the family.

When everything was ready, she arranged the bowls of steaming corn-rice, the small dishes of vegetables, and the plate of fish on the low wooden table and carried it to the main room. She set it on the floor, next to the mats where her mother and brother slept. Her gaze moved from the spread to the smiling portraits high on the wall above her. She felt the care emanating from their images, particularly the warm eyes of the Great Leader, who had become even more of a father figure to her since the loss of her own father ten years before. Her eyes pricked with tears as gratitude rose in her chest, for this food that would give her brother energy for the long school day, her mother strength to heal, and for herself, courage in her new job. So much goodness could come from this opportunity, if only she could continue to excel.

The martial music began to swell from the speaker on the wall. Behind her, she heard her brother stir. She turned to greet her family with a smile.

CHAPTER 2

When Mia walked into the dining room, Dad waved from one of the tables, his face lighting up at the sight of her. No sign of Simon.

"How's my girl?" Dad asked, kissing her forehead.

"Fine," she lied.

The breakfast offerings filled a long table. Rice, kimchi, small bowls of meats and vegetables. A steaming pot of some kind of soup. Mia liked the Korean food they served for holidays at Saturday language school, or at restaurants her parents took her to in Stamford or a couple times in New York, but she'd never had it for breakfast. At the other end of the table, a tray full of sliced white bread sat next to a toaster, with little pots of butter and jam. Two hooded silver containers with fires under them held fried eggs and some kind of processed meat. She toasted bread, poured a glass of juice from a can that had a picture of a peach on it, and scooped a fried egg onto her plate.

She looked Dad over as she moved to their table. Same scruffy corduroy jacket with the leather elbow patches. Same stray bits of hair sticking out. Same gray eyes peering over his glasses at the tour schedule. The least likely spy in the world. She wondered if she'd dreamed the whole thing.

As Mia picked up her fork, Simon slouched in through the doorway, heading for the buffet table. She took a bite of egg. It was rubbery and tough from sitting too long. The bread was just barely toasted, not crunchy the way she liked it, even though she'd put it through the toaster twice.

She glanced at Dad as she chewed, rehearsing ways to bring up the subject of last night. *How'd you sleep, Dad?* Or, *Funny, I thought I heard your room door open just after midnight.* Or point-blank: *Dad, what were you doing sneaking around the hotel in the middle of the night?*

There must be a simple, ordinary explanation for what he had been doing. Or he really had been doing something secret, in which case he wouldn't want her to know. If she brought it up, she could be making things dangerous for him. Especially in public, where someone could overhear. Even worse, in front of Simon.

Her brother plunked his plate down and slumped into his chair, avoiding eye contact. His earbuds were already in place, wires stretching to his MP3 player stashed in the pocket of his sweatshirt. Mia felt a little collapse within, a sinking sadness. Her brother was right here across the table, yet completely unreachable, like he'd been ever since the Trouble in August.

Simon had made the same choices of toast and egg. This was not likely to go well.

She continued the dutiful business of chewing and swallowing. She wasn't about to waste food, not in this country where floods, droughts, lack of farmland, and the government's bad policies meant that there were always hungry people. Without aid from other countries, the kind her father's organization brought in, the people would starve to death. An image flashed in her mind from one of the stories he'd told from his last trip, about a little boy in an orphanage, lying on his bed with his ribs sticking out. He was so weak he couldn't even lift his head, but his face lit up with a big grin when he saw the strange foreign man.

Mia pressed her lips together and shook her head to clear it. At least they wouldn't encounter any starving people on this tour. The government and their guides would make certain of that.

"They're still working out the Western food thing," Dad said at the look of distaste on Simon's face as he took a bite. Their father slurped from his white coffee mug, considered the taste, swallowed. "I've had worse." He smiled at his son and daughter and held up the schedule. "So, let's see, what's in store for this band of intrepid travelers today? First up, the statues at Mansu Hill."

Mia glanced across the table at her brother, leaning back in his chair, far away in his alternative musical universe. She reached for her backpack, pulled out her guidebook, and opened to the map of Pyongyang. "Here," she said, placing her finger on the site.

Dad's face bloomed with delight. "Mia! That's terrific! I didn't realize you had a guidebook."

"I found it on your bookshelf. It's got cool maps."

"Oh, that one. It's probably more than ten years old. But most of the maps should still be good." He peered at the page. "That's the place. Mansu Hill. It's the first stop on every tour. Every visitor has to pay proper respect to the Great Leader and the Dear Leader. Even when we're here on humanitarian missions."

"How many times have you been there?" Mia asked.

"I've lost count. But everything else is new to me. I've never been just a tourist here." He returned to the schedule. "Second stop, Juche Tower. Which, it says here, 'honors Kim Il-sung's concept of self-reliance.'" He looked up at Mia, then at Simon, whose eyes were on the tablecloth, fingers drumming to a beat only he could hear. "That's what *ju-che* means, self-reliance. And from the top you get a panoramic view of the city."

Simon slapped the table. Mia jumped, but her brother was glaring at their father. "I don't get why you're acting like this is a *normal* thing to do," he hissed, "going sightseeing in this messed-up country. How can you just go along with the program? You of all people, with all the stuff you've seen?"

Beyond cramming facts for his debate team competitions, Mia hadn't noticed that international politics had ever been Simon's thing. He was just grabbing any ammunition he could find against Dad for making him come on this trip.

As usual, Dad didn't bite. "You know what I always say: Giving your attention to something doesn't mean agreeing with it." His tone was mild, as if he and Simon were having a perfectly reasonable conversation. He took another sip of coffee. "I think there's a benefit to having foreign visitors in North Korea, learning about what it's really like, making contact with people, showing them that not all Americans are imperialist warmongers." He raised an eyebrow at Simon. Then his expression got more serious. "And of course there's the agency work. Showing respect seems a small price to pay to be allowed to help alleviate the suffering of hungry people. And I have to be particularly careful, because there's no American embassy here to rescue me if I mess up."

Simon huffed out a breath and turned away, but not before zapping his sister with a laser glance, though she hadn't said or done a thing. She was guilty by association, just for going along with Dad.

Mia could remember when Simon didn't look at her like she was his enemy. The last time had probably been late spring, before Randi broke up with him, before he ran off to New York. That escapade was one of the reasons they were on this crazy tour — the last thing in the world that Simon wanted to be doing. Randi was back home this week, and he'd been planning to see her. Instead, here they were.

A white-clad waiter approached their table, carrying a silver pot. He gestured toward Dad's cup. Dad nodded, thanking the waiter in badly pronounced Korean as he poured. Another waiter came by and picked up Dad's plate, then Mia's. He came to Simon's place but hesitated, his eyes on the food on the plate.

The waiter was lean. Mia wondered if he was hungry. Dad said that during the famines, it had sometimes been even worse for people in the cities, because there weren't any wild plants or things they could forage. How awful if the waiters had to serve all this food and didn't have enough to eat themselves.

Simon sighed heavily and shook his head. He placed the cold egg on the cold toast, folded it over, and crammed the whole thing in his mouth. After a moment, the waiter removed the plate.

Mia let out her breath.

．　．　．

The three guides who'd met them at the airport — Mr. Kim, Mr. Lee, and Miss Cho — were waiting outside the hotel. They herded their group into line to wait for the tour bus. Mia turned her head to watch the people passing on the sidewalk. The night before, it had already been dark when they'd driven into the city, so this was her first real glimpse of North Korea.

A couple of men in dark business suits passed by, one talking on a cell phone, both smoking cigarettes. A young woman in a stylish gray trench coat clicked purposefully along in high heels, carrying a designer bag. A mother held the hand of a cute little girl in a bright red jacket, her hair pulled into two ponytails. All appeared to be perfectly ordinary people going about their morning business, except that every single adult wore a small red badge near their heart, a waving flag or a circle, each with a picture of a smiling Kim Il-sung. Nobody looked brainwashed or robotic or starving. They just looked *Korean*.

That was by far the strangest thing to Mia: Here, *everyone* was Korean. In her Connecticut town, only a handful of people weren't white, and even fewer were Asian. Being surrounded by Korean people was surreal, like when she woke up out of a vivid dream and didn't know where she was for a bit. There'd been tons of Asian people in Beijing, obviously, but she and Dad and Simon had mostly been in the hotel recovering from jet lag or in the orientation meetings with the tour group, so she hadn't really been hit by it. And the people there had been Chinese. These people were *Korean*. Like she was. And no one noticed her. That was another strangeness. Their glances glided right past her, halting as they came to Simon and Dad and the other white Americans standing in line. She was used to having people's eyes stop when they came to her, to being the piece that didn't fit. Their family would be out together in a restaurant or a movie, and suddenly a stranger's look would remind her of the old *Sesame Street* song about one thing being not like the others, one thing not belonging.

The only other place she'd ever been surrounded by people who looked like her was at Korean language school on Saturdays in Stamford. But there she still stood out: The only one whose parents were white. The only one who didn't speak Korean at home. Here, she felt as if she could disappear. Just take a step away from the tour group and blend into the flow of people on the sidewalk. And as long as people were distracted by the white foreigners, no one would notice.

One older lady tilted her head toward her companion, talking animatedly, gesturing to her own black hair. Her eyes never left Simon's face. To a North Korean, he must look like a blond creature from outer space. But he was too busy complaining about having to line up to notice he was being stared at. His fists were jammed into the pouch of his navy hoodie. White wires still dangled from his ears.

"What the hell are we doing on this tour, looking at stupid sights?" he muttered under his breath.

Mia stiffened. He couldn't say things like that here. What was wrong with him that he couldn't go along with the simplest instructions? Simon in a place like North Korea felt like a dangerous chemistry experiment. Sooner or later something was going to explode.

The thing was, she had to admit that on this one point she actually agreed with him: It was crazy that they were here. As her brother had phrased it when Dad first brought up the idea: "Who in their right mind tries to bond with their kids by taking them on a tour of *North Korea*?"

Mia guessed that the real reason for the trip was to somehow make them a family again. But they could have come later when they had all figured out how to get along, especially since Mom had to cancel at the last minute, after Nona broke her hip. Instead, Dad, Simon, and Mia brought their problems overseas. At one point Dad mentioned that the trip would be an opportunity for Mia to connect with her heritage. But if it was for her benefit, they should be visiting *South* Korea, where she had actually been born.

Dad had looked odd after he said that, like maybe he regretted his words. But as usual, she hadn't voiced any of her questions or doubts. Simon had been making enough noise for both of them.

The bus pulled up and the line began to move. Dad turned back with a *Here we go!* grin, as if they were all just having a swell time.

Mia took a window seat halfway back. Dad slipped in next to her. Simon flung himself into the seat across from them, turning his scowling face away, toward the window. His expression reminded her of Stone Warrior, one of the villains from their childhood games of Knights and Castles. Simon would play the part with his body stiff, clomping around the backyard and uttering deep, hollow moans. Mia and the other little kids would run shrieking. Now her brother seemed to have gotten stuck in the role, anger running through his veins instead of blood.

The bus rattled along the city street, sounding as if something inside the motor had come loose. Mia pulled out the tour schedule and her guidebook, opening to the map of Pyongyang. With a finger, she touched the location of their hotel, then Mansu Hill.

"You always have been the family navigator," Dad said, leaning toward her. "I remember when we first noticed — I think you were three. We took a different route to the grocery store, and you piped up from your car seat, 'No, Daddy, turn left!'"

The bus turned. Mia searched for signs, trying to pinpoint their route. The broad streets seemed strangely empty, with only a handful of black cars, a few buses and electric trolleys. Pedestrians alone or in small groups looked tiny on the wide sidewalks, like people left behind when everyone else had gone somewhere more interesting. It made her feel sorry for Pyongyang, the city, as if it were one of those unpopular middle school kids that nobody wanted to hang out with.

Hulking concrete buildings lined the streets, many topped with huge Korean slogans.

"*In . . . Min . . . Gong . . . Hwa . . . Gook . . . Man . . . Sei.*" Mia slowly sounded out the syllables on one sign.

"You hot ticket," Dad said. She turned to see him grinning at her, his eyes shining. "What's that mean?"

Mia leaned closer for a moment, feeling warm inside. "I only know the last two, *man-sei*, which means 'ten thousand years.' People cheer '*Man-sei!*' like 'Long live our country.'"

Dad's expression was seriously pleased, like wasn't his daughter brilliant and hadn't they been great parents taking her to Korean school all those years and wasn't this trip such a terrific idea? But looking at him, Mia could only remember his hunched-over posture in the hallway after midnight. What if this tour was a cover for some other purpose?

She sat up and turned her face back to the window, frowning. Dad had always been her safe person, ever since she'd come home as a seven-month-old baby. For days after they'd picked her up, she'd clung to him, refusing to let anyone else hold her. He was the one she'd always been able to trust completely. She didn't like this feeling, being suspicious of Dad.

The bus cruised along the river for ten minutes or so before pulling into a huge parking lot. The three guides stood. The older, shorter man, Mr. Kim, gestured toward the young woman. He seemed to be directing the show.

Miss Cho stepped forward and cleared her throat. "Here we will visit Mansu Hill," she said. "The Korean people first erected this monument in April 1972 to the Great Leader, who is the Founder of the Democratic People's Republic of Korea. President Kim Il-sung, the Eternal Sun of Mankind, fathered the ju-che idea, under which he led the Korean revolution. 'Man is the master of everything and decides everything.' That is the main point of the ju-che idea."

Mia wondered what Miss Cho really thought about the things she was saying. The young woman's two front teeth were prominent, like a rabbit's. She flicked a glance at Mr. Kim, showing the whites of her eyes. A scared rabbit. She was hiding her anxiety well, but she seemed to be new at this guide thing.

"It is entirely thanks to the immortal idea that the DPRK is throwing radiant rays all over the world as the motherland of ju-che, a powerful socialist country, independent, self-supporting, and self-reliant in national defense. Indeed, the ju-che idea is a great and immortal revolutionary idea representing the future of the humankind." Miss Cho finished her speech with a smile and a bow. Though Mia didn't agree with what the guide had said, she felt an impulse to clap — *good job!* — just to encourage her.

Mr. Lee, the tall guide with thick black-framed glasses, held a bouquet of flowers in his hand. He was gesturing over the seats, smiling. At *Mia*. He beckoned for her to come forward. Why was he picking her? What did he expect her to do?

No. She did not want the spotlight on her. She did not want to be a poster child for North Korea. She glanced at Dad. He was smiling too. *That's a good girl.*

She huffed out a small sigh and clambered past Dad into the aisle. *Giving attention and respect does not mean agreeing.* Stepping off the bus, she shaded her eyes against the glare.

"Mi-a?" Mr. Lee stood with his garish bouquet of flowers, still smiling at her. So he knew her name already. Well, that wasn't too surprising. Of course the guides would have a list of the tour group members. "You are thirteen years of age?" He gestured forward and began walking across the pavement.

Mia shook her head as she fell into step with him. "Twelve." She kept her face blank, her eyebrows still when they wanted to go all squirrelly.

"Yes, I think so. But American age twelve is Korean age thirteen. You understand?"

She nodded. She'd learned at language school that Koreans counted the time your mother was pregnant in your age, so when you were born you were already considered one year old.

They were moving up a long, paved ramp that climbed a high hill.

"My daughter, she is thirteen also." Mr. Lee beamed at her.

Mia glanced back to see the other two guides shepherding the rest of the tour group up the hill, following her and Mr. Lee. Simon moved slowly, everything about him screaming, *I do not want to be here and you cannot make me do anything.*

"My daughter, she plays football very well," Mr. Lee was

saying. "Actually, you say in America 'soccer,' yes? Do you like soccer?"

Mia shook her head again. "No, I'm not really into sports." She wasn't acting very friendly. She tried to think of what she could share. Her favorite video game, *Quest*. Did North Koreans have video games? She liked making collages. Beading. Maps. All kind of hard to explain. "I like to read," she said.

Mr. Lee nodded, smiling even more. This was apparently a good answer by North Korean standards. "You must be good student."

Mia started to shake her head again, then stopped herself and just smiled back.

At the top of the ramp, an enormous open square led up to two bronze giants standing side by side: Kim Il-sung and Kim Jong-il, the two former dictators. On the left, the smiling statue with the raised arm, Kim Il-sung, looked like a tour guide, presenting the city of Pyongyang. Behind the statues, like a stage set, was a white building with pillars framing a dramatic mural of snow-covered mountains. To each side, in the wings of the stage, bronze soldiers and citizens charged forward under a huge flag.

The tour group crossed the square and climbed several wide sets of steps toward the base of the statues, peering up at the figures looming far overhead.

"Would you look at that?" Mrs. Blake, the plump, white-haired lady they'd met at orientation the day before, sounded awestruck. "They're enormous!"

"The way the North Koreans tell it, the first one they built is a monument to Kim Il-sung's modesty!" That was the professor-type guy in the horn-rimmed glasses. "Supposedly, they wanted to make the statue twice as tall, but Kim refused, said they should use the money for the 'people's needs' instead. And of course there's Kim Jong-un, who doesn't have any statues because he's too 'humble.'" His words were mild, but an edge to his tone alerted his American companions that he was being sarcastic. Mia figured he was referring to how these leaders acted like they put the North Korean people first, when in reality the dictators prospered while the people went hungry. She wondered if Mr. Lee would be able to pick up on his tone. Dad stood at the back of the group, looking distracted, not joining in the chatter.

As the stragglers joined their group, Simon among them, Mr. Lee moved forward. Mia, not sure what she was supposed to do, followed. Her head didn't even clear the platform on which the Great Leader and Dear Leader stood. It was not yet ten a.m., but already dozens of plastic-wrapped bouquets and wreaths lay at the feet of the two statues.

Mr. Lee bowed toward the statue, his back parallel to the ground. Then he handed the bouquet to Mia and gestured for her to place it on the pile. She did, and he bowed again before turning back to the group. Patriotic music blared from invisible speakers. Mr. Kim herded everyone into a more compact group and indicated that they should be silent for a show of respect.

Mia stood up straight, head bent, sort of like praying in church. She'd never admit it to Simon, but she actually liked being given a set of instructions, especially in a place as strange as North Korea. Following rules was easy, and it was how to stay safe. But Simon always hated being forced to do anything. Mia peered sideways through the curtain of her hair. Her brother stood on the outer edge of the group, his back to the statues, looking out toward the river. He wasn't causing a disturbance, but he certainly wasn't even pretending to show respect.

As the moment of silence ended, Dad moved quietly around the group, took Simon's arm, and moved him a little farther away.

"Okay, now you take photograph," Mr. Lee announced, gesturing an invitation. Everyone reached for their bags or shoulder straps or phones. At least no one was paying attention to their little family drama.

Mia, chewing her lip, watched Dad speaking to Simon, too quietly for anyone in the group to hear. She could tell from their father's posture that he was delivering a message, directly and urgently. Simon glowered and shrugged out of Dad's grasp.

He looked up then and caught Mia looking at him. An expression passed over his features, a flattening. His eyes went blank. Then he looked away.

Mia winced. He'd been mad at her ever since August. Not yelling-mad like he was with Dad. *You're dead to me* mad.

She closed her eyes for a moment. Then she sighed and turned around to look up at the monument, one hand shielding her eyes like a salute. The statues' heads seemed to touch the clouds. She took a few steps back, but she was still caught in their shadow. Mia remembered how she'd felt about the portraits in the hotel lobby. What if the statues had surveillance cameras in their heads? The Great Leader and the Dear Leader could still be watching over their people, even though they were dead.

The guides began herding the group back toward the bus. Moving away with her back to the statues, Mia could feel their gaze following her.

CHAPTER 3

"No, no! Please stop now!" Mia flinched at the loud voice. Mr. Kim, the head guide, was advancing up the aisle of the bus, shaking one raised hand like a scolding teacher. He stopped two seats in front of Mia, focused on Mr. and Mrs. Blake. "You cannot take picture."

From the aisle seat, Mr. Blake peered up over his glasses.

"Please give me your camera." Mr. Kim extended his hand, palm up. From the window seat, Mrs. Blake murmured apologetic sounds. Mia tugged on her necklace, putting the locket to her lips.

"What is it? What's the problem?" Mr. Blake asked as the guide examined the camera.

"No picture. You do not have permission." Mr. Kim's fingers manipulated the buttons, scanning the recent images, deleting. Finally, he grunted, then handed the camera back. "You must not take picture without permission," he repeated before marching back down the aisle.

Mia breathed out, feeling as if she'd narrowly escaped being sent to the principal's office.

"What did they delete?" someone whispered.

"All Grace did was take a few shots out the window." Mr.

Blake bent over the camera, clicking through the images. "Looks like he got rid of the ones of soldiers."

"Yes, they don't like anyone taking pictures of anything related to the military," Dad said, his voice low. "But sometimes they just want to remind us who's in charge. One day you can take pictures in one direction, the next day it's forbidden."

Mia leaned her head back against the seat. All these confusing feelings and impressions, all the tensions bombarding her. The tour had just begun, and she felt exhausted already.

.   .   .

"Mr. Andrews, guests for you." Mr. Lee stood at their table, looking expectant.

They'd just finished lunch with another member of the tour group, Daniel Moon. They'd first met him the day before at the tour orientation in Beijing, where he had told Mia she could call him Daniel. So far he seemed like the only interesting person on the tour. He was older — like thirty — but he was handsome, and nice enough to notice Mia existed. Even though he and Dad had spent most of the lunch talking about North Korean politics, it was a relief to have someone break up their little family triangle.

"Please come," Mr. Lee said, gesturing toward the lobby. Mia tensed. Maybe somebody had discovered what Dad was doing in the middle of the night. But Mr. Lee had said "guests."

In the lobby, two men in business suits rose from a cluster of couches. There were lots of bows and handshakes as Mr. Lee introduced Dad.

"They're saying they're from the Ministry of Agriculture," Daniel translated for Simon and Mia. "They're thanking your dad for all the work he's done on famine relief."

The man in the navy suit presented Dad with a large rectangular box. More bows and handshakes.

"A plaque of appreciation," Daniel said, talking low to Simon. "Koreans are big on those."

The men turned toward Mia and Simon as Mr. Lee spoke, probably introducing them as Dad's kids. Simon didn't step forward to shake hands, but he nodded his head. Once. With no expression. Mia bowed an extra time or two to make up for her impossible brother.

The shorter guy, wearing a black suit, held out a square package, about the size of a small bakery cake box, toward Mia and Simon.

Mia knew from Korean school that Simon should be the one to accept the gift. Firstborns and sons came first. But he just stood there, hands behind his back, face grim. She stepped forward, taking the box with both hands and a bow. "*Kam-sa-ham-ni-da*."

She stepped back and whispered to Daniel, "Am I supposed to open it?"

"No, that's not usually done. You can look at it later."

There was some lively discussion back and forth between the two officials and Mr. Lee. Mia heard two words she knew: *ddal* — daughter — and *ee-byang-ah* — adopted child. So they were talking about her. A South Korean adopted into a white American family must have seemed strange to the North Koreans. The ultimate victim of the "Yankee imperialists." Or the ultimate villain, siding with the enemy.

But the man in the black suit was smiling and nodding. She must have passed some kind of test. The men made their last bows to Dad, and the little group broke up.

. . .

At the end of their afternoon tour, the bus pulled up to the curb by the hotel. Everyone streamed off, heading to their rooms to prepare for dinner and the evening performance of the Arirang Mass Games. As Mia moved from the window seat, her backpack strap caught on the armrest, halting her. Pausing to untangle it, she ended up the last one off the bus.

Inside, she searched the lobby for her father. There he was, in the far corner toward the bar, standing with Daniel Moon. Mia started across to join them, then stopped. There was something about the way Dad was talking to Daniel that warned her not to call attention to them.

She stopped beside a pillar, pulled her guidebook from her backpack, and bent over it as if she were reading. She raised just her eyes from the page, watching Dad and Daniel. They didn't look like two men who'd just met, having a casual conversation. They stood close together, and Dad kept glancing up, scanning the area around them as he talked. They looked like they were sharing secrets.

Mia turned and walked back to the elevator. Was Daniel somehow connected to Dad — and to whatever it was he had been doing in the middle of the night?

. . .

That evening, Mia climbed on the bus to find Daniel with an empty seat next to him. He smiled up at her, and she surprised herself by sitting beside him.

"So how's the trip for you so far?" Daniel asked.

Mia wriggled out of her backpack and sat back in the seat. The bus rumbled and began to move. "It's . . . it's *weird*," she heard herself say.

Daniel burst out laughing. Mia felt her face getting warm. "That, Mia Andrews, is quite an understatement." Maybe he wasn't laughing *at* her. "North Korea is such a weird place, in so many ways. So what in particular have you found weird?"

"Well, first, all the Korean people." She blushed harder. Blurting out stuff was not what she did. "I mean . . ."

"Because you're Korean yourself? But you haven't been around many Koreans?"

It sounded almost shocking, hearing him state it so plainly and matter-of-factly. She gulped and nodded.

"So what's that like for you?" Daniel asked.

Mia put her head back against the seat and reached one hand up to touch her locket. She was familiar with invasive questions: "What *are* you?" "Are you Chinese or Japanese?" "How come your mom's white?" "*He's* your brother?" But once someone's curiosity had been satisfied, that was the end of it. No one actually wanted to have a discussion about her identity. People acted almost as if it was impolite to talk about it.

Except that Daniel was looking at her as if he really wanted to hear the answer. What *was* it like for her?

"I dunno. . . . We live in Connecticut, in a town where there aren't . . . many Asians. I go to Korean school, but we have to drive forty minutes to get there. I'm not used to see-ing so many Koreans. It's kind of overwhelming." Mia stole a quick glance at Daniel. He was watching her. Curious. Not like he was just being nice to some kid. Like she was an interesting person who had something to say. She was used to being stared at, but not to being *seen*.

"What's weird here is the feeling that I don't stand out," she said. "Nobody's looking at me like they do at home, like they're wondering what I am."

"How's that feel?"

She fixed her eyes on the seat in front of her.

"I like it that everybody's staring at Dad and Simon instead of me. I just feel like I have more . . . space. Like I can disappear for a little while. Like having an invisibility cloak." She wrapped her arms around her backpack, pressing it to her chest. There was something else she wanted to try to say. "But it's not disappearing into nothing, not being invisible like you don't exist. It's blending in . . . to something bigger that you're part of. Only . . . I don't really feel like I am a part of it."

Daniel was nodding. "Yeah, I get that. I'm Korean too. My parents moved to the States when I was nine. But every summer we'd go back to Seoul to see my grandparents. I know that feeling, that it's a relief to blend in, to be 'normal' for once." He made quotation marks with his fingers.

"At the same time," he went on, "everyone could see that I hadn't grown up in Korea, just by looking at me. There was something — my posture, my walk, my clothing — that said 'American.' And my accent wasn't right. Of course that's even more true here."

Mia sat in silence for a moment, letting the feeling of this conversation settle in her. Daniel wasn't just connecting with how she appeared on the outside, the fact that both of them looked Korean. He was reaching out and saying hi to the *person* she was, inside. Curious about her thoughts, her experiences, her feelings. Beyond her immediate family and Jess and Alicia, that happened so rarely that sometimes she wondered if there *was* anyone there. If her name was actually M.I.A. — Missing in Action.

The bus turned to cross a bridge over the river toward a small island, nearly filled with the inner-tube shape of an enormous stadium. Mia pointed. "Is that where we're going?"

Daniel nodded. The bus slowed as it pulled into a giant parking lot. In front, Mr. Kim, Mr. Lee, and Miss Cho stood up.

Daniel gestured toward the guides. "I feel such a pull when I'm here. There's the sense that everyone's Korean, these are *my people*." He placed his hand on his chest, near his heart. Then he dropped his voice. "But then there's the complete disconnect when it comes to the political and social realities. Like what we're seeing tonight."

The guides herded them off the bus, through huge doors, and toward bleachers overlooking an enormous indoor field. Filing into their row, Mia stuck close to Daniel, ending up between him and Dad with Simon on the other side.

"How's this for blending in?" Daniel gestured to the crowd of spectators. As far as Mia could see in any direction, the bleachers were filled with Koreans. Except for a few tiny clumps of foreigners, it was an unbroken plain of black hair.

Still, in this crowd of tens of thousands of people, Mia and Daniel were special. Different from the other Americans because they were Korean. Different from the other Koreans because they were American. But until Daniel had pointed it out, she hadn't noticed that space existed.

She scanned the crowd, trying out Daniel's phrase — *my people* — to see how it felt. Then she had a strange thought: It could literally be true. Somewhere in this huge crowd there could actually be someone who was genetically related to her. Of course her birth parents were from South — not North — Korea. But long before her parents were born, families had been split up when the peninsula was divided in the Korean War. There was actually a possibility that some relative of her birth mother or father could be here, some-where in this crowd.

She noticed movement on the other side of the stadium. A solid wall of schoolchildren — twenty thousand of them, the program said — had started warming up. Each child held up a large book of colored cards. Like mosaic squares, the cards merged to create an enormous picture of the North Korean flag, running the entire length of the sta-dium. Conductors made signals, the kids flipped their cards, and the image changed, sometimes snapping, sometimes rippling. Twenty thousand kids' voices shouted slogans as they flipped the cards in perfect unison.

Martial music swelled from loudspeakers, spotlights flooded the stadium, and the show began. The pictures shifted — flowers, a mountain scene, a sunrise — all in brilliant color. There was an enormous portrait of a smiling Kim Il-sung, then a group of workers holding up tools. Sometimes the cards formed words in the *han-gul* alphabet against a col-ored background, even a few that she could read — Kim Il-sung, Kim Jong-il, Kim Jong-un. *Man-sei. Ju-che.*

"The kids rehearse at school, every day, for months." Daniel spoke in low tones. "According to defectors, it's actu-ally pretty grim: They're forced to practice for hours and hours on almost no food, with no bathroom breaks. If a stu-dent performs poorly, the entire family gets punished. A strange form of child labor, all for the glory of the nation."

Mia couldn't take her eyes off the spectacle before her. But now she worried about the kids being hungry, needing to use the bathroom. What would happen if one of them made a mistake?

She tipped her head toward Daniel, keeping her eyes on the performance. The music was loud; there was no way the guides could overhear. "Do the kids really want to do this? Or do they have to?"

"Well, it's complicated. It's supposed to be a great honor to get chosen. But the children of the elite here in Pyongyang don't have to participate."

"So an ordinary person couldn't refuse to be in it? If they didn't want to?"

"Not without consequences."

Mia could only imagine what those consequences would be. It felt dangerous and exciting to be saying these things, surrounded by North Koreans, right in the middle of the Mass Games.

"How they get away with it," Daniel went on, "is convincing people that the greatest thing you can do is sacrifice yourself in service to the Great Leader. That's what this whole display is about."

Mia had to admit that the performance was completely amazing. On the green floor of the stadium, eighty thousand dancers, gymnasts, and acrobats moved together in waves, in ribbons, like flowing water or the wind through trees. There were thousands of women dancers in identical turquoise tops and billowing white skirts, then thousands in pink, thousands in yellow. After them came soldiers in olive-and-tan camouflage uniforms, brandishing guns and executing tae kwon do moves, shouting out fierce songs.

Daniel leaned over to her again. "The games also shore up the power of the state and its leaders. Watching something like this, the message is clear: 'Don't mess with us. We can get a hundred thousand people to do whatever we tell them to do.' People might take a lot of pride in the display, but in a way it feels like it's also a warning."

Mia tried to resist getting swept away by the show. She

wanted to stay in the conversation with Daniel, watching the performance but at the same time telling the truth about it. Usually, it was following instructions that made her feel safe. But breaking the rules here, talking about things that the North Korean government didn't want them to talk about, felt better than safe. It felt *right*.

"Can I ask you something?" Mia whispered during a lull in the loud music. Daniel nodded, leaning closer to hear. "About that meeting this afternoon, the ministry guys coming to see Dad? Who were they?"

"Well, that's funny. They introduced themselves as being from the Ministry of Agriculture. But I think that was a cover; based on how they were dressed and how they carried themselves, I'm guessing that they were actually from the Ministry of People's Security. That's basically the police here — regular police, not the secret police. They like to keep a low profile because they run some of the labor camps, the ones for people accused of crimes like theft and smuggling. People get nervous when they show up. But they're also in charge of the state food distribution system, so that's why they'd be aware of your dad's work."

Mia frowned, trying to puzzle it out. "But why would they thank Dad publicly for his work when he's providing aid from other countries? Isn't the whole *ju-che* idea that the North Koreans are doing everything all by themselves — growing all their own food, taking care of themselves? Wouldn't they want to kind of cover up the thing about people starving?"

"It might look like it from the outside, but the North Korean government is not all one, monolithic entity." Daniel was speaking directly into her ear. "There are actually quite a few competing factions within the government. Power struggles are going on all the time. This leader or ministry is in favor, this one's out. For instance, it seems as if the Ministry of People's Security, MPS" — he gestured with his left hand — "is almost always in conflict with the State Security Department, the secret police." He gestured with his right hand. "The SSD runs the worst camps, the ones for political prisoners that no one escapes from. They tend to be a lot more paranoid, always looking for threats to the state.

"But back to your question. No one wants to admit it, but everyone recognizes that the food distribution system doesn't work anymore. They know it only feeds a tiny percentage of the country. So foreign aid and the independent markets are the alternatives to another mass famine. In our experience, MPS people tend to be more pragmatic. They're willing to see what's actually helping — food aid from other countries. But they can't be up front about supporting it, or they risk displeasing other parts of the government. That could be another reason why they pretended to be from the Ministry of Agriculture. Maybe it's another form of ju-che: doing whatever it takes to survive."

Thousands of children were on the floor now, dressed in bright pastel gymnastic suits, their legs bare, prancing and somersaulting and doing back bends, the movements creating colorful designs against the green ground. Behind the children, the constantly moving backdrop of the card pictures, in perfect time with the blaring music and commentary, told the story of the Democratic People's Republic of Korea in ten glorious scenes. At the completion of each section, the mass of performers on the floor all jumped up and down, making brilliantly colored patterns undulating across the stadium. There was so much going on that Mia didn't know what to watch; no matter where she looked, she missed something. The entire thing was the most astonishing display she had ever seen.

She sat back and closed her eyes, her mind overwhelmed by a barrage of conflicting thoughts and impressions. The sense of connection with Daniel, sharing things that mattered. The mention of people in prison camps and people starving. The eye-popping spectacle of the performance. The idea that something awful might happen to one of these children if they missed a beat.

Everything seemed, impossibly all at once, so beautiful and so terrible.

YOO KYUNG-AE

✪ ✪ ✪

Kyung-ae would not, could not, make a mistake. She fixed her eyes on the conductor, afraid to blink lest she miss his flag signal and fail to flip the card at the exact right second.

This was the moment for which they had trained the whole year long, standing on the bare athletic field in the chill damp of autumn, the frigid cold of all but the worst days of winter, the icy rain of early spring, the hot summer sun. During daily gymnastics classes, and on the weekends. Hour after hour after hour. Drilling, until the flick of her wrist and the snap of the card into place was an involuntary response. She and all her schoolmates became one machine, at the command of the conductor, in perfect service to the Grand Marshall.

Now they were here in the stadium, in actual performance, standing in rows from the floor to the top of the bleachers, watched by tens of thousands of people. The Grand Marshall himself might come to one of these performances! Her terror at making a slip had mushroomed beyond anything she'd felt in rehearsal. A mistake here, now, in front of the crowds and the Party officials, could be catastrophic. She had hardly slept the night before, worrying about it. She'd heard rumors of one boy who had dropped his card book during a performance, creating a hole in the image of the Great Leader's smiling face. His entire family had been interrogated and had to attend weeks of self-criticism sessions.

The thought made her flinch, hands trembling as she held the cards. *Steady.* She inhaled fiercely through her nostrils, reestablishing her stance and aligning the edges of her book with those of the student on either side of her. *Flip. Flip. Flip.*

As she'd eaten breakfast at dawn that morning, her mother had watched, face drawn, the expression habitual since the day her father had come home early from work to report that the factory was closing. Her mother was the one who went to work now, selling noodles from a street stall from early morning until after dark.

"Remember not to drink too much," her mother had said, reaching out to straighten the red scarf around her daughter's neck. "And eat all your dinner so you have energy to perform well." Deep lines were carved across her forehead and on either side of her down-turned mouth.

But the final rehearsal had gone on so long that their break before the performance was cut short. There'd only been time to swallow a few bites of her dinner.

Flip. Flip. Flip. The music surrounded them, lights flashed and poured like liquid color, and the announcer's voice boomed across the stadium. She could sense the movement of thousands of dancers and acrobats on the floor below the bleachers, but she knew not to let her eyes be pulled by the spectacle. Focus on the conductor's flags. *Flip. Flip. Flip.*

She grew more and more tired but forced herself to concentrate, to think only of the conductor and the cards. She listened to the story the announcer told, the birth of the Great Leader, like the rising sun; his military prowess, winning battles against all odds to drive the foreign invaders from the homeland; and how he founded the greatest, most blessed country on earth. *Flip. Flip. Flip.*

Then her favorite part, the magical birth of the Dear Leader, in a cabin at the foot of Mount Paektu. The birds singing the glorious news, the double rainbow sparkling in the sky above, and at night, the brand-new star in the heavens. The music swelled to a crescendo.

"Mansei! Mansei!" The crowd roared their devotion.

The finale began. Fireworks exploded overhead. Acrobats flew through the air high above the stadium, then plummeted toward the ground to land in nets. On the floor, hundreds of performers formed the shape of the Korean peninsula, symbolizing the reunion between North and South. Eighty thousand more performers surrounded them. An enormous globe, like a giant turquoise beach ball, rose over the sea of people. The stadium erupted in thunderous applause. Adrenaline rushed through her body like electricity, connecting her to everyone in the stadium, one drop in a great tide of sound and light and movement. She thought her heart might burst with the majesty of it all.

As the lights came up, signaling the end of the performance, the students stood as a group, ready to file line by line out of the bleachers. It all crashed over her then, the tension of her empty belly and shallow breath, her exhaustion and terror and exhilaration. She slumped back onto the bench, then collapsed in a faint. Her card book slipped from her hands to the floor.

CHAPTER 4

OCTOBER 2

Mia woke early. 5:24 a.m. At least she'd made it till actual morning and Dad hadn't woken her with more spy games.

Only four more days left in North Korea. She could get through this.

After showering, she pulled on black jeans and a clean long-sleeved T-shirt and dried her hair. She tugged on the chain around her neck to make sure her locket was in place. Still not even 6:00. Breakfast wasn't until 7:00.

She pulled her daypack onto the bed, unzipped it, and surveyed the items: Water bottle. Guidebook. Korean-English/English-Korean dictionary. She probed deeper in the pack, unzipped a couple of pockets. Her useless phone. Her journal and colored pens. Her wallet. Snacks and two packs of gum she'd bought in Beijing.

The process reminded her of her favorite book from when she was two or three. It had brightly colored cloth pages, each with something to manipulate: buttons, zippers, Velcro tabs, buckles, pockets. According to Mom, Mia had made the book her bedtime ritual for most of a year, paging through it to unfasten and refasten every single thing until it was in order, where it belonged. She got that same sense of security from checking the contents of her backpack. Whatever happened, she'd have what she needed. She grabbed her blue nylon jacket from the chair and folded it on top.

Ready to go, and still a big chunk of time to kill. She'd read the guidebook cover-to-cover, and anyway, North Korea was the last thing she wanted to focus on right now. She'd foolishly read all six of the books she'd brought with her in Beijing while Dad and Simon were sleeping off jet lag. She didn't have a North Korean SIM card, so her phone didn't work here. She had her pens and journal, but she was all caught up in her account of the trip so far, and it was too early for her brain to want to do any more writing or even doodling.

Most of all, she wished she were back in her own room, on her laptop, immersed in her favorite video game, *Quest*. She always played the Scout, moving through the virtual deep, dark woods. Gathering food and tools and treasures. Discovering dangers to avoid. Finding the way for her team. Every time she shut the game down and reentered "reality," she felt as if she was coming back from another world, a very real one, and one that she often preferred to her actual life. If only she could play it now for an hour or two.

The gift box from the ministry sat on the bedside table. Mr. Lee had told her to wait and open it when she got back to the States, because of customs or something. Everything in North Korea seemed to be mysterious or forbidden. Or both.

She couldn't see any harm in taking off the wrapping paper. Dad hadn't gotten into trouble for sneaking out of the hotel in the night — at least not yet — so she was pretty sure there weren't any video cameras in the rooms. Even if someone was watching, it couldn't be that big a deal to unwrap a package.

Mia reached for the box, scooted back onto her pillow, crossed her legs, and placed it in front of her on the bed. She carefully peeled off the strips of tape without tearing the paper. She realized she was holding her breath, like a spy in a TV show stealing secrets or defusing a bomb.

The paper parted to reveal a cardboard box. Mia lifted the lid. Inside was another box, this one made of wood. She slipped it out with two hands, set it down on the bedspread, and studied it. The box was carved to look like a traditional Korean farmhouse, set on a thick platform about eight or ten inches square. The heavy tile roof was decorated with leaves and spherical fruit, some kind of pumpkin or gourd. She'd seen houses with vines of squash growing on roofs like that, in the ink paintings of the printed calendars Mom brought home from the Korean grocery store in Stamford. In fact, the whole box looked like one of those scenes, with an old farmer and his wife seated on the veranda. She smiled, charmed.

She lifted the roof lid, expecting it to be empty. But inside was a third box. This gift was like a set of nesting dolls, one thing after another to discover. The box had a picture of a phone. *A North Korean cell phone? Cool!* She knew she couldn't use it here; the tour guides in Beijing had explained that North Korean phones were only for citizens. But as much as she loved the wooden box, a phone would be a much more awesome souvenir to show her friends.

She lifted it out. One of the box tabs wasn't glued down all the way, which seemed like an invitation to open it. If she was careful, she could close it to look exactly as it had when it was given to her.

The phone inside looked like a real smartphone. To her surprise, when she pressed the power button, it turned on, already charged. That was weird. The people who gave them the phone knew they couldn't use it here. The screen lit, and there were the familiar icons in rows, over a photograph of a snow-covered mountain with a crater. This would definitely be something cool to show Jess and Alicia. Even the boys in her class, the ones who didn't seem to know she existed, might take notice.

She swished the screen with her fingers. Hey, it even came with some games — *Angry Birds! Yes!* It was a version she'd never played, with the title in *han-gul*.

She catapulted cackling birds into towers of pigs until 6:48. Finally, she could go downstairs.

Mia turned off the phone and reached for the boxes and wrapping paper. But wait. If she kept the phone with her, she could keep playing the game, as long as she was careful the guides didn't see her. She knew all the games on her own phone inside out, but everything on this one was new. If she was going to accept a present from North Korean officials, she might as well enjoy it. If the worst happened and she got caught, she could just pretend she hadn't understood Mr. Lee's instructions. She slid the phone into an inside pocket and hoisted her backpack.

As she started down the hall, the door of the next room opened and Simon stepped out.

"Squeak! You won't believe what I've got!" His face was open, excited, the first time she had seen him looking anything other than sullen since they left home. And he was even using her nickname, the one he'd given her because she'd been so easy to scare as a little child.

"What?"

Simon swiveled, showing his back. She looked him up and down, puzzled. "Your backpack?"

"On the left side. Check it out."

Pinned to a side pocket was a small badge shaped like a waving flag, with a smiling image of Kim Il-sung, the Great Leader.

"Simon!"

"Pretty cool, huh?" He turned around to face her.

"No! Not cool at all! Foreigners can't wear those!" Mia glanced both ways down the corridor to make sure no one was near. "Don't you remember? The tour people in Beijing said so! Where did you get it?"

"Don't worry, it's a fake. I went down to the bar last night, had to do something to get out of that room." The bar? Her brother was sixteen. Where had Dad been? Probably sleeping, after his middle-of-the-night wanderings the night before. "There was this other tour group there, a bunch of young guys from Australia and New Zealand and Malaysia or somewhere. They even bought me a beer!"

Mia started to shake her head.

"Oh, stop. It was nothing. They just bought a whole tray of bottles and slipped me one. Nobody saw. First time anything decent has happened since we left. Anyway, this one guy, from New Zealand, he was passing around this plastic bag and everybody was taking one — it gets to me and I see it's these pins! The guy is explaining to me how their tour came in by train from that Chinese city across the bridge —"

"Dandong?"

"Sure, maybe. Anyway, they were walking around the waterfront and there's a guy with a cart selling the pins — well, counterfeit versions, but it looks pretty authentic, doesn't it?"

"But you can't walk around with it pinned on your pack! Only North Koreans are allowed to wear them! You can't just treat it like a souvenir. It could even be dangerous."

"Oh, Squeak, don't be such a —"

"Simon. Really. I've read the guidebook. It's serious." Mia tried to sound authoritative, but mostly she was just scared. She knew Simon wanted to break the rules, with a pin he wasn't supposed to have displayed in an unsanctioned way. But this wasn't like wearing a T-shirt with an upside-down Stars and Stripes, and North Korea wasn't a democracy with protected speech for stupid Americans. He had to listen to her. "I know you'd be happy if we got kicked out or something, but something much worse could happen. To us. To the guides. To *Dad*. Remember that American college student who got sentenced to hard labor just for trying to steal a propaganda poster? You can't do stuff like that here. Really. Take it off. Put it in your pocket."

Simon scowled at her, but to her surprise and relief, he slipped his backpack off, unclasped the badge, and put it into an inside pocket. As he stretched one arm through the pack strap, his sleeve slid up, revealing a braided black cord around his wrist. Randi had made that. And he was still wearing it.

He stalked off toward the elevator before she could even thank him for listening. Mia blew out a sigh.

* * *

The tour bus halted in the middle of the street. Mia sat up and peered over the seats. Bright sun broke through thick clouds, spotlighting a blue uniform. A traffic lady, standing in a white circle in the center of the crossroads. There seemed to be one of them at every major intersection. Maybe in North Korea people were more available than electrical power.

At her signal, the bus began to rumble forward. Mia watched out the window as they passed. Like all the other traffic ladies she had seen, this woman was very pretty, neatly dressed in a military-style cap, jacket, and skirt, with white ankle socks and black shoes. In each hand she held red-and-white-striped sticks to wave at the vehicles. Arms up, arms out, arms down. Pivoting to the left, pivoting to the right, like a robot. Though there wasn't that much traffic, she performed her routine with total seriousness.

Mia sat back against her seat. The traffic lady looked like a model citizen: Following the rules. Playing it safe. Doing the right thing. But to Mia it seemed that in North Korea it wasn't possible to do all three. Not all at the same time. If she followed the rules, she might be safe, but it meant she was cooperating with a government that starved its people.

Last night Daniel had talked about factions and defectors and resistance to the North Korean government. All people who were breaking the rules. People Daniel seemed to support. Simon was doing everything he could to not follow the rules — disrespectful behavior, underage drinking, counterfeit pins — without actually getting caught.

She turned to look at Dad next to her, who was leaning forward, talking to the Blakes. When she'd seen him sneaking down the hallway two nights ago, it certainly didn't look as if he had been following the rules. Was he doing the right thing? If so, what was that? She still didn't have a clue. She hadn't had a single moment alone with him, and even if she had, she still wasn't sure she should let him know what she'd seen.

She had the smartphone in her backpack. Against instructions, she'd opened it and used it. She shivered, not knowing if she was scared or excited. She scooted a little closer toward Dad's comforting bulk and pulled out her guidebook.

"This afternoon we will tour Mangyongdae, the birthplace of the Eternal Sun, President Kim Il-sung," Miss Cho announced over the bus microphone. "There you may acquire a good knowledge of the glorious revolutionary history and ardent patriotism of the Great Leader, who was born into a revolutionary family and cultivated his great revolutionary will for the country and the people." Miss Cho pronounced every word very carefully, but it didn't sound as if she understood any of the phrases she'd memorized. "The endless stream of visitors worship the place as a sanctuary of the Sun."

In other words, *Here's where the Big Guy was born.* Mia bit her lip to hide a smile and looked past Dad toward Simon across the aisle, but he was focused on the *Sports Illustrated* that he'd pulled out of his backpack. She glanced back at Daniel, in the aisle seat behind Simon, exchanging a look of amusement with him, just in the eyes. A tiny act of resistance.

"Mangyongdae, or a place with ten thousand views, is situated a little over ten kilometers southwest of downtown Pyongyang," Miss Cho was saying. Dad leaned back in his seat. Mia touched her finger to their destination on the map in her lap.

"Oh, I get it," she told Dad. "*Man.* Ten thousand. Like *man-sei*, ten thousand years."

"They should make you the guide," Dad said. "So, ten kilometers, how many miles is that?"

Mia calculated. "A kilometer is five-eighths of a mile?"

He nodded. "So eight kilometers is five miles. . . . Then ten kilometers is . . . a little over six miles."

He grinned and gave her a thumbs-up.

"It was so named," Miss Cho was saying, "because its verdant Mangyong Hill, overhanging the famous Taedong River, affords a breathtaking panorama of ten thousand views."

The bus pulled into a huge, nearly empty parking lot.

"This traditional scenic wonder leaped to potentially foremost significance in the national consciousness on April fifteenth, 1912, the Day of the Sun, when the Eternal President Kim Il-sung was born at a plain thatched-roof cottage here, against a backdrop of Korea's national disaster in the colonial thrall of Japan." Miss Cho ducked her head at them in a bow as the bus shuddered to a stop.

The guides herded them down broad walkways bordered by trees, stopping at a cluster of small farmhouses that reminded Mia of the wooden box. The "birthplace of the Eternal Sun, President Kim Il-sung" looked brand-new. Throughout the park, plaques and painted wooden billboards described significant events in the Great Leader's life. It was the first spot on their tour that didn't include some gargantuan monument, although there were some portraits of the leaders. Those guys were everywhere.

The group followed the guides on a path through a wooded area, up to a rise where the ground opened, revealing a pavilion set on a cliff over the river. Far below, the calm water was a bright mirror under the afternoon sun. In the distance, the skyline of the southern section of

Pyongyang shimmered against the sky. Here was the "breathtaking panorama of ten thousand views."

"You see, so beautiful." Mr. Lee came up beside Mia, his eyes crinkling behind his glasses. "Many artists, many poets, they receive inspiration from this place. It is very dear to Korean people from olden times." He sounded like he was just talking, not reciting a rote speech learned for the tour.

"Do you come here with your family? With your daughter?" she asked.

His smile brightened. "Oh yes! This is favorite spot for picnic. My daughter likes to draw" — he pantomimed drawing on a paper — "beautiful landscape here. Also, I came here as young boy, with my father." He looked happy, remembering.

"I have a question for you," he said, tipping his head toward her.

"Okay."

"What did the little mountain say to the big mountain?" Mr. Lee asked.

"Uh . . ." She just looked at him, baffled.

" 'Hello, Cliff!' " He pronounced the *f* more like a *p*, but Mia caught his meaning. She giggled, mostly with surprise that Mr. Lee was telling her a joke. He grinned. "A British man told me this joke."

She nodded. North Korea just kept catching her off guard.

Miss Cho was shepherding the group from the pavilion to a nearby boulder with a plaque. She told them it commemorated an incident when the young Kim Il-sung stood up to a bully.

Mia heard chattering and turned to see a group of

students strolling up the path, all in uniforms of navy skirts or pants, white shirts, and red scarves. They looked about her age. Their eyes were on the light-haired, round-eyed foreigners. As if the Americans, not the boulder, were the tourist attraction.

"*An-nyung . . . ha-ship-ni-ka?*" Mrs. Blake tried out a greeting from her Korean phrasebook in her American accent, each syllable separate and clunky. The students dissolved in laughter, but Mrs. Blake just beamed.

"We speak English," one of the girls announced.

"What is your name?" the students called out. "How old are you?" "I am glad to meet you!" Though each textbook phrase made them giggle, they all seemed eager to practice.

"May we take photographs with them?" Mrs. Blake asked Mr. Kim.

The students took charge, pointing out the most scenic backgrounds, directing the shots. Mia stood, wrapped in her invisibility cloak, scanning the faces of the kids. They looked healthy and exuberant, with glossy hair and bright eyes. These students were certainly getting enough to eat. She studied the different shapes of their eyes, their hairlines, the profiles of their noses and chins. She wondered if any of them had the same family name — Han — as her birth relatives. As *her*.

All three guides seemed truly relaxed, joking with the students and the tour group members. Even stern Mr. Kim allowed them to wander about the pavilion, for once not hurrying them back to the bus. Dad was right where Mia could keep an eye on him. Simon was focused on taking pictures with his phone instead of on complaining. Mia let out a long breath. For the moment, they were all just a bunch of people, enjoying the scenery together.

She decided to head back to the bus so she could take her time. As she started down the path, she found Daniel next to her.

"So, Mia Andrews, do you have a Korean name?" he asked.

She nodded. "Han Sung-mi," she said, phrasing it the Korean way, with the family name before the given name.

"So that's where the Mia comes from?"

"Yeah. And my parents kept Han for my middle name." She focused on keeping up with Daniel's long strides. "At Korean school they call me Sung-mi. It means 'Success and Beauty,' something like that."

Daniel smiled. "You could choose another meaning for Sung-mi."

"Another meaning?"

"You know how traditional Korean names are based on Chinese characters?"

She nodded.

"Chinese is tonal," Daniel said, "but Korean isn't. Several different Chinese characters can have the same sound in Korean, but each one has a different meaning. *Sung*, like they told you, can be 'success' or 'achievement,' but it can also mean 'holy.'"

She wrinkled her nose. "That's worse than 'success.'"

"Well, there's a third character that's pronounced *sung*. That one means 'star.'"

"So . . . my name could be, like . . . 'Star and Beauty'?"

Daniel nodded. "Star of Beauty, Beautiful Star."

"Beautiful Star. I like that." Her cheeks got warm. Weird to be calling herself beautiful to Daniel.

"Got a piece of paper? I'll write the characters for you."

She pulled out her journal and handed it to Daniel. He

wrote the Chinese characters. Then the Korean letters. Then English: *Beautiful Star.*

"Here's what I do with two names," he said, extracting a white business card from his wallet and flipping it to one side, then the other. "Daniel Moon on one side. Moon Dong-won, in Korean and Chinese, on the other."

Mia examined the card. Name, contact e-mail, phone numbers. But no job title. He was Korean American, he spoke Korean, he had information from North Korean defectors. Daniel was a mystery. She slipped the card into her jeans pocket as they started down the path again.

She thought about the conversation they'd just had. She vaguely remembered the lesson in Korean school about the same Korean sounds having different Chinese sounds and meanings. But the problem with Korean school was that although she'd attended for six years, she'd never gotten very far. The hour she spent there was like visiting a foreign country, completely set apart from the rest of her life. All the other kids could practice all week with their parents, but there was no one at home who could help Mia absorb what she learned. Much of the time in class she just felt lost. And as soon as she got into the car for the long drive back, everything she'd been taught seemed to fly out of her head.

"Do you . . . do you ever feel . . . like you don't really fit either one of your names?" Mia asked. "Like 'Mia Andrews.' That's some all-American girl. Not really me. But I'm certainly not a Korean girl named Han Sung-mi. So . . . it's sort of like I'm not . . . either." She fixed her eyes on the ground as her cheeks got warm again.

"Yeah, I know that feeling." His voice had that turned-inside sound. "A sense of not really belonging in either group, being caught between. But you know, 'in between' — that's a place to belong too." She snuck a glance at him. He was also looking down at the ground, thoughtful. "You can look at both sides and choose the parts you want. Claim your own name: Daniel Moon, American and Korean. Or choose your name's own meaning: Sung-mi. Beautiful Star."

Mia felt suddenly exposed, as if the warmth of Daniel's attention had softened a hard scab, revealing something tender beneath. They were at the bottom of the hill, far ahead of the rest of the tour group. She couldn't think of anything to say to keep the conversation going.

She gestured across the parking lot. "Uh, I'm gonna use the facilities."

When she came out, Daniel wasn't in sight. Only a few members of the group had gathered in the parking lot. The guides would still have to round everyone up, herd them to the restrooms, then back to the bus. She headed for a shady bench tucked under a group of low trees. The guides would be able to see that she hadn't wandered off, but not that she was playing video games on a forbidden phone.

Sound off. Birds went flying through the air. Pigs tumbled. Mia glanced up to make sure nobody was watching. Some of the tour group members were just starting across the parking lot toward the restrooms.

When she looked down, the screen had changed. The colorful cartoon characters were gone.

A photograph, in black-and-white. A man, blindfolded. Tied to a post.

Mia sucked in her breath. Where had this come from? She zipped her finger across the screen. Another photo. The same man, still tied to the post, head slumped forward. Dark stains dotted his chest.

The two photos formed a terrible Before and After.

She wiped the screen, trying to erase the image. But it just brought up more photos. Other people.

A scrawny young boy, pushing a wagon heaped with coal. Barefoot.

A man digging with a shovel, his arms and legs nothing but skin-covered bones, his shirt open to reveal a skeletal chest.

A woman whose legs ended at her knees, leaning over a pile of corncobs, a tiny child tied to to her back.

A naked doll in the mud. No, a *baby*. Dead.

Mia closed the game and stared at the home screen, one hand clamped over her mouth.

CHAPTER 5

Simon came walking around the side of the bus. Mia leaped
to her feet, then stopped. She returned the phone to her
backpack pocket and left her pack on the bench. She didn't
want anyone near it. Crossing the parking lot toward the
bus, she forced herself not to run.

"I need you to see something." She lowered her voice
for only Simon to hear. She could barely get the words
out. "Over there." She gestured toward the grove of
trees.

"What is it, Squeak?" He looked annoyed.

"I can't — just *come*." He started to protest. She turned
to him. He caught her expression, let out a sigh, and followed her.

She pulled out her guidebook first. "Hold this and pretend we're looking at it," she said. "Turn around so no one
can see." He frowned. "Simon, please!"

Back at the bus, none of the guides was in sight and no
one was looking their way. Mia pulled out the phone, feeling as if she was holding a ticking bomb, touched the game
icon, and handed the phone to Simon.

"What . . . the . . . ?!" His eyes widened and his forehead

twisted. Then his mouth dropped open. His fingers jabbed at the screen. "Mia, what the hell —" He sounded furious.

"I don't know, I don't know. It was in the gift they gave us yesterday. I opened it this morning and there was a wooden box, and it had this phone inside it! I knew I couldn't use it here, but I tried turning it on and it was already charged. And it had *Angry Birds* on it. I was just playing a game and" — she gulped a breath — "these popped up." Her voice was ragged, near tears.

Someone called out. They both flinched, their heads snapping toward the sound. Some of the tour group members were moving across the parking lot to the bus.

"We gotta get someplace safer," Simon said, eyes scanning. "Behind the restrooms." He folded the guidebook around the phone and started off. Mia grabbed her pack and followed him.

As they crossed the pavement, Mia looked for Dad. There he was, over by the bus, talking to Mr. Kim. Or rather, Mr. Kim was talking to him, looking agitated. They couldn't risk calling to him while the guides were around.

The area behind the restrooms was completely out of sight from where the bus was parked. They'd be hidden, at least for a few minutes. Simon handed the guidebook back to her and squatted against the wall, his finger moving across the screen of the phone. Mia glanced down as she tucked the guidebook into her pack, squinting her eyes as if to protect herself from what she'd see. There were more photos. Ragged people standing in long lines, their faces hollowed like Holocaust survivors. Men staggering through the rain, bent under huge loads. Another dead baby. Mia heard herself whimper.

"These . . . are *messed up!*" Simon sounded stunned. "It looks like the kind of things that Dad says happen in the prison camps. But I never heard of there being any *photographs* from the camps. . . ."

"How did they get in the phone?" Her voice sounded high and scared, like a little girl's.

"Somebody put them there. It had to be on purpose." Simon slumped back against the wall as if exhausted. "So we have a major problem."

"Do they . . . do the North Koreans know . . . about the phone? That the photos are on it?"

"Well, someone knows, whoever put them on the phone knows. But we have no idea who that might be." Simon ran one hand through his hair. Took a breath. He gestured with the phone. "If these are actual photos of actual starvation and torture and executions in actual prison camps — that according to the North Korean government don't exist — then these images are *toxic*."

Mia gulped. "Dad talked about that guy who they said had a CD with photos of starving children, remember? He got sentenced to hard labor."

"If we get caught with these images . . ." The knowledge was breaking across Simon's face, changing his expression. "If we get caught with these, there's no way we're getting out of this country."

A violent shiver went through Mia's body. It felt as if everything was hurtling around her, like she was a balloon full of air that someone had just untied. This is what came of breaking the rules. She never should have opened the phone.

"But — but can't we just throw the phone away? Like bury it right here —"

Simon frowned, concentrating and talking fast. "If we could hide it so that none of the wrong people would find it, but where the right people could come back for it . . . Whatever we do, we have to do it immediately. They'll be looking for us soon."

Mia pressed her fist to her mouth.

Simon slipped around the side of the building and leaned to peer around the corner. His body tensed. Mia ran to look over his shoulder.

Dad and Mr. Kim stood midway across the parking lot, Mr. Lee and Miss Cho just behind them. Dad was leaning toward Mr. Kim, gesturing fiercely with his hands. Back at the bus, the entire tour group — including Daniel — stood in a cluster, watching.

"Dad's upset," Mia said. Their father never got angry.

A black car careened into the far end of the lot. It sped toward the group in the center, screeching to a halt, the doors flying open. Four soldiers spilled out and sprinted toward Dad and the guides.

The soldiers took hold of Dad's arms and began to walk him back toward the black car.

"Simon!" Mia grabbed his shoulder.

"They're *taking* him," Simon said, his voice cracking.

The knot of men, with Dad in the center, paused as they neared the bus. Daniel stepped forward. He spoke, then nodded at something Dad said. The soldiers continued their march, pulling Dad with them.

At the car, they pushed Dad into the backseat, one of the soldiers holding his head down, just like on TV cop shows. The doors closed. The black car circled forward and swept out of the parking lot.

Mia and Simon turned to look at each other. Simon's eyes were wide, his mouth open.

"What the — ?" He shook his head. "What was *that*?"

Mia pressed her clenched fists against her cheeks. They were in North Korea and soldiers had just taken Dad away.

"We definitely can't go back to the group, not now." Simon swiveled in his crouched position, looking behind them. "We've got to get out of here."

Mia stared at him. "Get out of here? But Dad —"

His head swung back. "Squeak, if we don't get away, they'll arrest us too."

"But we have to help Dad!" She had to work to keep her voice steady. "If we give them the phone, they'll let him go."

"Mia, think! If we give them this phone, *the photos will be used as evidence against Dad.* Maybe that's even why someone gave the phone to us, so Dad would get caught with the photos!" His voice cracked again. He was scared. Simon was *scared*.

Mia shook her head, forced the panic down. "We can dig a hole, bury the phone, then go back to the bus."

Simon stood and stepped toward her. "Don't be an idiot. They'll be looking for us any second. We can't hide the phone here; they'll be sure to find it. Someone knows we have the phone with those photos on it. Getting found with it would be the worst thing that could happen to Dad." He was talking fast. "And we can't go back. They just took Dad away. You've heard his stories: When they arrest people, they take their relatives too, send whole families to prison camps. When they execute people, they kill everyone, down to their grandchildren!"

Mia inhaled fast through her nose, eyes wide. Dad —

Simon tipped his head back and huffed out. "Okay, they don't kill Americans. But we could be held for ages." He glanced back toward the bus. "We have to go now. We've got to get behind that line of trees before anybody finds us." He pointed behind them. The trees looked impossibly far away.

Mia grabbed Simon's arm to keep him from moving. "Simon! *We can't run away in North Korea!* There's no way to hide here. Everyone will report us! And we'll only get Dad in worse trouble!"

He shrugged her off. "Listen! I don't have time to argue with you! We've got to get these pictures out of here now, to protect Dad. If we get away, maybe there'll be a way to hide the phone." He gestured toward the trees again. "You go back if you want, but I'm taking the phone that way."

Mia looked back at the bus. She couldn't see Daniel. A wave of nausea flooded her gut. She turned around, and Simon was no longer behind her. He had already started off, crawling low across the ground.

She could follow or be left behind.

Feeling as if she was being ripped in two, Mia dropped to her belly in the dry grass. Using her elbows and knees to propel herself, she slithered forward. The shoulder straps of her backpack snagged between her chest and the ground. She had to keep stopping to pull them free. She kept repeating Simon's phrase in her mind. *To protect Dad.*

She raised her head to see Simon disappearing behind the trees. She was alone, out in the open. The soldiers might come back. They could shoot her. Another wave of nausea and panic hit. She started forward again.

Finally, she was slinking between the trees and collapsing on the ground. She propped herself up against a tree trunk with her head back. Her breath came in gasps, as if she'd run for miles.

Simon was looking out through the trees on the far side of the grove. He was back before she'd caught her breath. "I think we can get down to the street from here. There are stairs. I don't think they can be seen from the parking lot."

Mia just stared at him, too winded to speak.

"C'mon, hurry."

"I can't," she moaned.

"No choice, Squeak. Unless you want to get arrested. This place will be crawling with soldiers any minute."

Every part of her protesting, she dragged herself to her feet.

No one was in sight as they crossed the lawn. "We have to look normal now," Simon said, "not attract suspicion."

Right. Two young Americans alone in the middle of North Korea. They might as well have had flashing neon arrows pointing at them.

They started down the wide stone steps.

At that moment, from behind them, someone spoke. Mia froze and felt Simon stiffen beside her. They were caught, not even halfway down the stairs.

Then, through the haze of her terror, she noticed the tone of the voice. An ordinary conversation. No one yelling a Korean version of "Halt, or I'll shoot!"

Mia stole a glance back over her shoulder. A couple — a man in a dark suit and a woman in a yellow *han-bok* — was heading down toward the landing on which she and Simon had paused.

"Simon?" Mia's voice wavered.

"Just look out at the city. Look like tourists."

Trees. Buildings. Blue sky. She tried to focus her attention, to look like she was just gazing at the panorama below them.

The couple's voices came closer. The voices stopped. Mia's stomach fluttered. *Don't look at them.*

"What a nice view." Simon made words, ordinary words, come out of his mouth. He had one arm up, pointing. "This is a beautiful area, isn't it?"

The couple passed them, heads craning back for one last glimpse . . . of Simon. The blond foreigner. They turned away quickly, good DPRK citizens with no interest in imperialist foreigners.

They never even glanced at Mia.

When the couple was out of earshot, she let her breath whoosh out. Simon was already several stairs below her. Each step felt as if she was wrestling against a force field. Leaving Dad, leaving Daniel, leaving the tour group — even leaving the guides — seemed like the worst choice in the world.

Except that Simon's terrible logic was convincing: It was their only choice.

CHUNG MIN-HO

✦ ✦ ✦

"I got a new one — a DVD!" Yoo-jin whispered as he passed Min-ho in the square that morning, moving to find their places in the neat lines of students. "After school!"

Excitement straightened Min-ho's back, adding an extra smartness to his step as they began the march to school. "Hold the red flag high, and solemnly vow beneath it!" he sang with gusto, conscious of gracing the passersby with his voice. Everyone always said his tone was beautiful, but he also took genuine pleasure in singing. It made him feel powerful and good and fortunate.

After school! Min-ho carried the promise all day, like a hidden sweet in his pocket. He stood even taller when called upon, reciting the answers in a clear, strong voice and seeing the approval in his teachers' eyes. Min-ho always imagined that the Great Leader

"No one will be home," Yoo-jin assured him. "But even if my father discovered us watching, he would not mind. He knows I am strong, and that it is only entertainment."

"But Soo-im's family . . ." Jae-hyun did not finish the sentence. Such things were not voiced openly, though everyone knew: Soo-im's family had been sent away for reeducation after her brother was caught with American DVDs.

"My father says the laws are essential for those in the lower ranks," Min-ho said. "They are already weak, and the foreign influence might corrupt them. But for the Loyal, it is no problem."

"It could be useful to learn about these things," round-faced Dong-nam added, "like . . . like a vaccination that . . . that prevents us from catching the disease of capitalism!"

Yoo-jin nodded. "In order to maintain our status as the most powerful country in the world, we must be familiar with how things are done elsewhere. That way we will be armed and not become prey to their corrupt ways." He sounded like one of their Juche Ethics instructors. No one said what everyone had heard, that even the Grand Marshall had a taste for foreign films and goods.

Entering the glittering lobby of Yoo-jin's apartment building, the boys fell silent, holding their breath with the daring of what they were about to do. As the elevator rushed to the eighteenth floor, they kept their eyes forward, just a group of students in their red scarves, white shirts, and blue pants, nothing on their minds but homework. It wasn't until they were inside the spacious apartment, the heavy door safely locked behind them, that their suppressed energy burst out.

"Where is it?"

"Let's see it, let's see it!"

"Yoo-jin! Put it on!"

"Don't you want a snack?" he teased, moving toward the kitchen. "There's fresh rice cakes. Belgian chocolate. Even American candies!"

The other three grabbed him and pulled him toward his bedroom, laughing. "Now!"

Yoo-jin slid open a desk drawer and extracted a slim DVD case from beneath a stack of notebooks. He held it aloft, like a trophy. "Look at this!"

"Big Bang?! You got Big Bang!"

"I can't believe it! That song just came out!"

"This is the best! Put it on! Put it on!"

On the TV screen, lights flashed, the crowd of fans screamed, drums and synthesizer pulsed, and there they were, all dressed in black, the five members of one of the South Korean pop world's most sensational bands. Their eyes riveted to the image, the boys crowded close, swaying and dancing and singing along,

CHAPTER 6

"We need wheels." Narrowing his eyes, Simon scanned the broad street in each direction. "Something to get us out of here fast, back to the city but in the opposite direction from the hotel."

Mia grabbed the shoulder straps of her backpack with both hands and hung on. She closed her eyes, studying the map from her guidebook in her mind.

"A bus. Or a streetcar. That way." She pointed left, her raised hand shaking.

Simon looked, then turned his head the other way, calculating his own answer. He pointed with his chin.

"So we need to cross to the other side." He started for the street.

Mia grabbed his arm and yanked him back. "The underpass." She gestured down the sidewalk. "North Koreans would never jaywalk. The traffic ladies, remember?"

Simon frowned but fell in step beside her. In the distance, two schoolgirls in their navy uniforms approached, carrying book satchels. Beyond them were several men in dark clothes and a middle-aged woman in a bright green blouse. Any one of them could turn her and Simon in.

Mia straightened her back, keeping her eyes focused forward. *Nothing to see here.* The men and the woman passed by on the sidewalk. But as Mia and Simon turned down the steps toward the underpass, the schoolgirls fell in beside them. Giggling behind their hands, the girls stared at Simon. Mia held her breath and lifted her chin, trying to look like someone who belonged here. She hoped the students didn't have cell phones.

They came out of the dark tunnel and climbed the steps up into the bright day. The schoolgirls turned right. Mia let out her breath.

"There's the bus stop." Only two figures stood beside it, not the long line she'd seen that morning. All they had to do was get to the bus stop. One step after another. Nothing in her mind except getting to the bus stop.

"We're going to keep walking," Simon said.

"What? Why?" She started to turn her head, caught herself. *Don't look anxious.*

"We can't just stand around on the street — anyone could see us. We're going to walk by it, to the next stop or the one after that if we have to. Time it so that the bus comes as we get to it."

"But Simon, what difference does it make, if we're standing on the sidewalk or walking down it? People can still see us."

"Squeak, think." His voice had an edge, as if he were talking to an idiot. "If we're walking down the street like we know what we're doing, we don't attract as much attention. No one knows who we are. It's only been maybe twenty minutes since we ran. They may not even realize we're missing yet."

He was striding along the sidewalk, forcing her to keep

up. She swallowed her panic and frustration. Kept her legs moving, counting each tree they passed as a marker, trying not to think about the fact that they were completely exposed out here.

The next stop was in sight when Mia slowed her steps. "Wait. How are we going to pay? We don't know how it works."

Simon was silent for a moment, studying the bus stop in the distance.

"Okay, there's one person there." He gestured toward the lone woman in a business suit. "So let me get on first. I'll watch and see what she does, but if I fumble a bit, it won't look too suspicious."

"Hang on." Mia stopped to slip off her backpack and pull out her wallet. "I've got some won that Dad gave me, change that he had from other trips. The guidebook said tourists aren't supposed to use won, but North Koreans and foreigners who live here use it on the bus."

Simon took the won she gave him, with a look like he didn't trust what she was saying. Then he resumed walking. "So I'll get on first and indicate that I want to pay for you. They won't expect me to speak Korean."

Mia nodded. Her whole body buzzed with fear. This had to work.

There was the roar of an approaching bus behind them. It pulled to a halt. The door swung open.

The businesswoman stepped up. Simon glanced sideways at Mia, then followed. He held his hand out, offering a handful of coins to the bus driver, gesturing to himself and then to Mia. She stepped up behind Simon, her heart pounding. She avoided the bus driver's eyes, praying he wouldn't speak to her.

The driver frowned and took some coins from Simon's hand. His expression was suspicious as she passed him. Maybe he knew who they were. Or maybe he just disapproved of her fraternizing with the enemy. He shifted the bus into gear, pulling away from the curb.

Mia followed Simon down the aisle to an empty section in the back. The driver wasn't reaching for a cell phone. As long as he was driving, he couldn't report them.

The bus rattled down the broad street.

Only minutes later, a siren began its pulsing wail. They both nearly levitated in their seats. In the opposite lane, a police vehicle sped by. Mia had to stop herself from ducking. Two more police cars followed. Just behind them, an army truck rumbled past, camouflage canvas top flapping in the breeze.

Mia turned to Simon, eyes wide. He pursed his lips in a silent whistle. She pressed back against the plastic seat. *Breathe in, out, in, out.* She tried to slow her racing heart. She glanced at her watch. 4:27. How long had they been running? It seemed like days.

She stroked the face of her watch for a moment, thinking of her grandmother, who'd given it to her. Nona had mailed one to Simon as well, for their trip. She'd explained during a Skype call the day before they left how the screen lit up when you pushed the button on the side, as if this were a new invention.

"It's for when you get caught in the blackouts," she told them with a touch of urgency. Though Nona knew their father traveled there regularly, she did not approve of him taking her grandchildren to North Korea, which she envisioned as a kind of war zone.

Warm, funny, caring Nona seemed a universe away now.

Mia scanned the passengers in the front seats. No one had turned to look at them, no one was talking on a cell phone. But any one of them could report them, foreigners in an unusual place, at any moment. The bus driver could pull up to a police station. Soldiers took Dad and —

Stop. She pulled her mind away from the fear list she was making. She was just scaring herself.

Focus. Make a list of what they needed to do next: *1. Don't get arrested. 2. Get to a safe place. 3. Hide the phone. 4. Find a way to save Dad.*

It all seemed — it all was — completely impossible.

Mia opened the zipper on her pack, looking for a distraction. She pulled out her guidebook and flipped to the map of Pyongyang. A map!

"I can figure out where we are, where the bus is going!" she whispered.

Simon glanced at her map, then at her. "Yeah, right, Mia. How the hell are we going to know what street we're on? Have you noticed the signs are in *Korean*?" Though his voice was quiet, the scorn came through clearly.

"Simon. I can read them." She turned and faced him. "What did you think I was doing at Korean school every weekend?" He'd seen her go off, all those Saturdays. She had a vivid memory of standing fully dressed, Simon lounging on the living room carpet in his pajamas, her favorite cartoon playing on the TV screen in front of him. "Have fun at school," he'd called, too softly for Mom to hear, as she was pulled out the door to the car.

Now he looked momentarily surprised, recalculating. Then he turned his head away.

She scanned the map, trying to make out the small print. "I think we must be somewhere around here." She ran her finger back and forth over a small area.

Simon kept looking out the window. Not even listening to her. Even now, when they were in such danger, it was all about him. His way. Well, like it or not, they were in this together. There was one thing she could think of to do. So she might as well do it.

She tried to catch sight of a street sign, but between the glare of the sunlight and the speed of the bus, she couldn't see well enough to read them. She could have switched to the window seat, but she didn't feel like talking to Simon.

Several times they stopped at a crosswalk long enough for her to make out the syllables, but she couldn't find any of those names on the map. Then she caught sight of a railroad track, visible in the gaps between buildings. She scanned the map for railroad tracks. *There.*

They pulled up to an intersection with a much wider street, stopping long enough for Mia to decode the letters. *So . . . Chun . . . Ryo.* She peered at the map. There it was, running right alongside the train tracks. Sochon Street.

Simon gestured toward the other side of the bus. "The sun's traveling that way. So we're traveling north, northeast."

"I know!" Mia could barely contain her excitement. "Look, I just found our location on the map!"

Simon's jaw tightened. He turned his head back to look out the window. Mia's face went hot, but she just took another breath. Studied the map again.

"There's a train station coming up." She made her voice as calm as she could. "It looks like about six blocks."

His tongue worked in his cheek. Then he nodded. "Let's get off there. We'll see if we can sneak on a train. That'll get us out of the city."

"Out of the *city?*"

Simon turned his head, giving her a warning frown. Mia lowered her voice. "But you said . . . I thought we were just finding a place to hide the phone."

"There's no place to hide anything here. We have to get out into the countryside. It's the only way."

She stared at him. But there was no way to discuss it now. Not on a public bus in the middle of Pyongyang, with a manhunt probably being organized at this very minute. They had to disappear first, get somewhere safe. Then they could plan.

There was a more immediate problem: getting off the bus and walking into the train station without getting caught. Simon couldn't possibly blend in. And even though Mia looked Korean, her clothing was all wrong.

Clothing.

She pulled out her jacket and put it on. Zipped up, it felt a little more like a uniform. A little less American. She took an elastic out of her backpack and smoothed her hair back into a ponytail. All the North Koreans she'd seen seemed very neat and put together.

Then, as she closed the pack, she had another thought.

"Your badge," she said, turning to Simon.

"What?"

"That North Korean flag pin you got from the guys in the bar. Give me your badge."

Simon shook his head, as if she wasn't making any sense.

"People keep looking at you," she said. "Not at me. Here, any North Korean who's with a foreigner is a guide. So now" — she gestured to the jacket — "I can look like your guide, at least for a quick impression, if people don't look too closely. But I need a badge."

Simon frowned, but he fished the badge out of his backpack and handed it to her. She pinned it on her jacket, over her heart. He watched her, then shrugged.

The bus slowed, curving around the circular driveway in front of the station. Mia closed her eyes for a moment. All she wanted to do was open them to find that she'd imagined all of this. To see Dad. Or Daniel. Someone who would take over and put things right again.

But there was no one else. She and Simon had to save themselves.

Ready or not. She opened her eyes. 4:46 p.m. She stood up. Arranged her posture. Marched off the bus, trying to cover the shaking in her knees.

Four red banners hung from the front of the gray stone station. The flat roof was topped with the usual display of slogans. No one challenged them as they walked through the center doors, beneath the portrait of Kim Il-sung.

A crowd milled about inside. Under her pack, Mia's back felt incredibly exposed, as if it had a bull's-eye on it. She held up the guidebook, poking the map with her index finger.

"There's no way we can buy tickets," she said from behind the cover of the book. "You'd have to do it and it wouldn't look right. Dad said they never let Americans travel in the countryside except on an officially approved trip."

Simon nodded. "The thing is, do they collect tickets before you get on the train, or can we just walk onto the platform and board one?" he asked. "That way we'd be out of the city before they discovered we didn't have tickets."

"And then what? That would get us caught for sure."

"Well, have you got a better idea?" Simon's whisper was fierce.

"Don't —" Mia caught herself. She held up the guidebook again, making sure her badge could still be seen. "People are looking at us. Some of them must have cell phones."

"Okay." He sounded as if he was working to calm himself down too. "Let's walk out on one of the platforms as if we're going to take the train. The track closest to the end, not the ones in the middle."

They lined up behind a knot of passengers moving slowly through a door. Country folks, their clothing rougher and less stylish than that worn by people in Pyongyang. Maybe there was less of a chance that they'd have cell phones. As people caught sight of Simon, they pointed and nudged and turned to stare.

No one gave Mia more than a glance. But it was still terrifying to be out in the open. Seen. Any moment she expected to hear the shouts of someone discovering them.

Through the doors, a train stood to the right alongside a platform. Simon nudged her ahead of him, following the passengers down the pavement. A wheeled cart, piled high with cardboard boxes and cloth parcels, was parked next to a pillar. The crowd flowed to the right, toward the train. To the left of the platform the first track was empty; on the far track stood another train, dark and deserted.

"Go to the left." Simon's voice was in her ear. Mia veered left, away from the people in front of her. They passed behind the pillar and the cart, which momentarily blocked their view of the train. Simon grabbed her arm.

"Stay here. Anyone who saw us will just think we're boarding at the front."

Mia's heart was pounding. She couldn't see anything from their hiding place.

"Okay, here's what we're going to do. *Mia. Focus.*" She focused on his eyes. "We're going to jump down on the empty track. There's probably an overhang that we can hide under. Then we can run along the track, maybe find a freight train or something to hitch a ride on."

No way! Jumping. Running. Catching a train. Fine for Simon. He played touch football and soccer and baseball. He went to wilderness survival camp. He put himself at risk for fun. Mia was the clumsy one. She'd stumble and fall and blow their cover. Even now, someone could come around the corner and catch them at any moment.

Without giving her a chance to argue, Simon slipped over the side of the platform, disappearing below it in one fluid motion, as graceful as a cat. Mia stood alone on the platform.

She could not do this.

The top of Simon's head rose above the edge of the platform, just enough for him to see over the side.

"Okay, coast is clear. Move now!"

She moved, scraping her ankle on the rough concrete edge, Simon helping her over the side. Then she was down, under the overhang, low on the track beside him, out of sight. Bent almost double, they staggered along the edge of the track bed.

By the time they reached the end of the platform, Mia's thighs and back were screaming. Ahead was the train yard, covered with a maze of tracks. There was nothing out there to hide behind. She watched Simon, trying to push down her panic. He was scanning the area slowly with narrowed eyes, studying every corner of the train yard.

"We're gonna have to cross to that one." He pointed toward the train on the end track. It was much longer than the one that was boarding, its engine far ahead in the yard. "We'll have to move fast. We're going to go straight across and under the car; I think that's safer than running to the end of it."

Mia's eyes widened. What planet was he on?

"No one's looking down here, Squeak. They're busy boarding the train, getting settled. And the train conductors and the crew, they're busy too. They don't expect anyone to be here, and people often don't see things they're not looking for."

A low warning whistle made her start. Simon tensed. "We've got to move, now, before that train pulls out."

Somehow, they got across. Mia kept her eyes glued to the ground, keeping as close as she could to Simon, willing herself not to stumble on the rails. As Simon reached the other train, he went down, rolling under the car. Mia scrambled after him, feeling as if her purple backpack were a blinking neon sign.

They had just gotten into the shadows beneath the train, crawling over the oily black dirt and gravel between the tracks, when they heard shouts and piercing whistles. Every muscle in Mia's body seized.

Simon flattened himself on the ground. He twisted around to peer back at the platform where the train had started to pull out.

"Soldiers! They're on the platform!"

CHAPTER 7

There was a screeching of brakes, more loud shouts.

Mia squeezed herself as small as she could, trying to make herself disappear.

"They're stopping the train! They think we're on the train!"

So they hadn't seen them. Yet.

"The whole place could be overrun," Simon was saying into her ear. "I think we stay here till it's dark."

Mia dared to open her eyes. They lay in the shadows, watching the soldiers swarming in and out of the railcars. Men in uniforms paced up and down the pavement, barking angry orders.

"They knew which train to search," she whispered, trying to breathe normally. "Someone turned us in."

"They could be searching all the trains for all we know. But you're probably right."

"They've already caught up with us?!"

"Yeah." Simon said. There was a long pause. "But they haven't caught us yet. So it ain't over . . ."

"Till it's over," Mia finished automatically. It was a favorite phrase of Dad's.

Dad. Where was he? If anything happened to him — Nope. She wasn't going there. Things were terrible enough. They were like prey backed into a corner, hiding there under the train.

Except, as Simon said, they hadn't been caught.

Yet.

. . .

Mia came to, her body cramped, head pillowed on one arm. Her eyes flew open. She peered out through the space between the track and the bottom of the train car, scanning the opposite platform. Empty and dark. So was the station. That was one factor in their favor: the darkness of North Korea at night. Except for the spotlights on the monuments, they didn't use lights that weren't needed, and it looked as if the station was deserted.

The search had continued for more than an hour after sunset. Finally, as Mia and Simon had watched, the other train had pulled out of the station.

After that, the soldiers still milled about. For one heart-stopping moment, a young soldier had stretched out on the platform and peered beneath the overhang. But he had quickly pulled himself upright and fallen into conversation with the other soldiers.

"How come they're not searching over here?" Mia had whispered.

"So far we're just lucky. They had this idea in their heads that we were on that other train, so nobody's thought to look over here. Maybe no one has imagined that two Americans would actually run across the tracks and climb under a train. But somebody might think of it at any moment." Which hadn't helped her calm down.

But the light had dimmed in the sky and no one had come. Mia would never have believed that she could've fallen asleep under a train, knowing people were out there searching for her. But apparently exhaustion had won out over fear.

She pushed the button on her wristwatch to light it. 9:17. Her stomach growled. They hadn't had anything to eat since their big Korean lunch at a traditional restaurant. Dozens of colorful side dishes covering a long table. Bowls of rice and hot soup. How good that soup would taste now.

She reached back and pulled her arms out of her backpack. Beside her, Simon stirred. He must have been sleeping too.

"What are you doing?"

"Getting something to eat."

"You've got food?"

Mia's hand rummaged in her pack, feeling for the shapes of things. "A little. Some chocolate, some dried fruit. Some little packages of nuts, I think. Here." She reached for Simon's hand and placed a few dried apricots in his palm.

"Just a couple. Save the rest of it."

His words brought her back to reality, nearly spoiling the sweetness of the apricot she was chewing. They'd just run, because they had to. There was no plan. There was no guarantee that they'd get out of this mess today. Or tomorrow, or days from now. If at all.

Then Mia noticed a more immediate problem.

"Simon?"

"What?"

"I need to pee."

He was quiet for a moment. "Okay, it's dark enough — I think it'll be safe if we crawl out of here. But I'll go first, this way." She followed him out from underneath the car into the dark space between the train and the last platform. The train hid them from view, even if someone had been in the station or on one of the other platforms.

"I'll keep a lookout while you go."

"Go where?"

"Just squat over there."

Mia moved down the track. Even though it was so dark she could hardly see her own legs, she still felt self-conscious pulling down her pants with her brother so near.

After Simon took his turn, Mia handed him her plastic bottle of hand sanitizer. He gave a little snort of laughter.

"You are too much." A tiny ray of light appeared. "Hold this. And lemme see your guidebook." Simon handed her his pocket Swiss Army knife with a miniature flashlight. He paged through the book, to the map of Pyongyang, studying it for minutes.

"Where do you think we are?" he finally asked.

Mia smiled to herself in the dark. *Gotcha.* She put her fingertip on the northwest corner of the city. The train tracks led north.

"Okay, let's get going. We're gonna just follow the tracks."

No, no, no. The tiny island of safety they had, hiding there in the dark, sank away as fear washed over Mia. Nothing in her wanted to go north. From the moment that image of the prisoner had appeared on her phone, the day had felt like a kind of torture. Going north would only prolong it. The farther they got from the hotel, the farther they were from Dad. And the harder it would be to get back.

But they couldn't stay here. In the morning, their hideout would be exposed. Maybe outside of the city they could find a place to disappear for a little while. Hiding seemed like the least bad option right now.

Mia followed Simon on the trackway, feeling a mess of conflicting emotions, all bad: Miserable that they were leaving Dad behind. Desperate to run, not walk, toward any place that might offer them a place to hide. Annoyed that there wasn't enough light to see, as she kept stubbing her toes on the crossbars.

They passed between old railcars resting or abandoned in the train yard. Beyond, there was nothing but open tracks. On either side, the city slept in near total darkness. Overhead, a sea of stars glittered, hard and brilliant. Mia craned her neck to take in the sweep of it. The stark beauty seemed almost cruel, as if the sky didn't care about the trouble they were in. This same sky hung over the people who were suffering in prison camps, like the ones in the photographs.

Simon pointed an arm, solid black against the inky sky. "You follow that side of the Big Dipper, there's the North Star. So at least we can always tell what direction we're going in."

The stars were like a giant map. How could she not have noticed that before? At camp she'd always gone for the cozy, indoor activities rather than anything out in the wilderness. Now she wanted to fix her eyes on the constellations. Maybe she could detect patterns, give herself a moment's distraction from the nightmare they were in. But walking with her face turned up made her stumble.

The temperature was dropping, the night air cold on her face. She concentrated on the warmth of her jacket. *Whoever invented nylon, or whatever is keeping out this wind, thank you.*

And thank you, thank you, thank you that she'd stashed this jacket in her pack. And the food. And everything else.

Except the phone. If she hadn't opened the phone and brought it along, none of this would've happened.

"Simon?"

"What?" He was a dark shape in motion, up on the track to her left.

"What do you think is going on? Why did Dad get arrested?"

"I've been thinking and thinking about it. I can't come up with anything that makes sense."

"They know who he is, right? I mean, that he's been here before, that he works with Food for the World?"

"Remember all those papers we had to fill out in Beijing to get the visas? Of course they know what he does, how many times he's been here, everything."

"So why would they let him in the country and then arrest him?" Mia asked.

"Well, that's what I keep asking myself. The only thing I can imagine is that it has something to do with the people who gave us the phone."

She raised her head to look at him, though she couldn't see anything but his silhouette. "How?"

"Well, Dad says the various government bureaus and ministries don't always work together smoothly. There's lots of infighting between different factions."

"Daniel was talking to me about that." It was comforting to remember: Daniel was still out there. Maybe he could help them somehow. "That there are always power struggles."

"So I've been wondering: what if the guys we met —"

"The ones who said they were from the Ministry of Agriculture. But Daniel says they were probably from the Ministry of People's Security," Mia said.

"Yeah, whoever they were, what if they wanted to make another group look bad?"

"Daniel said the Ministry of People's Security, the MPS, is the regular police, and they're always fighting with the secret police who run the political prisons. The ones no one escapes from."

"Okay, so that could be it. What better way to one-up the secret police than getting photographs of their secret death camps?"

Simon's voice was raised, like he was arguing in debate club. Mia glanced around nervously. Nothing but darkness. But someone could be hidden, listening.

"Maybe the regular police somehow get these photos of what's going on in the political camps, which they want to use to embarrass the secret police," he went on. "And maybe the other ministry, the secret police, gets the idea that Dad is somehow connected with the regular police, maybe meeting with them. It's the only idea I have to connect the dots between the phone they gave us and his getting arrested. Which cannot be a coincidence."

Mia suddenly connected some dots herself. "Simon! Dad was wandering around in the middle of the night. The night before last."

"Squeak, what are you talking about?"

She told him what she'd seen.

"You sure it was Dad?"

"I saw his jacket. And I heard him come back, sometime after one o'clock."

"Huh. That's weird. I wonder what he was doing."

"Meeting somebody."

"Hmm." She could practically hear him thinking. "In which case, maybe the arrest really *is* some power play by one group trying to make another one look bad." Simon sounded as if he was trying to assemble a puzzle. "Because holding an American — that isn't going to make the US happy. It will only make things difficult for North Korea. So what's the purpose?"

"I thought you hated all that political stuff, when Dad would talk about it back at home." Mia was wishing she had paid more attention.

"Yeah, well, I still heard a lot of what he was saying."

Just ahead the tracks split, one veering off to the right, the other bearing left. Simon followed the left fork without hesitating.

"Where are we going?" Mia stepped faster to keep up.

"Right now we're just getting out of Pyongyang. It's incredible that we managed to hide this long. If we stay in the city, we're sure to get caught. But the bigger plan is: We're going to follow the train tracks north to the Chinese border."

"To the border?" She stopped short. "You never said any-thing about going all the way to the border!"

"It's the only way."

"Simon! We can't —"

"Keep it down." He sounded closer, facing her in the dark. He got to raise his voice, but she couldn't.

She spoke in a fierce whisper. "We can't make it to China! And we can't leave Dad!" And he might have discussed the plan with her! "We have to go back."

"Go back?!"

"Yeah, to the hotel. To . . . get some help. To save Dad. Daniel's there. He'll help us."

"Daniel? Are you kidding? Daniel's probably working with the North Koreans."

"What are you talking about? Daniel's our friend!"

"No way, Mia. I've been watching him since we met him. I'm sure he's connected to this somehow."

"Well, I've actually talked to him. I know he would help us. Anyway, we can't walk out of North Korea! It's impossible! We have to go back —"

"And what happens after that?"

"What do you mean?" She could feel the setup; no matter what she said, it would be wrong.

"What do you think will happen if we just show up at the hotel again? I told you, they arrested Dad; they'd arrest us too. Especially now that we've run away. There's no way Daniel or anyone can protect us, not while we're still in this country." There was steel in his voice. "And the phone? If we keep it, things are even worse for Dad. If we get rid of it, the images are lost. No one will ever see the evidence — the executions, the beatings, the starvation, the murdered babies —"

She put her hands over her ears.

Walking out of North Korea was completely impossible. Totally crazy. And it felt so wrong to be going away from Dad. Not to mention that Simon was presenting this as a done deal. He had set her up, from the moment he decided they should run.

But the way he posed it, it was the only choice. The only way there was a tiny chance they could help Dad —

"Okay, so now can we get back to getting out of here?" Simon's tone was mocking, like he was talking to a whining child. "As I was saying, the train tracks go north from Pyongyang all the way to the border. That's how those guys I met got here. Their tour came down by train from China." He'd started forward, his voice once again trailing over his shoulder.

Mia's hands dropped, shoulders slumping. She took a step. *For Dad.*

"We just have to make sure we keep to the west coast. Going northeast, it's about three times as far to the border. We follow the tracks, heading northwest, all the way to — that city on the river, across from China, I can't remember the name —"

"Sinuiju." She said it automatically. Before the trip, she'd pored over the maps.

"Whatever. It's about a hundred and twenty miles, I think."

One hundred and twenty miles. About two hours driving. But walking one hundred and twenty miles? Her feet became blocks of cement she was dragging.

"We can't go south, though it's much closer," Simon went on. "We'd never get through to South Korea. The DMZ is way too tightly guarded and there are minefields." He'd thought the whole thing out. "East or west, in either direction there's an ocean. Going north is the only way. We should be able to do it in about ten days."

One hundred twenty divided by ten was . . .

"*Twelve miles?* We're walking twelve miles a day?!" Mia was squeaking.

"Once we get to China, I figure we'll call the American embassy. We could even call Mom."

Mom! Mia felt her heart squeeze with longing. If Mom

were here, she'd figure out a way to fix things. Of course if Mom were here, they wouldn't be in this mess in the first place.

A lump formed in her throat. If she kept thinking about Mom, she was going to start crying. She forced her mind back to Simon's plan. "But what about the river between North Korea and China?"

"There have to be bridges. The train gets across somehow; like I said, those guys I met in the bar came in that way."

Mia trudged along behind Simon, saying nothing. It was typical of her brother that he was just making it up as they went along. Assuming he could figure it out when they got there. She liked to make advance preparations. Plan A and Plan B. Especially when they were being hunted by people who might arrest them and throw them into a North Korean prison.

But her brother's ideas were like those hardy plants in Mom's garden that just kept growing and grabbing space. Pretty soon they crowded out the smaller, more delicate plants. Survival of the fittest.

Mia felt her forehead tightening into a scowl. Everything hurt. Her back and hip from lying on the hard gravel under the train. Her feet from her shoes rubbing. Her legs from the endless tramping. Her stomach from the acid terror that had spilled through her gut, again and again, ever since they ran. Or maybe because she was so hungry she could kill something.

Her heart hurt too. Like she'd actually torn it, leaving Dad behind.

The cold air stung her cheeks and the tip of her nose. She yanked the sleeves of her jacket down over her fingers. The whole thing was Simon's fault. He was forcing her to go along with this crazy escape plan. She hated that he was right all the time.

And Dad. As fiercely as she missed him, she was mad at Dad too. For being so obsessed with starving North Koreans that he had done something to get himself arrested, instead of just paying attention to his own kids.

And Mom had chosen to be with Nona instead of with them on the trip and now she wasn't here when they needed her so much. None of this would have happened if she had come with them.

Tears were trickling down, chilling her cheeks. She was glad it was dark so Simon couldn't see. But another part of her longed for him to notice. To stop. To do something to let her know that she wasn't just extra baggage he had to drag along.

There was nothing to do but keep moving forward. Even though it felt like slowly, slowly tearing a bandage off a nasty wound. The excruciating agony of it going on and on and on.

And on.

CHAPTER 8

OCTOBER 3

Mia bolted awake to a shrieking, deafening roar. She almost screamed, then caught herself. It was just a train passing. The rumbling faded into the night, but her heart still raced.

She and Simon were huddled in the corner of an old railway shed. They'd come to it when Mia was sure she couldn't take another step. Simon had managed to separate the door from its rusty hinges. Inside, in the narrow beam of his knife light, the shed had looked abandoned, full of old machinery, straw mats, and dust.

Now it must be near sunrise. She could see the outlines of stacks of machine parts. In her sleep, she had slid to the ground, knees drawn up to her chest. Her right hip and shoulder bones pressed into a stiff straw mat against hard concrete. The air in the shed was frigid. Her back, the only place she felt warmth, was wedged against Simon's leg. Even the train practically running them over hadn't wakened him.

She was cold.

She was scared.

But most of all, she was *hungry*.

She wondered what came after hunger pangs. If it hurt. Maybe she'd start feeling dizzy. Maybe she wouldn't be able to walk anymore. Then they'd never get to China. They could *die*.

She didn't know how long it took to starve to death. They could end up looking like skeletons . . . like the people in the labor camp photos.

Stop. She didn't know anything about hunger. They'd missed one meal. Those people had been hungry for *years*.

Mia remembered Dad's accounts of babies who wouldn't stop crying because their mothers didn't have any milk. Families that had to choose which child to feed. Which to let starve.

She wasn't starving. But reminding herself that other people were didn't make her hunger go away.

Slowly, trying not to disturb Simon, she unzipped her backpack and rooted around for her snacks. Her hand closed over a Snickers bar. She unwrapped it as silently as she could.

The heavenly flavor of chocolate flooded her tongue. She tried not to chew, to just savor the taste. It would be gone all too soon. But she couldn't hold back. Her teeth gnashed at it. She slid her tongue over each tooth to find every trace of sweetness.

Then she lay curled in a rigid ball on the ground, one hand squeezed around her locket. Her cold and fear and hunger were just as fierce as before. And now she had more to feel terrible about. Eating without giving any to Simon. Wondering how soon the snacks would run out. Imagining what people in the labor camps would have done for a candy bar.

And missing home so much it hurt.

" " "

The air on Mia's back was cold. Simon was up, moving around, opening the shed door. She groaned in protest and raised an arm over her eyes as a shield against the assault of light. She turned over and curled her limbs together more tightly, wanting nothing more than to crawl back into the dark cave of sleep.

"I'm going to scout around outside." Simon's voice came from above her.

Mia grunted. The tin door creaked closed. She could feel the emptiness of the shed without him. Good. Just a little bit more sleep . . .

Within moments, she knew it was hopeless. She couldn't get comfortable on the scratchy straw and hard concrete, and there was no way to get warm. Worse, the hunger in her gut was getting more insistent, demanding *breakfast*!

Yesterday, there had been breakfast at the hotel. How she would savor a piece of that cold, chewy toast, that rubbery egg.

And there had been warmth. If only she could be warm again . . . She'd follow the guides anywhere. Bow at the feet of a hundred statues. Visit a thousand monuments, sitting on the cushioned seats of the tour bus. Next to Dad.

Dad! All the events of yesterday flooded her brain. If only she could turn back the clock. Be waking up yesterday, with the day to do over. She would never, never, never open the package with the phone.

She sat up then. *The phone.* If there were no photographs, there'd be no reason to attempt an impossible escape. There'd be no evidence against Dad. And even if they did get arrested, there would be food. And warmth. And something soft to sleep on.

She clambered onto her knees, reached over for Simon's backpack, and pulled out the phone. There must be some way to get rid of the photographs. Quickly, before he came back. He would be furious. But she could say she'd just wanted to look at the photos again, and they had gotten deleted by mistake.

She pressed the power button. *Hurry, hurry.* She scrolled to the *Angry Birds* game. There was the first photograph. The blindfolded man tied to the post.

All she had to do was find a way to delete them. All their problems would disappear.

She paused. If she got rid of the photographs, the people in them would disappear too. No one would ever know about their suffering. No one would ever know that baby had lived, even for a few short months.

She'd seen them. She couldn't pretend they didn't exist.

She startled as something moved outside, along the wall of the shed. Her arm jerked. The phone flew out of her hand and landed with a crack on the concrete floor. As she scrambled to grab it, Simon slipped through the door.

"What are you doing?"

"Uh, I just wanted to see the pictures again. . . ." She looked down at the floor to hide the heat in her face.

"Mia, don't be stupid! They might be able to trace the signal." He grabbed the phone from her hand. "Damn, why didn't I think of that before? I should have taken the battery out." He bent over the phone, popping off the back to remove the battery, then putting it in his pack.

"The highway runs alongside the tracks as far as I can see," he said as he worked. "I could make out some buildings way up the road to the north, but no sign of people. You can go down the side of the track to pee — there's a couple of bushes in the field."

Mia stepped out the door into the filmy light. Dun-colored fields stretched to distant low hills in every direction. Deserted. Desolate. A cold bit of sun broke through the cottony cloud cover overhead. She shivered and hugged her arms.

Squatting in the field behind a bush, she realized there was one advantage to not having anything to eat. In a day or two, there'd be nothing left inside.

Back in the shed, she knelt to search her backpack for the hand sanitizer. Above her, Simon was corkscrewing his body to stretch out, swinging his arms to one side, then the other.

Out of habit, she started her inventory. Guidebook. Journal. Colored pens. Two plastic-wrapped packages of tissues. Her phone. The Korean-English/English-Korean dictionary. Her water bottle — half full. She took one big gulp, wanting more but stopping herself. Her hairbrush. When she ran it through her hair, bits of straw and dust floated to the ground. Her wallet, with old photos from before she had a phone: a Christmas portrait of their family, including Nona and Poppy, and school pics of Alicia and Jess.

She stacked everything in front of her on the straw mat. Each object looked both dear and strange. Proof of an ordinary life, the life she'd had until yesterday afternoon. She could hardly imagine it now.

At the bottom, her snacks. The bag of apricots, about eight pieces left. Two airline bags of peanuts. A package of Starbursts. The other Snickers bar, the one she'd saved for Simon. Two packs of Chinese gum and one of sesame candy.

After what she'd seen in the photographs, it seemed as if

she shouldn't feel hungry. As if she didn't have the right. But her body wasn't listening.

She reached for the apricots, one bag of peanuts, and two clean tissues, laid out two apricots each, and carefully poured out two small piles of peanuts.

"Breakfast."

"I think we should save it." Simon was leaning into a lunge, stretching out his back leg.

"I've still got some apricots and another bag of peanuts and some candy. We need to eat a little. So we can walk farther today."

Simon shrugged, reached down, and scooped his portion into his mouth. He continued stretching while chewing, then took a swig from his water bottle.

Mia chewed one peanut at a time. Slowly. Alternating with bites of the apricot. When she was done, it felt like she'd actually eaten something. She took a small sip of water, then tucked the bottle back into her pack.

As she repacked, her hand touched something else. Something she'd rolled up and stuffed down there, two days before in Beijing, and then forgotten: a clean pair of socks and underwear, the clothes wrapped around a tiny hotel bottle of shampoo and a small rectangle of soap. She'd put it there in case the North Korean airline lost their luggage and it didn't turn up for a day or two.

She felt her spirits lifting a bit, despite everything. If they ever found water, they could wash. She could change into fresh underwear and socks.

So when they got caught and thrown into prison, or starved to death, at least she'd be clean.

She'd done every task she could think of doing. Mia turned to her brother. "Now what?"

"I'm trying to figure out if we should risk traveling in the daylight or not. There don't seem to be any people around, and I think we'll go crazy if we have to spend the entire day in here. And there's no guarantee someone won't come along and find us."

It seemed like he was using her as a sounding board. She nodded. She wouldn't be able to stand it, spending the day locked in this tiny tin shed. Walking would give them something to do. Something else to think about. The sense of going somewhere.

Somewhere there might be food.

"I think we should try to make a little progress, maybe find a better place to hide."

She nodded again.

As they stood by the door, ready to start out, Simon glanced back at the shed floor.

"Squeak!"

Mia jumped. "What?!"

He pointed to the little foil bag that had held the peanuts. "That's how they'll be able to trace us!" He was shaking his head, as if he couldn't believe her stupidity.

She bent and picked up the bag, then stuffed it deep into her jeans pocket, her lower lip jutting out.

Outside, Simon carefully inserted the rusted bolts back into the hinges to look as if the door was still locked.

"Walk along the edge of the field," he ordered, leading the way down the slope. "We'll duck out of sight if a car comes." He set off along a path that ran below the tracks and the highway to their right, level with the rice fields on their left.

When Mia didn't respond, he glanced back. She avoided his gaze, keeping her eyes on the fields. Every time Simon opened up a little and acted like they were in this together — like the moment when he'd actually seemed to be asking her opinion — she thought things might be changing. This was a really big, really hard thing they were doing together. She wanted — she *needed* — to do it as a team. Like real partners.

Yelling at her about the trash was a little thing. But that wasn't how you treated someone who was your partner. And each time she got her hopes up and he pushed her away, the rejection felt sharper.

Even worse than when he just shut her out all the time.

When they were younger, Simon seemed to like hanging out with her. They'd played endless backyard games of Knights and Castles, built forts and tree houses, lain side by side on the floor in Simon's room reading his comic books, spent countless hours playing Parcheesi and Chutes and Ladders with their grandparents. Of course, that was when Nona and Poppy still lived with them, when they'd been a real family.

Then, the summer before Mia started seventh grade, everyone went off and left her alone. Nona and Poppy moved to Arizona. Dad got a promotion and his trips got longer. Simon wanted to spend all his time with pretty Randi, his new girlfriend. Mom was technically home, but distracted, responsible for everything by herself. Before, it was like they'd all been traveling together inside in a cozy, shared bubble, like a space shuttle. Now they were each solo astronauts, tethered to the shuttle but floating out in space on their own.

In August, Simon had disappeared for three days. Mom had made frantic calls to all Simon's friends. Dad had come home early from his trip. There were police officers at the kitchen table.

Afterward, when it turned out he had just gone to New York to see a concert with some friends, Simon blamed Mia for ratting him out to Mom. The memory was fresh, him banging open the door and storming into her room.

"Why did you tell on me?" His eyes had glittered like blue ice.

She'd looked up from her video game, trying to figure out what he was talking about. Her failure to respond was evidence enough to convict. He'd whirled and stalked out the door.

She jumped to her feet then, chasing him down the hall. "All I said was that you weren't at Nathan's! How was I supposed to know you didn't want them to find out? You didn't tell me anything!" Too late.

She didn't get why he was so angry with everyone anyway. He had a pretty great life. At school, he shone like a sun, with groups — his sports and debate teammates, his friends, random girls — orbiting around him like planets, just to be in his light. She'd seen the girls at the mall looking sideways at him, heard her classmates' squeals, "Omigod, Simon Andrews is your *brother*?!" There'd even been a couple of older girls who'd tried being nice to her, just to get near Simon. As if she had some special access. Since August, all she shared with him was a last name and a street address.

Maybe he was still upset about Randi breaking up with him. They'd gotten together his sophomore year, when Mia was in sixth grade. It was really fun at first; Randi was friendly and laughed a lot and she and Simon even took Mia for ice cream or to a movie once in a while. But at some point Mia crossed some line — or they did — and they were no longer interested in her. Then last year Randi dyed her light brown hair black and got her freckled nose pierced. Next she stopped smiling, got really skinny, and started dressing in all-black clothes. Finally, just before summer vacation this year, she said she didn't want to be with Simon anymore.

Mia remembered he was still wearing the black cord bracelet Randi made for him. The whole thing might be a bigger deal for him than she had realized.

The rubbing of the sore spot on her right heel brought her back to this drab day, this endless walking. Her legs felt heavy, her back stiff from sleeping all cramped up. She should have done stretches like Simon.

Another uncomfortable thing was being able to see what a distance they had to go. In the night, walking had felt kind of timeless, just moving along under the stars. Now, she could see the countryside stretching in all directions, and how slowly they covered it. She could feel the weight of — what was it — at least a hundred and ten miles to go? Forever.

To keep herself going, she kept telling herself they were getting out of North Korea so they could save Dad.

After a while, her mind went into a kind of trance and she just trudged along behind Simon. Only a few vehicles passed. She ducked into the ditch when her brother ducked. Got up and started walking again when he did. Just another game of "Simon Says" she would play until she dropped.

The railway tracks had just brought them back to the highway when a truck came around the bend before they had time to hide. Simon dropped to his knees in the ditch, Mia right behind him. A rattling rumble as it passed. Then a *putt*, *putt*, *putt* and the sound of squealing brakes.

CHAPTER 9

There were no running footsteps. No accusing voices pointing out their hiding place. And no sound of the truck starting up again.

Simon lifted his head. "I'm going to crawl up there, see if I can see anything."

Before Mia could protest, he was scaling the slope like Spider-Man. Her heart lurched. He paused at the top to peer over the tracks, up the highway.

A moment later, he was back beside her.

"It's two guys. Doesn't look like they saw us. They've stopped for a picnic."

A picnic? They had picnics in North Korea? A picnic meant food.

"There's a pond on the other side of the expressway. They're sitting there, facing away from us. There's a bunch of stuff in the back of the truck. I think we can sneak on and hitch a ride."

Now her stomach lurched. "Won't they see us?"

He shrugged. "It's all a crapshoot, whether we're walking along the tracks or in the back of a truck."

"I thought you said we were going to walk all the way."

"I didn't want to get your hopes up, in case we couldn't find a ride. But there's no way we can make it walking all the way; it would take more than a week and we haven't got any food."

Her shoulders came up. Simon was still keeping secrets.

"Look, Squeak, we can't keep this up forever. Sooner or later, someone's bound to see us. I just figure, the farther we are from Pyongyang, the better. If we're going to risk exposure either way, it seems better to do it riding than walking."

She was dead tired. Riding sounded wonderful. And if Simon was right, if they were in equal danger either way . . . He wasn't really asking, but she nodded.

Bent low, they ran along the ditch beside the field until Simon raised a hand. He crawled up the embankment again, then beckoned for her.

An old rusty pickup truck that had once been turquoise was parked in a small section of pavement on the far side of the train tracks. Mia peered through the gap between the truck wheels. Across the empty expressway, two men squatted on the bank of the pond, facing away from the truck. One wore a dark sweater, the other a tan jacket. They were eating with chopsticks. Mia's mouth watered.

"Okay, let's go." Simon stood, darted across the tracks on silent feet, and was up and into the back of the truck. His hand flashed over the side, waving her on.

She ran then, as silently as she could. The truck sides were horizontal boards with narrow slits between them. Crouched on the truck bed, Simon watched the men.

"Now!"

Mia slipped around the truck, grabbed the rope tied across the back, and pulled herself up into the truck bed.

Simon halted her with a hand signal. She froze for a long moment, certain she'd blown their cover. But then he waved her to keep moving.

Old tires filled the front of the truck bed near the cab, stacked in piles, each tied with rope. Mia peered though the slats on the sides. The men were sharing a cigarette.

"I think they're almost done." Simon pointed her toward the front stacks of tires. More slats of wood blocked the view through the back window of the cab, as long as no one looked through the cracks. Mia slipped down onto the floor in one corner, between two stacks. She caught her breath at the sound of the men's voices approaching. The doors opened, then slammed shut, and the truck started up. Simon twisted his head around to catch her eye.

"Here we go," he mouthed.

It was not a comfortable ride. The metal floor was hard. If they made any noise, they could be caught. But it felt fantastic to be moving so fast, the pavement smooth under the wheels of the old truck. If the men were going far enough in the right direction, they could be at the border in a few hours.

At this rate, Mia thought, they might even survive long enough to get out of this country. That would be something people would notice: two American kids who escaped from North Korea. Maybe they'd be in the news, on talk shows, be celebrities.

Everyone Mia knew had something that made them stand out — in a good way. Alicia loved to act and sing. She studied for fun and was always at the top of their class. Jess was all about horses; she rode on an equestrian team and even won ribbons at riding shows.

Mia was . . . their friend.

In the library last month, she'd overheard two kids from her class, Jared and T.J., talking on the other side of the shelves near the table where she was studying.

"Do you see Mia Andrews?" Jared had said. "Miss Gerald said she had the book."

"Who?" T.J. had asked.

"You know — Mia? That Asian girl who hangs out with Alicia and Jess?"

If she and Simon got out of North Korea on their own, Mia wouldn't be just "that Asian girl" anymore.

But even better, they might be able to save Dad. That was the only thing that really mattered. If they could help get Dad home.

Through the cracks between the slats, Mia glimpsed flat brown fields stretching out across a plain. In the distance, a lone farmer followed a plow pulled by an ox. A line of men dug with shovels in the brown dirt. Schoolchildren carrying backpacks walked along a path between fields full of yellow stubble, as if the crops had gotten a crew cut. Mia held her breath as the truck passed through a town, praying they wouldn't stop.

The land began to rise in dusty hills. She pulled out the bar of sesame candy, broke it, and tapped Simon on the shoulder to hand him a piece. She tried to pretend it was dessert, after a filling lunch, but her stomach wasn't fooled.

When the truck turned, it was 3:11. Mia felt the wheels bump across the tracks and then slope down onto an unpaved road, leaving the highway.

"Simon?" she whispered.

"I know. We'll have to figure out a way to get out as soon as we can."

There were more turns, onto rougher and rougher roads, climbing steeper hills. It was exceedingly uncomfortable, hanging on and trying to stay upright and hidden. Left, right, left again. Mia's heart sped faster. She tried to memorize each turn so they could find their way back to the train tracks. They needed to get off this truck.

The slopes rising on either side of the road were covered in dark green pines, dotted with trees flaming like bright torches, gold and yellow and red. The truck sped on, stirring up a swirling cloud of dust. Every bump jarred Mia's sitting bones on the metal floor as she clung to the edges of the tire stacks.

Finally, the truck slowed down and squealed to a stop. Mia froze. A door creaked open, then another. The men's voices, conversational. In front of her, Simon twisted to peer between the truck slats.

"They're peeing. C'mon." Simon uncoiled himself and moved stealthily to the back of the truck bed. Mia squeezed her way between the stacks to crouch beside him.

"Wait until we hear the door close, then jump. We'll only have a second. Watch the rope."

She poised on the edge, straining to listen.

"They're taking a long time," Mia whispered.

"Probably sharing another cigarette."

"What if they see us?"

"Just keep your head down and hope they don't look back."

The voices again, nearing. Mia's whole body tensed. The doors squeaked open; one slammed shut, then the other.

"Go!"

Simon hurled himself into space. She was just behind, the rope slowing her, the truck starting forward as she leaped, tossing her to the ground, rolling her over. She lay in the dirt.

Simon was on his feet. "You okay?"

Mia scanned her body. Nothing seemed broken. She pulled herself up, brushing the dirt off.

An engine whine came from the direction the truck had gone. Simon grabbed her sleeve and yanked her off the road as the noise grew. He threw himself down behind a clump of bushes, but she was still half standing as a motorbike sped around the corner. Mia couldn't stop herself from looking at the driver, a man in a leather jacket. His eyes met hers, his expression puzzled, before he sped by, raising a dust cloud.

"Did he see you?" Simon whispered from the ground.

Mia nodded.

Her brother swore and jumped to his feet.

"We've got to get out of here! C'mon!" Simon charged up the hillside into the cover of the trees. Mia plunged after him, her heart pounding. They wove through thick brush and among tall trees until Mia was sure they were so lost that no one could possibly find them. She glanced back a few times, but there was no one anywhere in sight. She was panting hard by the time Simon slowed his pace.

"You should have moved faster!" He swore again, turning his head to vent at her. "What the hell?! We're walking along the train tracks, along the main highway, for *hours*, and there's not a car in sight! Then we're on some godforsaken country road in the middle of nowhere and all of a sudden there's traffic?"

"Where are we going?"

No answer. Mia scuttled after him.

"Simon, don't we want to go back to the road? I don't think that guy is coming back. I didn't see any sign of anyone following us. . . ." She gasped the words out. "He didn't have time to really look at me, he probably just thought I was some North Korean girl. If we go back to the road and I can find a road sign or a village name or something, then maybe I can find it on the map. . . ."

He ignored her, stomping up the hill. She scrambled to keep up. They reached the top of the rise and started down the other side.

"Simon, wait, I think we can figure out where we are. There's a map —"

He whirled on her, face fierce, mouth clenched. "Mia, will you just *shut up* about your stupid map?"

Something in her burst.

"What?! What did I do? I'm just trying to help, and you're acting like I'm the problem!" she shouted. Everything she'd been holding inside came to a boil. "It's *your* fault that we're out here! You're the one who made us leave Pyongyang! You're the one who made us get a ride on that truck! But you keep getting mad at *me*!"

Her throat was raw, her breathing ragged. But the words, shut up inside for so long, were a flood she couldn't hold back.

"I've been following you for two days! Doing everything you said we had to do! No matter how hard I try, I'm still this stupid little sister who's such a bother. It's like you wish I wasn't here! Why don't I *matter* to you?" Her last words came out in a wail.

That seemed to be the last straw for Simon.

"Is that all you can think about? How about looking at it from *my* side, Mia?" He leaned toward her, eyes blazing. "I'm responsible for you here! You play games with some stupid phone, and all of a sudden we're in the middle of a freakin' international incident, running from soldiers, police, and who knows who else? We don't know where we are, we've got no food, and I have to figure out what to do!" He shook his head. "I've been kinda busy trying to *save your life*, so *sorry* if I happened to hurt your feelings! How about you shut up and let me concentrate so I can get us out of here alive?"

He turned and continued his relentless march, deeper into the woods.

It was all she could do to keep from screaming at him. She was never going to share food or maps or anything with him ever again. He was selfish and arrogant and mean and she hated him. And they'd never save Dad if they got lost in the woods.

Mia clomped along, her frustration building as the foliage grew thicker and harder to navigate. Branches scratched her. Her thigh muscles burned. Her ankles felt rubbed raw.

Finally, Simon halted.

"We need to find a place to camp out." He didn't look at her. "There won't be light left for long." She didn't look at him.

Out of the corner of her eye, she saw him stick his index finger in his mouth, then hold it up, turning his hand around from one direction to the other.

"Wind's coming from that direction." He pointed. "So we want shelter on that side. Maybe on the other side of that hill."

Mia said nothing.

On the next rise, they found a cluster of boulders that Simon grimly approved as a windbreak. "We should get some pine needles, grass, stuff like that for a little insulation. It'll be pretty cold by morning." His tone was flat, as if he could barely bring himself to care.

By the time they had a thin layer of cushion, it was nearly dark. "You lie against the rock," he ordered. "Might be a little heat left from the sun."

He was being "responsible" for her, like she was a burden. Mia pressed her lips together.

With her backpack for a pillow, she tried to find a comfortable position for her bruised body on the hard ground. All she wanted was to escape into sleep, away from the storm of feelings raging inside. At the moment she'd rather be caught by the North Koreans than spend another day following her brother.

She lay spooned against his back. Trying to steal warmth from his body. Trying to unknot her rigid muscles. Trying to ignore the gnawing in her belly.

Dad's voice spoke in her head, saying, "Things always look better in the morning."

It sounded like a lie.

CHAPTER 10

OCTOBER 4

It was morning. It was cold. And water was dripping on Mia's face.

The small pine trees overhead provided some shelter, but a little rivulet of rain was running off the needles right onto her brow.

She sat up, wiping her eyes, shivering. Walking in wet socks and shoes, they'd have blisters in no time. Maybe she should just go off to find shelter by herself. Leave Simon there.

She shook his shoulder.

"Simon. It's raining."

He was deep asleep. Not pleased to be disturbed. "What the hell, Mia —"

"We have to get out of the rain. Everything's gonna get wet."

He groaned and rolled over. His forehead landed right under the little stream of water. He cursed and sat up, spluttering, wiping his face.

Mia put her mouth under the stream and let it spill down

her throat, gulping a few mouthfuls. Trying to stand, she found that it hurt to move. She struggled into her pack. Simon was already off between the trees, leaving her behind. As usual.

Her sore legs and feet tripped on rocks. Back muscles strained as she ducked under trees. Her face got splashed with icy drops from pine branches. Soon her jeans and jacket were damp and she was shaking with cold.

It all matched what it felt like inside her. In the night, the heat of her anger had cooled. Now she felt enveloped in a deep gray numbness. The odds that they would get out of here alive were terrible. She would never see Dad or Mom again. Things did not look better this morning; they looked worse.

Simon stopped before a slanted wall of rock. It jutted out over a low stone shelf, forming a shallow cave, big enough to hold both of them. The covering of dead leaves and moss and the ground beneath were dry. They climbed in under the rock and huddled on the ledge.

Within moments the rain picked up, falling steadily. Mia leaned back against the rock, pulled her knees to her chest, and wrapped her arms around her legs, trying to hold in the little warmth she had left.

Simon's arms were folded. He stared out at the sky, his mouth clenched. As if it were raining on purpose to annoy him.

Mia's stomach growled. She was too miserable to care, but her body wasn't. She unwrapped herself, pulled off her backpack, and took two apricots out of the package. She opened the last bag of peanuts and dumped half on top of the remaining apricots. Without looking at him, she held out the apricot package to Simon.

"How much stuff do you have in there, anyway?" He sounded annoyed, as if having the foresight to pack snacks was a fault.

"Why are you being such a jerk?" she burst out, angry again. "What's in your pack? Have you got anything in there that could actually *help* us?"

Simon's face tightened. Then his expression shifted. He started rummaging around in his pack.

"I just remembered. . . . Yes!" He held up one hand. Clutched between his thumb and folded fingers was — wonder of wonders — a book of matches. "It's from the hotel in Beijing, from the bar."

Mia's eyes widened. She didn't ask what he'd been doing in a bar. For all she knew, he'd been in lots of bars, like in Pyongyang and when he ran away to New York.

"I think it's safe to make a fire," he said. "The rain will keep the smoke down so nobody will see it."

They swept the litter of dry leaves, twigs, and grass from the rock shelf into a pile on the patch of sheltered ground. Simon tore some pages out of the *Sports Illustrated* in his backpack, crumpling them into balls. From a nearby thicket of trees, he gathered an armload of dead branches and built a triangular construction on top of the bed of leaves and paper, like the frame for a log cabin.

"Okay, here goes." The little match looked so flimsy, its cardboard stem so short. Simon struck the head on the strip and the match flared to life.

It immediately blew out.

"Damn!" he said. Mia counted: only about twenty matches. They had no idea how long they'd need them to last. "Get over here next to me. Block the wind."

The second match caught, flickered, then went out. Finally, on the third try, the flame held long enough for Simon to bring it down to the leaves. He cupped his hand around the tiny fire as he touched it to the brush. Mia held her breath, willing it to grow.

The brush ignited, the dead leaves curling. The pine needles glowed like orange wires before they turned to ash. Then the branches caught and a small, steady fire began to burn.

Warmth on her face and hands was a miracle. Mia's tensed shoulders loosened a little. All it took to feel better was some heat.

"Oh, Simon," she breathed.

He glanced at her sideways, a hint of a smile tugging at the corners of his mouth. "We've got to dry our clothes so we don't get hypothermia." His voice had lost its hard edges. "When you're warm enough, take your jacket off and hold it up. It'll dry faster that way."

The fire did its work efficiently. Mia stripped off her jacket and held it up to the heat on each side, careful not to get it too close to the licking flames. Then she took a turn holding up Simon's heavy, damp sweatshirt while he added fuel. When she was tired of squatting and standing, she stepped back to the ledge over the fire.

"The rock is warm!" She was dry. The surface below her was hard but heated. Her knotted muscles began to relax.

Now if only they had some food. And, of course, a way to escape from North Korea, save Dad, and get home . . .

But just for a moment, there was this little bubble of comfort. She could imagine that things might possibly turn out okay.

Her stomach growled louder. The few apricots and peanuts had worked as an appetizer. "Time for room service. Hot chocolate. And a cheese omelet. With buttered toast and jam."

"And sausages, still sizzling," Simon said. "And hot, strong, black coffee."

"And a big glass of orange juice."

They stared into the flames. Mia tried to picture each bite. The cheese melting out of the edge of the omelet. The toast brown and crunchy. She could almost taste it.

Simon peeled a twig with the blade of his knife and put it into his mouth. Mia remembered one of Dad's stories about people eating bark during a famine in North Korea.

"What are you doing?"

"Cleaning my teeth. You know, after that great meal."

"What if . . . what if that's some kind of poison bark or something?"

"*Poison* bark?" He raised a skeptical eyebrow.

"I don't know, like poison ivy. . . ." She trailed off.

"Squeak, it's just plain birch. And anyway, I peeled the bark off."

"Oh." Her own teeth felt fuzzy. She hadn't brushed them since . . . the morning before last. Two days. "Can I have one too?"

"Aren't you afraid of getting *poisoned*?" But he sorted through the pile and found a twig, peeling it before he handed it to her. It felt good, using the broken end to scrape the surface of her teeth, the point to probe between them.

The flames danced. The rain pattered on the leaves. It was falling more gently, a pleasant sound now that they were sheltered around a fire.

Mia played with her locket between one thumb and finger.

"Do you still have that old family picture in there?" Simon sounded honestly curious, not critical.

She nodded. "Plus my baby picture. The one Dad and Mom got with my adoption referral." She held the locket for a moment. Then she pried open the tiny door.

In the locket's left half, a wide-eyed baby peered out, wrapped in a blanket. Mia couldn't read the card pinned to the blanket, but she knew what it said: Han Sung-mi. She held it out for Simon to see.

"How old were you?"

"Four months." The tiny face looked unformed, an image that hadn't come into focus yet. Her hair stuck up in a point.

Mia studied the picture in the right half. The six of them on the beach at Silver Sands State Park, when she was about three. Dad. Mom. Nona and Poppy. Simon, grinning, his head cocked to one side. And in the center, Mia. Safe in her daddy's arms.

If something happened to Dad, she couldn't bear it.

She closed the locket, pressed it to her lips for a moment, and let it fall against her chest. She and Simon sat in silence, watching the fire.

*　*　*

"Rain's letting up." Simon's voice roused her. "We should be ready to go when it stops. I've let the fire die down; I'm going to put it out now so no one sees the smoke."

Mia stretched out her hands to feel the heat one last time. She felt a stab of grief as Simon gathered a handful of wet debris from the ground nearby and smothered the fire. He stomped on the ashes until they stopped smoking.

As they moved out of the clearing and in among the trees, Mia glanced back at their shelter, missing it already.

"From what I remember of where the sun was when we started climbing the hill yesterday, we were traveling west, maybe northwest," Simon was saying. "Then we got all turned around." He pushed aside a large spray of dripping branches and held it for her to slip through.

"Obviously, we can't get back to the railroad tracks where the truck turned off. It's like twenty, thirty miles back, maybe more." He sounded like he was figuring it out as he talked. "So I think we should keep pushing northwest. No matter where we are, until we hit the coast, the border crossing will be to the northwest. As long as we don't get turned around to the south or east, we can't miss it."

He stopped and pointed. "The sky seemed to get light from over there, so that's east, more or less. We'll get a better bearing if the sun actually breaks through these clouds. I'm hoping if we just keep going northwest, eventually we'll cross a road and find a signpost you can read, and then maybe we can figure out a general sense of where we are."

He was actually assigning her a task, including her in his plan.

Maybe the fire had melted Stone Warrior's heart.

. . .

"If we get the photos out, what will that mean?" Mia asked. "Could it help anyone besides Dad, like the people in the labor camps?" They were moving through a patch of dark evergreens broken by an occasional blaze of red or orange. The wet leaves gleamed as if they'd been polished. Birds chittered, chirped, and trilled in the distance.

"I guess it's a possibility. It could maybe put pressure on the regime to make changes so that more people don't starve or get executed." Simon made a path for them through a thick tangle of brush and started down a slope.

Mia skidded downhill, dislodging pebbles. "What about Dad?" Her voice sounded young and scared. "You don't think they'd . . . hurt him, do you?" It was the thing she'd been trying not to think about.

"I can't see how that would help them in any way." Simon spoke over his shoulder. "The North Koreans might interrogate him; they could try him in court and sentence him to hard labor. But if they really mistreated Dad, they'd have an international incident on their hands. Which is the last thing they need. Probably what they really want is to use him as bargaining power with the US."

Mia grabbed a branch to slow her downhill plunge. "Daniel could be helping. Dad stopped and talked to him, remember? Maybe Daniel figured out how to get him freed."

Simon shook his head. "If Daniel Moon is working with anyone, I think it's with the guys who took Dad away."

"Yeah, well, I think you're wrong." They'd reached the bottom of the slope. "Daniel's our friend. There's no way he's helping the North Koreans."

"Don't be so dense, Squeak. He glommed on to us from the beginning, introducing himself at the airport, always hanging out with you or Dad, having meals with us. Why would he do that if he didn't have some ulterior motive?"

"We had all these things to talk about. Like about being Korean and American at the same time. It was cool."

Simon turned as he ducked under a low-hanging tree limb, giving her an *oh, please* look.

"Just because you're not interested in what I have to say doesn't mean someone else wouldn't be." She felt like punching him.

"Get real." Her brother's voice was full of scorn. "You're a twelve-year-old girl. Why would a grown man want to spend time with you?"

"I still think you're wrong." She couldn't keep the pout out of her voice. "I think Daniel's my friend. And yours too. And I bet he's trying to help Dad right now."

"Okay, you believe whatever you want to, if that makes you feel better. But the truth is, there was more going on there than friendliness. He's connected to this whole mess somehow, I know it."

A branch he'd just moved past whipped back into place, scattering raindrops and grazing her face. Mia nearly cried out in frustration. Simon always had to have the last word. It reminded her of how he'd teased her when they were little. Enraged, she would lunge at him, pummeling with her fists, and he would hold her at arm's length, his body just out of reach. Once, he'd even picked up a book with his other hand and started reading while she swung at him.

She moved several steps to her left. It was harder going, but she'd rather make her own path than follow her brother's.

They stumbled across the road without meaning to. They were pushing through dense growth when it opened up to a grassy bank, right above a dusty road. Mia hardly had time to register the sight before Simon turned and pushed her, hard. She toppled like a falling tree back into the brush.

She landed on her backpack with a *whoomp*, the air knocked out of her. Simon hit the ground beside her face-first.

"Don't make a sound!" he hissed into her ear. *"Soldiers!"*

CHAE SUNG-MIN

✦ ✦ ✦

As Sung-min rode in the back of the canopied truck, his stomach rumbled. The daybreak meal of thin maize gruel hadn't filled him up — it never did — and the next meal wouldn't be until evening. A whole day working on the roads with nothing to eat. It was all he seemed to think of now, the constant calculating of where and how and when he could find something to satiate the gnawing in his gut. He wasn't starving — he knew the difference — but he was hungry enough to never be able to release his mind to other thoughts.

The truck rattled and bumped over the rough road, surrounded by open fields. The day was clear and bright; that was a blessing. Even if the early-morning rain had continued, they'd have still headed out to work on the roads.

They passed a stream where a young woman squatted over a large rock, wringing and pounding her laundry, her short braid shiny black against the white of her shirt. Sung-min thought of his own sister, helping their mother with morning chores before school began. She was only twelve, but with their father down in the mines and her brother gone to be a soldier, she'd carry a heavier load. When would he see her again? With luck and leave granted, he might get back to the village once or twice a year. By the time he finished his service, nine long years from now, she would be out of school, possibly married, perhaps even a mother herself. The thought made him tired, as if he were an old man whose life had already passed him by, instead of an eighteen-year-old on the brink of adulthood.

He knew this thinking was wrong. He should be happy for this chance to serve. It was all he'd dreamed of as a young boy, to be on the front lines ready to defend the homeland from invading Yankee imperialist warmongers. Back in kindergarten, he'd felt strong and powerful during field day games, smacking imaginary foreign invaders with toy guns. From the age of nine, he'd marched proudly as a Young Pioneer, and with his friends, reenacted thrilling scenes from the movies the whole village watched in the theater each week, of North Korean spies outwitting the treacherous Japanese, and brave guerrillas winning impossible battles against the invading long-nosed Americans and their South Korean puppets. He'd been thrilled, as a teenage member of the Socialist Youth League, to practice on the shooting range with live ammunition.

Now he'd achieved his vision of being a soldier — but all he could think of was food and where to find it.

Next to him on the wooden benches, some of his fellow recruits murmured together in low voices while others dozed, heads lolling back against the green canvas. Even Chul seemed subdued, lacking his usual energy to devise torments. One small reason to be grateful for their inadequate rations.

The rain had dampened the dirt of the road, so the truck wasn't raising a cloud of dust. He had a clear view out over the rice paddies and beyond to the hills thick with trees, a bordering ribbon of autumn color. He saw how he could paint the scene, washing in yellow gold for the expanse of fields, filling a brush with color for the bright foliage, adding more water to sketch in the far blue hills. Finally, a brush tipped with dry ink would stipple in the rough stubble of the shorn stalks, as if the fields had been shaven.

That was a job he hadn't minded, helping the farmers with the corn harvest. There was always the chance of stray kernels to be palmed as he bent to lift an armload of stalks, then slipped into his mouth to soften and surreptitiously gnaw, or a grasshopper when no one was turned his way. He preferred them roasted to bring out the nutty crunchiness, but they were tolerable raw.

A truck with a load of crushed stone was following their caravan today, so he guessed the detail was filling potholes. He'd be lucky if he could snag some grass stems to chew on. He thought about the day ahead, shoveling and spreading rock, summoning strength from a body winded by lack of fuel, and he wondered, again, about a way out.

A few of his comrades, so malnourished they could barely climb out of their bunks, had been sent home to regain their strength. He had thought of pretending to be too sick to eat, played out the vision in his head of being shipped back to the village, of seeing his father and mother and sister again. Of finally eating a meal that filled him. Of resting, and of painting. But two things stopped him: The extra mouth to feed would be a burden for his family, as would their anxiety about his health. And when faced with a mess hall meal, no matter how unappetizing or inadequate, his hunger always overcame his resolve.

They reached the hills, where the road met the forest. The truck slowed, pulled to a halt. Another group of soldiers was already there, carrying shovels and pickaxes. He rose to his feet and clambered out of the back of the truck to join his comrades.

CHAPTER 11

Mia froze. Above them, the grass and bushes grew waist high. Enough to hide them from the road, she hoped. She tried to breathe, calm her racing heart.

"They're just down the road, about fifty feet," Simon whispered. "A couple of trucks. I'm pretty sure no one saw us."

They waited, still as stones. No one could possibly know they were here, unless . . . maybe the motorcycle driver had gone straight to some official and reported the strange girl. But then they should be searching the woods, not the road.

"I'm going up there a little, see if I can find a place to watch them, find out what's going on."

"I'm coming too!" Mia mouthed.

He shook his head. "No way."

Simon wasn't the boss here. Even if he had saved her from getting caught. When he started forward, she followed. He glanced back with an annoyed look, but there wasn't much he could do to stop her.

They crawled through the wet grass and bushes parallel to the road, as close to the ground as the brush would allow.

A sharp sprig scratched Mia's ear and she flinched, swallowing a cry.

In the distance, faint voices called. On his belly in the grass in front of her, Simon held up his hand. He pointed his index finger at himself, then the road. Mia nodded. He slithered forward, heading toward a thick cluster of bushes still in full green leaf. Reaching the screen of foliage, he lay there, looking to the right, then for a long time to the left. Finally, he turned his head back to her. He lifted a finger to his lips, then beckoned her forward.

The soldiers were just boys her age. Skinny middle-school boys, five feet tall or so, shorter than Mia. About twenty of them, all dressed in olive green uniforms and caps. They carried shovels and seemed to be filling holes in the road, not searching for foreign escapees.

An engine roared, coming up from Mia and Simon's right. Several of the soldiers turned toward it, facing in their direction. Mia gasped.

They weren't boys. They were young men. Older than Simon, maybe nineteen, twenty.

But they were the *size* of boys.

She'd seen Dad's photos of little children who never got enough to eat, with bloated bellies, sores, and hair like straw. This was what childhood famine did to bodies that survived it.

Simon turned to look at her, his jaw tightening. He caught her eye and tipped his head back. *Let's get out of here.*

Soon they were hidden in thick foliage and could stand upright. Mia fell in behind Simon, feeling spent. He seemed to be walking a line parallel to the road, so they could return to it when the soldiers were gone, she guessed.

The ground was uneven, suddenly falling away, then rising up, jarring as her foot hit solid mass sooner than she expected. She felt jittery and trembly, each step an effort. Her mind was muddled. Maybe it was being so tired and hungry. Or maybe it was the sight of those young men, the thought of their hunger as children. Or their hunger now.

"*Mia, keep up!*" Simon called in a fierce whisper, turning to frown at her.

She stopped dead in her tracks and folded her arms, glaring at him.

He gaped at her, arms outstretched. She stood her ground.

Simon dropped his head back in exasperation, then stalked back toward her. "Mia, what the —"

"You could go a little slower, so I *can* keep up! We were working together for a little while back there. Now you're back in that stupid cave of yours. Surrounded by 'Trespassers Will Be Shot' signs."

"What are you talking about?" He was staring at her as if she'd lost her mind.

"If we're going to save Dad, we have to be a team. You're only willing to accept me as a team member when you're in charge of everything!" she raged at him. "You keep shutting me out!"

"Squeak, I have no idea what this is about, but we don't have time for this. If you'll remember, we're trying to escape from North Korea. And trying to help Dad get out of prison. So could you just keep up?" He turned his back on her and started off, still at the same pace.

She felt like something in her would explode. She stomped along, pounding each step as if Simon were underfoot. She kept her eyes on the ground. He could just wait for her.

After a bit she glanced up again. Her heart lurched. She couldn't see Simon anywhere. She swallowed. *Don't panic.* He had to be nearby.

Then she caught a glimpse of his gray sweatshirt moving through the leaves, down at the bottom of a gully. Relief flooded through her. But he had gotten really far ahead. She didn't think she could catch up unless she sprinted, and she was way too tired to run.

This was dangerous. He should've checked to see if she was behind him. He was too far away to hear unless she shouted, and shouting was obviously a bad idea.

Simon was moving around the base of a small hill ahead to her right. If she went over it rather than around it, maybe she could come out in front of him. That would show him.

She turned and started up the slope, relishing for a moment the feeling of choosing her own path. The Scout, that's who she was.

By the time she was halfway up, she saw her mistake. The hill was covered with dense undergrowth, with tree trunks and boulders she had to weave around. It would take longer than going around. Maybe the other side would be faster, going down.

The summit of the hill was a long ridge, covered in piles of flat rocks. She was out of the thicket but had to watch her step on the precarious piles. At least it looked as if the ridge was taking her in the direction Simon had headed.

To her right, the ground fell away, rock platters spilling down the slope, as if the top of the hill had caved in. As Mia stepped on a large rocky sheet, she felt it wobble under her weight. Her body tipped to the right, then her feet slid out from under her. She tumbled off the ridge and down the steep side, dislodging loose rocks as she fell. She landed hard near the bottom of the scooped-out center of the hill, an avalanche clattering around her.

A cloud of dust rose. She lay still, checking her body for damage. She was on her back, head pointed downhill. It smarted where she'd banged the back of her skull on hard rock. She was scraped and bumped and rattled in a dozen places. But she was okay. Her first reaction was giddy relief.

Then she noticed pressure on her legs and pelvic bone. Several large, heavy pieces of slate had slid on top of her.

She pushed on the rocks with her hands. They didn't budge.

She tried to raise herself. It was like trying to do sit-ups on an angled board with someone holding down her legs and hips. She tried to twist on her side to slip out from under the rocks. A sharp pain in her lower back stopped her. She lay back, the blood rushing to her head.

Simon! Help!

She stopped herself before the scream left her throat. He might not be able to hear her anyway. But if he could, so could someone else. He might have heard the rocks falling, but he wouldn't know it was her. Or where to look. He was probably still forging ahead. How long would it take him to notice she wasn't there behind him?

The weight of the rocks pinned her down. She didn't have the strength to lift them off or to crawl out from under them. She was trapped.

CHAPTER 12

The panic rose, a tidal wave submerging her. She could die here. She'd never get home, never see Dad or Mom or Simon again. And the longer she lay trapped, while Simon moved farther away, the more likely it was they would not survive. Simon could spend days looking for her, until he died of thirst or starvation. . . . She hiccupped a sob, tears leaking down the sides of her forehead into her hair.

If Simon hadn't been so awful, this never would have happened. He was the one who'd made them run, who'd made them get into that truck. He was the reason they were lost in the middle of a forest on a mountain in North Korea! He left her behind. If she died here, it would be all Simon's —

Stop.

If she kept wasting her time blaming Simon, she would die here.

She had opened the gift box and the phone against Mr. Lee's instructions. She had followed Simon when he said they had to run. She was so busy being mad at him she hadn't noticed him getting ahead of her. She chose to take the shortcut over this hill.

She had gotten herself into this.

She felt the weight of the rocks again. It was true. She was completely trapped. There was nothing she could do.

This time, instead of panic, she experienced a sense of emptiness. Not like depression, like outer space. Vast and endless. And somehow, free. Her hand slipped off her mouth and dropped to the ground below her head.

She lay there, still. Not fighting it. Just letting go.

A picture floated into her empty mind: a bottle of soda. And a bottle opener, popping off the cap. It seemed so random.

Then she saw.

Her feet, legs, and hips were pinned, but her arms were free. If she could grab something to wedge under the rocks, lifting them enough to free herself . . . It would be like popping a cap off a bottle.

She felt around until one hand found a medium-sized chunk of rock. Thin enough, maybe, to slip under the rocks pinning her. Strong enough, she hoped, not to shatter.

The pressure in her head from being upside down was increasing. She focused on the image of the bottle opener. Find a place the rock would fit between the layer on top of her and the one below. Find something she could balance it on so there was room to maneuver it. Find the strength to wedge it in.

She pressed the rock into the opening. Nothing happened. Then she felt it — a tiny bit more space. She shifted her body down an inch. She shoved the small rock in a little deeper. Pushed down on it. Shifted her body again. This would take forever.

Her hips were freed for a moment, but her knee was now

pinned. Then her ankle. Her backpack caught on the rocks beneath her. She rotated her body in tiny increments, looking for some bit of space where she could move. She remembered, with a shudder, a short story about a cave spelunker caught in a tunnel deep underground, working and working to get his body free.

Sweat pooled at the back of her neck. She took a deep gulp of air. At least she was out in the open. She was going to do this. She was going to get out of here. She was going to save Dad.

And then all at once she was free. Her legs slid out from under the pinning rock. The sudden lifting of the weight was glorious. She rolled over onto her side, hugging herself and laughing. She had done it.

Mia clambered shakily to her feet and stumbled back to sit on a rock, letting her head clear. She was dusty and bruised and scraped, but her clothing and pack had protected her from getting badly cut.

Her watch read 1:17, but she had no idea what time she'd started up the hill. She needed to find Simon. Fast.

She started picking her way up the slope, careful not to set off another avalanche. Along the ridge and down the hillside. Her legs felt wobbly after all the exertion. She forced herself to move slowly and carefully.

As she started down toward the gully where she'd last seen Simon, she peered through the brush and trees, looking for any sign of movement, any blond hair or gray sweatshirt. Nothing.

At the bottom, she turned in a circle, scanning the woods all around. No sign of Simon. He could have gone on ahead. Or retraced his steps to look for her. She sank to the ground against a small tree trunk, completely spent.

There was a crackle in the underbrush. She leaped to her feet, whirled, looking wildly in every direction.

Simon's light hair flashed in the sunlight, coming down the hill toward the gully. She staggered to him, relief washing over her. He looked like the best thing she'd ever seen.

"Mia! What the hell —" Simon's expression was furious.

"I went over the hill, but I fell and got pinned under some rocks. I couldn't call out to you. It took me forever to get out!"

He was shaking his head, swearing, eyes wild. "What were you thinking? Do you know how dangerous that was? I've been searching for you for ages! I might never have found you! You could've died up there!" As if he had rescued her.

"I know, I know, I'm sorry! I got so far behind and I thought I could catch up! It was dangerous, I know!"

Simon stamped about for a few more minutes, continuing to swear, occasionally turning on her. For some reason, his anger didn't bother her at all. She had to clamp her lips together to keep from smiling.

It was okay. She hadn't died. They had found each other again. And his fury — it sounded like caring. About *her*.

As they started walking again, a triumphant little song played in her mind: *I saved myself. I saved myself.*

. . .

"I'm going to climb a tree and see if I can get a bearing," Simon said.

They were at the top of a long slope. All around them, great pines rose, blocking the light from reaching the forest floor. They'd been walking on a spongy carpet of rust-colored pine needles. The space was like a vast ballroom, with dozens of towering pillars supporting a sky-high leafy ceiling.

The whole place felt as if she'd stepped into the world of *Quest*, only it was real. She half expected to spot a ring of toadstools pointing to a treasure hidden among these tall trees, or magical beings waiting to help them in their cause. In the aftermath of getting herself out from under the rocks, she felt even better and stronger than when she successfully completed a chapter in the game, the Scout bringing her team — the Archer, the Wizard, the Alchemist, the Prince, and the others — safely to the next milestone on the quest to rescue Queen Aditha.

The tree Simon had chosen was enormous. He was already moving up the trunk with ease, stretching from one limb to another, his hold as sure as if he had sticky webs on his hands and feet.

Mia sank carefully to her knees on the soft ground, trying not to bump her worst bruises. She watched until he was out of sight on the other side of the massive trunk. She didn't want to think about how high he was off the ground, how long a fall if . . . She lay back on the needle-covered ground to rest, reaching a hand for her locket.

There was nothing there.

She sat up and felt her neck with both hands. No chain. No locket pendant. She stood up and shook out her jacket and T-shirt, searched her jeans pockets. Finally, she opened her pack, emptied everything onto the ground, and shook it upside down. She examined each item as she repacked. No necklace.

The rocks. The chain must have broken when she got trapped. Or when they were crawling through the brush beside the road. She felt like crying. All that work saving herself, and she had to go and lose her necklace. Of course it was nothing, compared to everything they were going through. But she wanted her necklace, all the more *because* of everything they were going through.

Her hand went to her throat again, searching for the locket to hold, to comfort herself because she had lost it. She gave a shaky little laugh. Her mind knew it was gone, but her body hadn't gotten the message yet. Her hand opened on her chest and patted it, like soothing a crying baby. *There, there.*

There was a scrape above her, Simon's shoes on the bark. He was navigating the lower branches, still high overhead. He was almost down when he gave a stifled cry, then a sharp exhalation. A moment later he dropped to the ground and lowered himself beside her. His hand went to the inside of his left calf.

"Damn! I stabbed myself! There was this broken branch, really sharp, slipped under my jeans —"

He bent forward and rolled up the cuff. Mia gasped. His leg was covered in bright blood.

Simon reached for his pack and pulled out his water bottle, unscrewing the cap. He poured a stream of water over his leg, his breath hissing through clenched teeth. It was a long, nasty scrape, like a channel down the length of his shin and ankle. Mia winced, then shivered. Pale watery blood streamed down his leg onto his sock.

"I've got to bandage it somehow, stop the bleeding," Simon said.

"My underwear, the clean pair." She grabbed her pack. "I haven't worn them."

Simon made a face, but he took the underwear. With the blade of his knife, he cut a long strip of the lavender cotton, then started to wrap it around his leg.

"Wait!" she said. "I've got soap!"

Simon gave her a look, but this time he didn't make fun of her. He cut off a section from the leftover scrap of cloth and used it to wash the wound with soap. Red-tinged water dripped onto the orange pine needles.

The wound cleaned and wrapped, Simon got slowly to his feet. He put his foot down, shifted a little onto it, then more fully.

Mia's eyes widened. If Simon couldn't walk . . .

"Okay," he said.

She let out her breath. "Do you think we should try to get back to the road? So it's easier to walk?"

He shook his head. "The last thing I need is to run for cover if someone comes along." He was scuffing the wet and bloody spots into the dirt, covering them with more pine needles.

"Did you figure out what direction we're going?" She leaned down to gather their water bottles and search the ground for any trace of their presence.

"I couldn't see much when I was up there, but I could tell which way was west. The sky's brighter over there." He gestured to their left.

They walked side by side down the gentle slope, then up a steeper rise. Mia caught Simon wincing from time to time. Maybe he was in pain and not telling her. She felt a little light-headed herself. Her arms and legs were heavy and her bruises ached.

"It looks like some kind of trail over there." Mia broke through the brush and found herself in an open green tunnel, as if someone had mowed a pathway through the undergrowth. "Simon, come see!"

There, in the grass at her feet, were two rusting metal rails. They ran straight ahead, deep into the forest, nearly covered by grass in spots.

"Weird." Simon shook his head. "Maybe there was some kind of factory in the forest, for some forest product, and they sent the freight out by rail."

"Let's follow it!" She traced the enticing path with her eyes.

Simon was calculating, looking up at the sky, turning around in a circle to get his bearings. "It's running more or less west. It'll take us away from the road, but it's gotta go somewhere eventually."

In spite of everything, Mia felt her mood lifting as they set off uphill along the tracks. Despite the overgrowth, it was much easier walking. That must be better for Simon's leg. And there was something about following a path. . . . Bushwhacking didn't necessarily go anywhere but more wilderness. But a path led *somewhere*. And she had found it. She was a real, true Scout.

As the brightness of the day dimmed, they still hadn't come to any kind of shelter. The trees were smaller and spaced wider apart, and there were open stretches of barren land: dry, brown dirt covered only in browning grass. It was looking less promising that they'd find anywhere good to rest for the night.

Then, around a bend, they came to a structure framed in a little group of trees. An old boxcar on rusted wheels. Gray wooden sides rotted in a rusty metal frame, one side open where the door had disintegrated.

When they looked inside, they found a tree growing up

through a corroded hole in the metal floor, pushing out through a missing section of roof. The far end of the roof was still in one piece, sheltering one corner of the boxcar.

Simon leaned forward and placed both hands on the metal floor, testing. "Seems like it's solid."

"Let me try. I'm lighter." Holding the side of the car, Mia climbed up carefully. They didn't need her falling through, scraping her leg on sharp metal. She walked around, then stamped, and finally jumped up and down.

"It'll be dark soon. Guess this is our motel room." Simon started to lower himself to the edge of the car floor. Mia jumped out of the boxcar and reached to hold some of his weight as he sat.

"Mia, I'm fine. Back off." His tone was short, annoyed.

"Hey, I'm just trying to help."

"Well, don't."

He leaned against the edge of the doorway and shut his eyes, frowning. She stepped back.

"Knock it off, Simon. I know you're frustrated —"

His eyes flew open and his head came up. "You don't know anything." His mouth turned down in an angry sneer. "You wanna know what's going on for me? Well, let me lay it out for you. As you pointed out yesterday, *I'm* the one who got you into this. *I'm* the one who said we had to run. It's *my* fault that you're in danger. What would Mom and Dad say about that? And speaking of Dad, oh yeah, he's stuck in some prison somewhere, and I have absolutely no idea how to help him."

Mia let herself slowly down to kneel on the ground, eyes on Simon as he went on.

"Then, to top it all off, I have to go climb a tree and injure myself! And ever since this started, it's like my perfectly ordinary, scaredy-cat little sister suddenly morphed into some kind of Spy Girl!" He was talking to the ground now. "You've got a map, you've got a dictionary, you've got dried food, you can read and write freakin' Korean! . . . I mean, you're like some Special Forces operative who's been training for months!

"Meanwhile, I'm totally *useless*." His voice was ragged by this point, the words torn out of him. "I stick out like a neon sign. I don't know how to do anything that can actually help us get away."

He looked across at her, eyes blazing. "We are *lost*, Mia. In a freakin' totalitarian country! They're looking for us everywhere. I can't walk fast. We haven't eaten in twenty-four hours, except for your stupid snacks. I've been terrified since we ran. I'm afraid I can't get you out of here." His voice cracked.

Mia stared.

Simon sat up, pulled his MP3 player out of his pack, and put on his earphones.

Mia stood up and walked a few steps, then sat down on a large rock near the boxcar. She felt a little dizzy. It was as if somebody had slipped into her mind and rearranged all the furniture.

She had been so focused on herself that she hadn't thought that Simon would be blaming himself for everything. He was used to being the champion, the bright sun that every-one — his little sister, his classmates, the fans at soccer and baseball games — looked up to.

She knew better than to try to reassure him by remind-ing him of all the amazing things he'd done. He'd known they had to run, which had kept the North Koreans from finding the photos on the phone. He'd led them out of

Pyongyang. He'd found places to hide. He'd gotten them a ride. He kept figuring out what they needed to do. It was because of him that they hadn't been caught.

She knew none of that would be enough in his book. It was all or nothing for Simon.

She remembered a baseball game last spring when he'd hit two home runs. Mia had run up to congratulate him afterward, bouncing with excitement. He'd just looked at her and said, "We didn't win, did we?"

Another thing she understood now: Simon was *scared*. All that Stone Warrior stuff was just a cover. When he'd forced them to run, seeing his fear had made her panic more. But now, somehow it helped to know they were both afraid.

Then there were the things he'd said about her. It was as if he'd held up a mirror with a reflection of someone she didn't recognize. She wasn't an invisible girl in the shadow of her competent big brother. She wasn't a heavy burden dragging him down. She was someone who had something to offer.

She couldn't help smiling. Spy Girl, he'd called her. A Special Forces operative. Her mind began to make a picture. She'd need a superhero uniform — it would have to be black, like a wet suit. With a pull-up ninja-style mask. And tight, black, thigh-high boots with stiletto heels, like Catwoman.

Simon opened his eyes then and caught the look on her face.

"What's so funny?" His voice was loud over the music. He sounded like he might eat her.

She cocked her head and gave him a little grin. "I was just kind of imagining that Spy Girl thing, what the costume would look like." She shrugged an apology. "But Simon —" Her voice was serious now.

"What?" His tone was a little less aggressive. He pulled out one earbud.

"Getting the photos out isn't stupid. The people in the photos matter. It may not be much, but it's the only thing we can do to help them, and Dad."

"Yeah, well, that's not going to help us get out of here, is it?" Simon put his earpiece back in and climbed into the boxcar.

Mia felt exhaustion coming over her in a great smothering blanket, pinning her to the ground. She made herself stand up. She gathered a few armloads of grass and leaves and piled them in the corner of the boxcar. She slid to the floor on top of the pile, feeling as if she would never move again.

Simon was propped against the side of the car near the opening, where there was still some light. He bent forward over his leg and pulled off the bandage. In the center of the lavender cloth that used to be her underwear was a large, dark red stain.

"How is it?" She tried to sound casual.

"I can't really tell. At least it's clotted some. I'm going to let it air out for the night and dry out the bandage. We don't have enough water left to wash it." He reached forward to drape the bloody cloth over a branch of the little tree at the center of the car. It hung there, a grisly decoration in the dusk. Simon crawled across the floor and stretched out beside her.

Mia gathered her strength to sit up and pull the pack from underneath her head. She took out the Snickers bar and handed it to Simon.

"This is for you."

He glanced over, then turned his head sharply away. "No way, Mia. It's yours."

"Simon, I saved it for you. You lost some blood today —"

He exhaled loudly, scoffing. "Well, you did, a little. But more than that, you need more fuel than I do. I still have the package of Starbursts. I'll eat some of those."

He finally saw that she wasn't going to back down. Watching him eat the chocolate was even sweeter than the taste of the candy melting in her mouth.

He carefully folded the wrapper and handed it back to her. "Thanks."

Her face warmed with pleasure. She took a swig from her bottle, restraining herself from gulping down the rest. "Do you still have water?"

"A few swallows. We'll have to find some tomorrow." Simon picked some dry twigs off the floor of the car, carved the bark off, and handed her one. They lay side by side, working on their teeth.

"Simon?"

"What?" His voice sounded bleached out.

"We really need some food." Mia thought of the young soldiers who would never grow to their full height. The many nights they had gone to bed feeling this hollowness — or something much worse.

"I know. We'll find something tomorrow, somehow."

She chose to believe him.

SON JI-HOON

"Agent Son, the chief wishes to see you in his office. 18:30." The call came from Chief Yoon's secretary as Ji-hoon was packing up to leave.

A warning stirred in his gut, like the faint rumble of a far-off storm. Prepare for trouble.

Of course it didn't necessarily mean catastrophe. The bureau chief often requested face-to-face meetings, to update him on investigations or to pass on instructions in particularly delicate operations, such as the one that had presented itself the day before. But Ji-hoon was on high alert these days. The director of his agency, the Ministry of People's Security, had chosen to work in direct opposition to the State Security Department. And even more deadly, he had decided to bolster their efforts by involving foreign contacts. Ji-hoon knew that as a senior agent, he'd have a target on his back if anything went wrong.

He checked his watch. 18:22. He had eight minutes to collect himself, in case he wasn't coming back to this office. Rubbing the raised rope of scar on the back of his right hand, he scanned the surface of his desk and did a mental inventory of the neat stacks of papers and the drawers of his file cabinet, ensuring once again that there was nothing that could be used to incriminate him or any of his associates. Not that any of that would matter if the agency needed sacrificial lambs. The only recourse in such an event was to jump ship before it was too late. Equally important, though, was not taking action too soon; premature movement could have immediate, deadly consequences.

He put on his suit jacket, slipped his cell phone into his pocket, stepped through the office doorway, and started down the corridor.

His survival instincts remained keen, honed in the famine days when he'd had to scrounge, steal, and fight for his life as a kotchebi — a flower swallow, one of hundreds of street children who haunted the markets, public squares, and rail stations of North Korea after their adult relatives had starved to death, left to find food, or abandoned them once they could no longer feed them. He carried more than just physical scars from this harrowing experience. Perhaps the most useful thing he'd acquired was the ability to read nuances of expression, gesture, and speech, like an early-warning system, detecting vulnerabilities to be exploited or threats to be avoided. And the habit of always having a Plan B, like a stowed-away life raft.

In the corridor he passed Baek and Ahn, talking intently. He felt a kind of pity for his fellow agents, a bunch of boys whose families' wealth and prestige were as responsible for their current positions as any personal merit. For once he was grateful for his early losses, and to be yet unmarried, childless. He could make his choices without worrying about a family.

Pausing before the door to the chief's office, he took a breath, stilling his face: a quiet pool reflecting a clear sky and bright sun, not a ripple to suggest the tumult beneath the surface. 18:30. He stepped forward and knocked on the door.

"The two young Americans," the chief began, without even greeting him. "They've been spotted."

CHAPTER 13

OCTOBER 5

Something was wrong.

Simon was groaning.

He stood near the opening of the boxcar, his back to Mia. Balancing on his right foot, he held on to the edge of the doorway, left knee bent, foot dangling.

"Simon?" It came out as an anxious squeak.

"It's okay, Mia. My leg just hurts a little."

She rubbed her eyes. He was trying to reassure her, but this was bad. If his leg was hurting this much, when he wasn't putting weight on it, he shouldn't walk on it.

It hit her again, how desperate their circumstances were. No water. No food left. They hadn't had a meal in nearly three days. They were getting weaker, or at least she was. Simon was wounded and needed to rest his leg. They'd never get out of the country if he didn't heal.

Oh, Dad.

Mia wanted to curl up on the floor of the boxcar and go back to sleep. She forced herself to stand. She stretched out her legs, brushing the bits of dead leaves and grass from her clothes.

Simon had slid to the floor by the doorway with his left foot on his right knee, examining his leg. She crawled over to him.

"Simon! It looks terrible!" The blood was dried and dark, the nasty line of the wound black at the center. Around it, his shin was purple and swollen, the skin pulled tight. "Is it infected?"

"Not badly, not yet. The redness is only around the wound itself. I think the swelling and bruising could be from the trauma, and from walking on it."

"You've got to rest."

There was a silence. Simon shook his head and sighed. "Yeah, I'm afraid so. I need to elevate it." He leaned his head back against the door edge, as if he didn't have the energy to hold it up anymore. Mia sat down beside him, her legs dangling toward the rails.

"I need to go look for food and water."

His head swiveled to her, sharp. "No, Mia, uh-uh. No way are you going alone."

"But we've got to get something to eat and drink. Maybe I can find something."

"Like what? A grocery store? *McDonald's?*" He closed his eyes.

Really, Simon? Is being right and in charge more important to you than being alive? Mia caught herself. She remembered what she had learned last night: He was being a jerk because he felt helpless. They couldn't afford the time or energy to fight about this.

"Water, at least. We really need water."

Simon still had his eyes closed, as if it was too much effort to keep them open. Resting against the doorframe, her tough, athletic brother looked utterly spent. If she didn't get water, his leg might get really infected. He needed her help.

"Simon, we don't have any choice."

He opened his eyes, his face stony, resisting.

"Listen, I'll stay on the tracks, or within sight of them. We haven't seen a single sign of anyone since we left the road. And remember, I look Korean. And I've got the badge. If I see someone — *which isn't going to happen* —" she added quickly as he flinched, "but in the highly unlikely event that I see someone, I'll pretend I'm mute or something."

"Jeez, Mia, no! *N-O*. It's too dangerous."

She was on her feet now, facing him. "Simon, it's already dangerous. Look at you." She gestured to the woods around them, keeping her eyes on his. "I've got to go. You can't stop me."

He calculated, the emotions playing over his features. Finally, he turned away, let out a breath. "One hour. You have to be back here in one hour, whether you find anything or not."

Mia nodded and collected both their water bottles. They checked that their watches were synchronized. 7:46 a.m.

She started down the tracks, turning once to wave at Simon. From this distance, he looked small and alone, sitting in the opening of the dilapidated boxcar. Mia wanted to run back to him, but she turned to the tracks, to her quest.

Her head felt woozy, with a faint ringing in her ears. Walking was more like floating, her body curiously weightless. The colored leaves were brilliant in the early morning light. It was beautiful, but it felt completely different from being in the woods behind their house in Connecticut or finding a path through the forest in *Quest*. Instead, it seemed strange and sinister that the day could be so lovely when they were in such terrible trouble.

She moved as quickly as she could, peering from side to side for any signs of a stream. There had to be water around here somewhere.

After she'd walked for about ten minutes, she caught a flash of movement to the left, just past her vision. She froze, swiveling her head in a broad circle, surveying the woods.

She waited, holding her breath. Nothing moved.

She made herself move forward. If she was in real danger, there wasn't anything she could do about it. One step, then another. Nothing seemed to be following.

At twenty-eight minutes, she found it. Water, flowing right under the tracks and down to her left, carving a thin slice out of the hillside.

It was a beautiful stream, a perfect stream, a burbling, babbling brook right out of a fairy tale. She'd never seen anything more lovely. She knelt on the grass below the tracks and plunged her hands into the flow. She splashed handfuls of icy water on her face, then drank big gulps, only admitting at that moment how thirsty she had been.

Hurry. She took out the two water bottles and filled them to the brim. She should have brought the bloody cloth to wash. Well, they had water, that was miracle enough.

She checked her watch. 8:17. She'd been gone thirty-one minutes. She calculated. She wouldn't need quite as much time for the return trip because she wouldn't be wasting time searching. If she followed the stream downhill for just a few minutes, maybe she'd find something they could eat. Anything. Wild berries. A tree with nuts. That's what people were always eating in wilderness stories.

Mia grasped branches and saplings as she made her way downstream, crossing back and forth on rocks, careful not to slip and fall. She scanned the ground cover, the bushes, the foliage. Some of these wild plants must be edible, but she wouldn't know them if she saw them. And she wasn't ready to try tree bark.

Thirty-four minutes. Just ahead, the stream curved to the left, out of sight behind the trees. She'd go just around the bend. If there was nothing, she'd start back.

There, around the turn, was a crumbling low wall and a gnarled tree. And high in the tree among the nearly bare branches, a few orange dots shone against the bright blue sky. Mia blinked and shaded her eyes. Still there. Round, orange dots.

Her eyes swam, looking up into the sun. She shook her head to clear it. How could there be a tree with fruit in a country where people were starving?

The wall was a disintegrating pile of stones and packed mud. Beyond it was a structure of earthen walls. Once a one-room shed, now missing its roof. Nearby, another crumbling wall surrounded a larger building. A farmhouse with a porch. Pieces of straw matting still clung to the damaged roof. Clearly no one lived here anymore.

But the fruit was still there up in the tree. Maybe fifteen or twenty pieces, squat and round, like bright orange tomatoes. She'd seen those before, on the October pages of Korean calendar paintings: country boys perched in the trees picking the fruit, while girls waited below with their skirts held open to catch the harvest. Persimmons.

Maybe she could climb the tree.

No, she'd run out of time. But this was food. A few fallen

persimmons lay scattered on the ground. She could come back later to get the rest.

Mia scooped up the fruit from the ground. Three pieces were split, and one was half-mashed, but she slipped them into the empty outer pocket of her backpack. Bits of the persimmon flesh clung to her fingers. She licked them clean. It tasted like the best thing she had ever eaten.

Then she ran.

Up the stream bed, splashing a little in the water, hanging onto branches to keep herself from falling. She got to the tracks, panting. 8:27. She had nineteen minutes to travel a distance that had taken her twenty-eight. She was already out of breath. She couldn't run anymore.

She took long strides, moving along the rails as quickly as she could. The distance seemed so much longer than it had coming. Eleven minutes left. Seven. How far was she from the boxcar?

At 8:45 she called out, "Simon! It's okay! I'm coming!" But she couldn't get enough breath to make her voice loud. He'd never hear her. But someone else might.

Mia made herself run again, her legs rubber. Her heart beat painfully against the walls of her chest. Her breath was ragged, tearing her throat.

Then, finally, there was the boxcar. Simon wasn't in the doorway. Where was he? She stumbled to the edge of the doorway, gasping.

Simon was lying on the floor, turned on his side away from her. Not waiting and worrying. She could have walked instead of killing herself running.

Then she realized that he was asleep. A little zipper of fear ran through her. If Simon were well, he would have been watching for her. Counting the minutes. Angry when she was late. To have passed out at a time like this meant he must be completely overcome with exhaustion. Or weak with hunger or dehydration.

She sat watching him for a few minutes until she had her breath back. Then she shrugged out of her backpack and pulled out one of the bottles of water.

"Simon?" He stirred but didn't wake. Mia got on her knees and reached over to gently shake his arm. "Simon, wake up. I found water."

He grunted and turned over onto his back. As his hurt leg hit the floor, he moaned. He raised his head and looked at her, as if through a haze. "Huh?"

"Water. I got water." She held out the bottle. He reached his hand out to take it, but his eyes closed and his head went back to the floor. Her heart pounded. This was bad.

She shifted closer to him and unscrewed the cap. With one hand she lifted his head, put the bottle to his lips, and let a little water trickle into his mouth.

That woke him. His eyes opened, and he raised himself on one elbow, took the bottle, and drank. Mia watched with satisfaction as he downed half the container. He wiped his mouth with the back of one hand, sat up, and scooted back to rest against the wall of the boxcar. At least he was awake.

"Whew, I needed that. So you found something."

A smile spread slowly across her face. "A stream. And more." She unzipped the outer pocket of her pack and pulled the flaps open to display the fruit.

"What's that?"

"Persimmons."

"Wow, Mia, seriously?"

She pulled off a mashed piece and held it out. "Try it."

Simon dipped a finger into the pulp and licked off the dab. His eyes widened.

They ate all five persimmons, every bit of flesh and skin, licking around the stems, spitting out the few seeds. The pulp was soft, deeply sweet and tart at the same time, with a kind of puckery aftertaste. It was heavenly, eating.

"There's some still up in the tree." She told Simon all the details of the stream and the abandoned farmhouse. "It's about a thirty-minute walk, but we can eat the persimmons and use the house for shelter. We'll have all the water we need while you rest your leg. And then, when your leg is better, there must be a path from the house that goes somewhere."

■ ■ ■

The sun was high overhead by the time they reached the farmhouse, Simon leaning on a stick Mia had found for him. Everything was still there. The stream. The persimmon tree. The crumbling walls. Following Simon as he limped into the overgrown yard, Mia was grateful she wasn't alone. It was the kind of place that made her think of ghosts.

Now that she wasn't in such a desperate hurry, there was time to examine the farmhouse. It consisted of a single room with a raised wooden porch under an overhang. A door hung at an angle off one hinge. Inside, wooden rafters framed the sky where sections of the thatched roof were missing. Fixed up, the structure would have looked a lot like the carved box the Ministry officials had presented as a gift.

"Kinda small, isn't it?" Simon said, letting himself down slowly onto the edge of the porch.

"In farmers' houses, the whole family lived in one room." Mia remembered the pictures she'd pored over in a book at Korean school. They showed traditional homes — from peasant cottages to royal palaces — with layouts like little maps, with all the details of how the houses were built and how people lived. "They'd eat in here, sleep in here, everything. They didn't have any furniture, just quilts they folded up in the corner. A table that was carried in to eat on. That door would have been covered with rice paper, to keep the wind out but let a little light in." She pointed to a passage to the right of the porch, under a lean-to roof. "And that's the kitchen. See that clay shelf with the hole in it? I think it goes under the house, like an oven. They'd build a fire to cook with and it would also heat the floor of the room."

Simon winced as he lifted his leg to the porch. Mia hurried to help him. He leaned back against the porch pillar, jaw muscles clenched. She bit her lip.

"It hurts, doesn't it?"

"I just need to rest." He sounded completely drained. Mia climbed onto the porch and stepped gingerly into the room. She knelt and ran her hands over the section of the clay floor that wasn't cracked and crumbling.

"I think you can lie down in here. There's still some shelter." She moved into the corner. "We can sleep here. Even if it rains."

"It sure is tiny. But it must have been a good place to live." Simon's voice sounded faint, half asleep, as he gazed out at the view. "It's facing south, so they got sun all day."

The farmhouse perched on an open hillside, looking across at other tree-covered hills. The stream ran along the field behind the house, tumbling down toward a small valley. Everything was overgrown now, but there must have once been a few terraced plots for corn or vegetables.

"I wonder why they left," Mia said.

"Dad said people got sent off to labor camps for doing anything against the regime," Simon said. "Like hoarding food. Or being accused of it. And people starved to death, whole families."

She made a moan of protest, imagining the skeletons of a farmer, his wife, and his children in this space.

But Simon was shaking his head. "People who have crops, fruit trees, a whole forest to hunt in, they're going to be the last ones to starve to death. They might go hungry in the winter, but there's always something to eat. The really desperate ones were in the towns and cities." His head dropped back against the pillar, as if that bit of thinking had used up all the energy he had.

Mia stepped back into the room and used her hands to sweep a corner clear of dust, dried leaves, and crumbled clay. Then she helped Simon onto the floor, propping his head on his rolled-up backpack. He leaned forward, hissing through clenched teeth as he pulled the cuff of his jeans up over his shin.

Everything about his injury looked worse. The redness was a deeper scarlet, the swollen skin shiny where it pulled tighter, the bruising darker. A disaster zone.

"Nice." Simon's tone was grim.

"We have to wash it. With the soap."

"What it really needs is heat. And raising it up, that will help with the pain, maybe the swelling. . . . But first I just need to sleep. . . ." He lay back, spent, his hurt leg bent, foot on the floor.

Fear flickered in her stomach. Simon's wound was getting worse, not better. He was losing strength. She knew that people could die of blood poisoning from infected cuts.

If only they could trade places. Simon would be so much better at handling this. But it was up to her to figure something out. Or they were both doomed.

CHAPTER 14

Out in the yard Mia found a large rock with a flat top. Squatting, she got her fingers underneath it and gradually pried it out of the ground. She brushed off the dirt, then lugged it across the yard and into the room next to Simon.

"Here, I'm going to put this under your foot." He grimaced as she lifted his heel and placed it on the rock. His foot was raised up about six or seven inches. Maybe it would help a little.

He mumbled, already drifting off.

Mia could feel the beginning of panic at the edges of her brain. *Do something. Keep busy.*

Their water bottles were empty. Kneeling by the stream, she filled them. She splashed cold water on her face again and again. She needed to stay alert.

She washed Simon's cut. He winced a lot and sucked in his breath, but he let her clean it. She managed to soak some of the scab off and get the cut to bleed a little. But it wasn't enough. Like Simon said, it needed hot water.

She'd found water. The next step was to find a way to heat it.

She examined the layout of the lean-to kitchen. She'd been right, there was a firepit. The woods around the farmhouse were full of kindling. They had matches, and paper from Simon's magazines.

All she needed was a vessel that could hold water and withstand heat. All they had was two plastic water bottles, a container of hand sanitizer, and a tiny bottle of shampoo. Nothing that wouldn't melt.

Maybe she could make something. Some kind of pot, out of whatever she could find around the farm. She might be able to mix dirt and water into clay. But that would take ages to dry, and she needed the hot water as soon as possible.

She could try weaving something. She gathered handfuls of long dry weeds and some twigs. She was the arts and crafts camper; she understood the basic principle of over and under, over and under. But nothing would stay together long enough to be woven. She threw down the mess in exasperation.

She needed something that would hold a round shape. When she took Simon's knife from the pocket of his jeans, he didn't even stir. She yanked her mind back from the fear to her task.

Mia cut three U-shaped lengths of some woody vines. Back on the porch, she hit on the idea of lacing their middles together with some tough pieces of grass. The brittle strands of grass kept breaking until she tried braiding several into a rope. Finally, she had a claw shape, with six long fingers tied together at the bottom. Two more curved stems formed a circle at the widest point, which she lashed to the ribs. Then another smaller circle to connect them at the top. A skeleton of a bowl.

It seemed to take forever to weave the grasses in and out through the vines to fill in the bowl. How had ancient people managed to survive, when everything took so long to make? Of course they had nothing but time. Mia was working against the ticking bomb of Simon's infection.

The final vessel was lopsided and scraggly. Pieces of grass stuck out in every direction. And there were holes, lots of holes. No way was it going to hold water. She could line it with mud. But then the water would get dirty. Mia sat back on her heels, hands covering her face. Her stifled scream came out in a long moan.

The emptiness gnawing at her belly was making it hard to concentrate. Except for the out-of-reach persimmons, there wasn't any food. But at least she could have something in her mouth. She retrieved her packages of Chinese gum, put a stick in her mouth, and began to chew. Two pieces left in the open package; seven total. She smoothed out the silver foil wrapper, then began to fold it.

There was the answer, right in her hand. The wrappers. She could use them to line the basket. And maybe some of the gum, to fill the cracks, or hold the wrappers in place.

Excited again, she pulled out all the food, candy, and gum wrappers Simon had made her save. The foil peanut packages. The plastic bag that had held apricots. Two plastic wrappers from the candy bars and one from the sesame candy. Three foil squares from gum. Three small plastic Starburst squares. Plus the piece of gum she was chewing.

She lined the inside of the basket with the wrappers, sticking the sides and corners down with tiny bits of gum. She had to chew two more sticks to cover the bottom. It was the saddest specimen of a craft project she'd ever seen. But it didn't need to be beautiful. It just needed to work.

Time for a trial.

She reached for her water bottle and slowly, carefully poured a trickle of water into the basket. A little seeped out the bottom, darkening the ground around it, but it was a slow leak. Some of it stayed in the basket, on top of the wrappers. A partial success. Maybe she could keep adding water as it leaked out, and there would be enough in there to heat. All she needed was enough to get the cloth hot so she could wash Simon's cut.

Next, heat.

It took two of their precious seventeen matches for the fire to catch. As the flames grew, Mia studied the basket in her hands. She should have made a handle. She'd have to put it right on the edge of the fire pit.

She inched the basket onto the clay shelf. Immediately, some of the sticking-out pieces of grass caught fire. She cried out, yanked the basket away from the fire, and dropped it on the ground, smoking. The little bit of water in it spilled on the ground. She stuck her singed finger into her mouth. She wanted to scream, kick the damn thing, stomp it into the dirt.

But Simon needed her to make this work.

She sucked her finger while the basket cooled, then lifted it to examine the damage. Amazingly, the wrappers were mostly still in place inside. She carried it out to the stream to a wet patch of bank. Scooping with her hands, she smeared mud over the bottom of the basket, careful not to dislodge the wrappers on the inside. The cool goop soothed her burned finger. And, she realized, the mud on the bottom should make it more watertight.

In the kitchen, she carefully slid the basket back over the flames. This time, it didn't catch fire. She poured in a little water, watching the level with fierce concentration. It lowered a little, then held.

She poured in a bit more. It was holding, about two inches in all. She stuck her finger in the water. On the third try, she could feel it warming. It was less than a cup, but she had done it.

Eventually, the water began to steam. She washed the scrap of underwear bandage clean in the stream and dropped it into the water. Then she carried the dripping, steaming basket to Simon.

A line of yellowish liquid ran down the length of his cut. Pus. She shivered.

"Simon, I'm going to put a hot cloth on your cut." She lifted the cloth out of the water with a stick and waved it to cool it a little. She touched the wet bandage to her cheek — hot, but not too hot — and slowly placed it over his leg.

"Aaaaaa!" He came to, arching his back, teeth gritted.

"Sorry, sorry! Are you okay?"

"Yeah, yeah, it's fine." Teeth still clenched, he grimaced in pain. "How'd you . . . get it hot?"

"I made that." She pointed to the basket.

"Impressive." Maybe he was being sarcastic. She felt too triumphant to care. She soaked off the rest of the scab, poured a dribble of hot water over the open wound, and washed it with soap until the blood ran clear. She used her spare pair of socks to soak up the mess on the floor. Then she folded the bandage, dipped it into the remaining hot water, and laid the compress over the clean cut.

More fire, more heated water. Let the heat do its healing while Simon slept. She put her mind to the next task. Food.

Out behind the farmhouse, she studied the high branches of the persimmon tree. She could climb it, but . . . Her mind ran a little disaster movie, seeing herself hurtling to the ground. Lying there with broken bones, unable to move.

She shook her head to clear it, then examined the tree again. There was one branch with two persimmons that might be low enough to reach.

She worked her way up the trunk and shimmied along the branch. Clinging to it with one arm, she reached out with her other hand to grasp one persimmon. She slipped the fruit into the unzipped pocket of her pack, then grabbed for the other. From her high vantage point, she scanned the trees, turning in a full circle. Still no other sign of life.

Back on the ground, she studied the remaining persimmons. It was maddening to see them hanging there, so tantalizingly close, yet impossible to reach.

She fed one of the persimmons to Simon, fingerful by fingerful. She ate the other.

Twilight. The fire had gone out, so she made another one to heat more water. Fourteen matches left.

Except for when she fed him, Simon had barely stirred since the first time she washed his wound with hot water. She laid the hot cloth over his leg again, but he didn't move. He seemed so far away. As the light dimmed, Mia sat on the floor beside him, clutching her elbows.

Her brother could *die*.

She reached for her locket, encountered the emptiness where it had been. A sob rose in her throat. *Simon, come back.* She'd take him exactly as he was — bossy, know-it-all, angry, withdrawn.

If only he didn't leave her here alone.

. . .

In the dark, looming, menacing figures came for her. She tried to run, but couldn't make her legs move. Her mouth opened to scream, voiceless. She was overwhelmed by a heavy sense of doom. She sensed Dad's presence, but always just out of reach.

Then it wasn't Dad anymore. It was a woman she longed for but couldn't get to.

She came to, grasping for consciousness like a swimmer trying not to drown.

As she lay in the dark, she realized reality was worse than the nightmare. At least you could wake up from a dream. But the list of real terrible things right now was so long, she didn't know where to start. Simon's leg was infected. They had no medicine to cure him if it got worse. If he didn't get better, they couldn't travel. They hadn't eaten a full meal in nearly four days. They had nothing left for tomorrow except a few out-of-reach persimmons.

Night by night, it was getting colder. They'd been lucky to have two days of sun. But it was October. If it rained again, they could get dangerously chilled. The farmhouse could shelter them for a night or two. But winter was coming.

To reach the border, they had to leave the forest. That meant crossing through areas where they could be seen. Traveling at night. No shelter. There were people out there looking for them. Dangerous people. If they caught her and Simon, they'd arrest them and take the phone. It would be clear that the photos were connected to Dad. He — maybe all three of them — could be held for months, put on trial, even sentenced to years of hard labor. The photos would never get out to the world, to pressure the North Korean government to treat its people better.

She wondered for the first time who had managed to take the pictures. Who could have possibly smuggled a camera into a prison camp and secretly taken photographs? A guard? An inspector? How did that person choose what images to record?

The image of the baby flashed into her mind, dead in the mud. She could only imagine the suffering of that short life. The other images crowded in, each one clamoring for her attention, as if competing for the title of Worst Terror. She twisted on the floor, feeling the horror flooding her limbs. She saw herself in a prison camp, pushing a heavy cart of coal, barefoot in the snow. Watching Simon — or Dad — being tied to a post and blindfolded. Before . . .

At the bottom of the pit of horrors in her mind, she found this one: It was all her fault. If she hadn't told on Simon back in August, they wouldn't have come to North Korea to try to fix their relationships. They'd still be in Connecticut together, safe at home.

In the dark, there was nothing between her and the monster terror, which had a life of its own. It wanted to consume her.

CHAPTER 15

OCTOBER 6

Mia woke up, grateful that she was still alive. The fear hadn't killed her.

Next to her, Simon moaned. So he was still alive too. She sat up and examined his leg. The redness and swelling and bruising didn't look any worse.

She needed to start a new fire and heat water. And figure out some way to reach those persimmons in the high branches.

Simon moaned again. He looked flushed, and his lips were dry. She scooted closer to him, lifted his head, and brought a bottle to his mouth. He gulped water. She lay his head back on the pillow of his pack, put her hand to his forehead. It felt like he was burning up inside.

Simon had a fever.

Mia grabbed her spare pair of socks, scrambled out of the room and across the porch, and ran for the stream. She rinsed the socks in the icy water and came running back to place the cool, wet fabric on her brother's forehead.

Now, hot water. But when she picked up the basket, she saw that it was ruined. The mud had dried and cracked, and most of the wrappers had come loose. It would never hold water now. She felt a moment of complete defeat.

Then she took a deep breath and blew it out. She had to help Simon get better. She'd make another basket. At least she knew how to do it now.

Searching for weaving materials in the long grass near the stream, her foot caught on something. It was dark brown, half buried in the dirt. A fragment of a large curved vessel.

She knelt and began to claw at the dirt with her fingers. Finally, she lifted the vessel out of the ground. She recognized it as a jar for holding kimchi. Cabbage and red pepper were mixed together and buried in jars through the winter to ferment. One whole side of the jar was missing. But the bottom was intact. The unbroken section came nearly to her knees. Leaned on its side, it looked as if it could hold at least a gallon of liquid.

Careful of the broken edge, she carried the fragment to the stream and scrubbed it clean. Then she lugged the vessel, filled with clear, cold water and cradled in her arms like a heavy baby, back to the lean-to, inching along so the liquid didn't slosh out. She arranged it at an angle in the fire pit so that the surface of the water was level. Her heart was pounding now. A little hope mixed with the dread.

She filled the fire pit with wood and dry grass and lit it with a single match. Thirteen left. Squatting in the lean-to, she watched the fire. It was going to take forever to heat that much water.

Maybe she could wash her clothes — the inside ones — while she waited. She took off everything in the lean-to, then quickly pulled her jeans, jacket, and shoes on over her bare skin. Squatting beside the stream, she tried to imitate the women in another one of the Korean calendar pictures, washing clothes by pounding them on rocks.

When she got back to the kitchen, the water was starting to steam. She helped Simon hobble out of the room and across the porch to pee in the yard. Put a hot cloth on his wound, cool socks on his forehead. Got him a long drink of water.

When he was sleeping again, she went back to the persimmon tree. Since impossible-to-climb was no longer an option, the next choice was what was possible. And safe.

There was a nub of a branch that might hold a foot. And maybe she could use a stick to knock the fruit down.

It took six tries, but finally, she had a pile of ten persimmons on the ground. Some of them were even still whole. She'd gotten every piece except the few out of reach on the highest limbs.

She fed three persimmons to Simon and ate three herself. More rounds of hot and cold cloths. He barely moved through all of it. Mia had to keep stopping to take little rests, feeling the toll of all the activity on so little fuel.

She draped her wet clothes over a section of stone wall to dry in the sun. Back at the fire pit, the fire was down to ashes, but there was still a lot of water and it was still hot.

She realized then. A lot of hot water. Enough for a bath.

She checked on Simon again. His wound was clean and covered with the hot compress. She'd given him food and water. What he needed most was rest.

She stripped off her jacket, jeans, and sneakers again and stood naked in the lean-to, shivering. The bruises on her hips and thighs were purple, but the edges were already fading to yellow. Dipping her water bottle into the hot water, she lifted it above her head and poured. As the warm stream cascaded over her body, she nearly screamed with pleasure.

She completely wet her skin and used a little soap where it counted. Wet her hair and shampooed it. Then she poured bottle after bottle of hot water over herself, wanting it to go on forever. The only uncomfortable part was letting her body wind-dry a bit so she wouldn't soak her jeans and jacket. She'd never again take a towel for granted.

Dressed, she went back to the room for her brush. As her bare feet touched the floor, she flinched in surprise. The floor was warm.

She moved her foot, testing. Of course: The fire in the lean-to was heating the floor. She'd explained to Simon how the system was set up, but it hadn't occurred to her that anything in the crumbling house would still work. The fires she'd built yesterday must have been too small to fully heat the thick layer of clay.

Mia moved across the floor, trying different spots until she found the perfect temperature. She stood still, letting the delicious warmth seep into her feet. This would help Simon rest.

Now that she was clean and the floor was warm, she wanted it clean too. She got her wet socks from the stone wall and put them over her hands. She poured warm water from her water bottle over the floor and scrubbed it with her sock mittens, shifting Simon a little to get the parts under him. Mom would be so amazed to see her at work, the daughter who hated to clean her own room.

Mia had always been more her daddy's girl. Mom was brisk, in constant motion, bustling and fixing. It wasn't easy to relax around her because Mom kept thinking of things that needed improving. Such as her daughter. When Dad read to her, he just read. Mia could disappear into the story. Mom would get to an exciting part, then stop and ask, "What does this word mean, Mia?"

It was weird to find herself acting like her mother, putting things right — and actually enjoying it.

She collected another load of sticks and branches and stoked the fire for the day's last batch of hot water, and to make sure they'd have a warm floor to sleep on. Then she gathered her sun-dried clothing from the stone wall and dressed. The stiff, clean T-shirt, bra, underwear, and socks felt great against her skin.

On her way back from filling the jar at the stream, she caught sight of a dark shadow in a patch of sun on a low section of the farm's outer wall. She gasped. A snake! Large and black with yellow rings. Backing up, with the water sloshing in the jar, she stumbled to the lean-to and set the jar down on the fire. Her eyes darted nervously around, making sure the snake hadn't followed her into the kitchen area.

She shivered. Snakes made her squeamish. It could be poisonous. Maybe it could even kill her.

But . . . people ate snake meat. Even poisonous ones like rattlesnakes. That slithery reptile out on the stone wall was a long rope of protein. They could really use some protein right now. Each day she had a little less energy. And meat would help Simon heal.

But that meant she would have to kill it.

No way could she kill a snake.

Simon would know how. But he was lying comatose on the floor, with a fever. If any snake slaying was going to happen, she'd have to be the one to do it.

Mia peered at the wall from a distance, almost hoping the snake had slipped away. Still there, exactly where she'd seen it. Maybe it was sluggish from the autumn cold.

She couldn't do this.

But she had to. She just had to be tough enough to do what needed to be done.

She crept a little closer. Maybe she could throw a rock at it, without getting too close and scaring it away. Or getting bitten.

Across the yard, one corner of the wall had tumbled down into a pile of stones. Mia sorted through the debris to find one big and heavy enough to kill a snake.

She moved within range and raised the stone over her head with both hands, shaking. She had only one chance. If she missed, she'd scare the snake away. Or maybe it would leap at her. *Get ahold of yourself, Mia.*

She took a deep breath and hurled the stone as hard as she could. It struck the snake and bounced off, tumbling down onto the ground by the wall. Suddenly, the snake was a coiling, writhing mass. She shrieked. She'd only wounded it! Desperate — for the meat and to stop the snake's suffering — she ran to the wall and picked up the stone. She brought it down again on the snake's mashed head, once, twice, three times. The body stilled, then went limp. A tremor of revulsion went through her. Tears filled her eyes.

"Sorry," she whispered. She felt like throwing up.

But she didn't have time to be sick; she needed to cook.

She left the carcass on the wall, went back into the lean-to, and stood for a moment, shivering. Then she put her mind to the problem. She couldn't just put the snake's body in the fire. It would only burn. The jar was like a giant cooking pot. There were four or five inches of water in it, beginning to steam. She could use the water to cook the meat. Snake stew.

Medical treatments first. The water was hot, but, she hoped, not yet hot enough to melt plastic. She dipped her water bottle into the jar and filled it with steaming water, carried it into the room, and reheated the compress on Simon's leg. She lifted the warm cloth from his forehead and returned with it wet and cool.

"Mmmm," Simon murmured as she laid it over his face. He reached up one hand to press the coolness in.

C'mon, Simon, get better.

Back at the wall, she touched the carcass gingerly. She stretched it out lengthwise on the stone wall, avoiding looking at the bloody mess of the head. The thick body, minus the head, was longer than her outstretched arm.

Once, when she was nine or ten, Dad had taken her fishing and showed her how to clean the fish she caught. She closed her eyes, trying to recall the process.

She pushed her jacket sleeves up to her elbows, held up Simon's knife, and sawed off the snake's head. Then she made a slit down the length of the body to the tail. She pulled out the slimy guts and dropped them to the ground, trying not to gag. She sliced crossways through the skin and bones, cutting the meat into big chunks. By the time she was done, the top of the wall, her hands, and her forearms were covered in blood and guts and bits of raw flesh and skin. *Meat*, she kept telling herself, pushing down the impulse to puke. *This is meat.*

She carried the pieces, two handfuls at a time, into the lean-to and slid them into the steaming water. Then she ran to the stream to scrub her hands and arms over and over until every trace of the grisly operation was gone.

If she survived this trip, she was going to become a vegetarian.

When she returned to the lean-to, the most amazing aroma of cooking meat reached her nostrils. Her mouth started to water. Her stomach, which had given up and gone to sleep, woke up, clamoring to be fed. Mia pulled out hunks of the meat and arranged their feast on a thin platter of rock.

Inside the farmhouse, Simon was leaning up against the wall, eyes open. She nearly dropped the platter.

"Hey, Squeak," he said.

Tears sprang to her eyes at the relief of seeing him awake. She hadn't realized until this moment how worried and desperately alone she'd felt without him.

"You're better!" she said.

"Yeah, I think the fever's broken. Was I out a long time?"

"Since we got here yesterday morning. It's late afternoon now. The next day."

"Whew. I had such weird dreams." He had his hands flat on the floor now. "I thought it was the fever, but — how come the floor's warm?"

Mia grinned. "I made a fire in the kitchen. It heats the floor — it's set up that way. And that's not all —" She slowly lowered the flat stone to the ground in front of him. "Ta-da!"

"What is that?"

"It's meat. Snake meat."

Simon's eyes widened. "Where — Squeak, you killed a snake?"

She nodded, grinning at the disbelief in his face.

The meat was bland, but it was by far the best thing she'd tasted in her entire life. Even better than persimmon pulp.

"Mmm, tastes like chicken," Simon joked.

It actually sort of reminded her of chicken, and also a bit of fish. Plus something else she couldn't place. The best part was the meatiness. The sensation of sinking her teeth into something solid and nourishing. Chewing.

Maybe she wouldn't become a vegetarian.

When she'd finished gnawing the bits off the little bones, she sat back. Her stomach was actually full. The floor beneath her was warm. It was the best she'd felt since the moment she'd found the photos on the phone.

She told Simon about everything she'd done.

"You're blowing my mind," Simon said, shaking his head. "All I did was sleep."

"How's your leg?"

He pulled off the cloth and together they examined the wound.

"Colorful," Mia said. Some of the red had faded to pink. The bruises bloomed in purple and blue and even a bit of green.

"Definitely better. Look how much the swelling's down. I'm gonna try to sleep some more."

She helped him prop his leg on the rock and lie back, then stood with the remains of their dinner.

"Squeak."

"What?"

He closed his eyes. "You're a hot ticket."

She caught her breath. It was a favorite phrase of Dad's. Gratitude and longing, relief and fear swept through her. She hiccupped a sob.

In the kitchen, she dumped the skin and bones left from their meal back into the kimchi pot with the remaining snake meat. Bones could make soup. She added kindling to the fire for the night. Then she washed her hands and filled their water bottles at the stream.

Completely spent, she rested on the porch. The late afternoon sun cast a bit of warmth. A breeze tossed the branches of a nearby grove of trees, dancing the leaves in a shimmer of yellow confetti. If she didn't turn around to see the half-gone roof, or look down to see her jeans and jacket, she could imagine that she was a young woman living on this farm with her brother in times past, when Korea was all one country.

She saw herself carrying a low table with the meal she'd prepared, placing it on the floor in front of her brother — and nearly burst out laughing. She'd pictured Simon sitting cross-legged on the floor in traditional clothing, but his skin and eyes and hair were all wrong for this daydream.

She was no farmer's daughter in long-ago Korea. She didn't have any real cooking or cleaning or homemaking skills. Everything she'd done today she'd had to make up along the way. But Simon was better, because she'd found a way to heat water. She and her inside clothes were clean. Her belly had meat in it. Parts of her were actually warm. And she had done it all. All by herself.

Simon was right: She was a hot ticket. Spy Girl and Katniss Everdeen, rolled into one.

She pulled out her journal and made a few notes, the first she'd been able to write since they'd run. She was too tired to do much more than make an outline of what had happened each day, but it was impressive when she saw, all at once, what they had managed to do. It was completely, unbelievably astonishing that they had made it this far; what were the chances?

Later, lying in the darkness against the warm floor, feeling her muscles unknot, she wasn't comfortable by any standard she'd known before. The floor was brick hard. They had no pillows or blankets. The room had a hole in the roof and no door. Whatever part of her was on top was soon chilled. But compared to straw pallets in a railroad shed, compared to a pile of leaves on a mountainside or the metal floor of a boxcar, this clean, flat, warm surface felt blissful.

They were going to have to leave the farmhouse soon. They still had an impossibly long journey. Dad was still under arrest. There were people chasing them. It might get bad. But right now, there was a little bit of good.

Time to rest and get strong for what was coming.

KANG SOON-OK

✱ ✱ ✱

It was raining when she woke, but Soon-ok decided to spend the day gathering wild roots. The moisture would loosen the soil, making the plants easier to pull. Winter was on the way, and it wouldn't be long before she'd have to dig through the snow and chip the roots from the frozen ground.

Her favorite spot to harvest was a secluded grove high on the mountain, a place that seemed all her own. She gathered her basket and tools and went quickly, before anyone could appear with some request or demand to delay her.

As she started up the path, the misty rain helped clear her head. She felt the relief of getting away from the village, away from the always-watching eyes, the calculating, judging, and sometimes outright hostile glances, from faces that had once been friendly but now feared contamination by association.

Soon-ok's father, a farmer, had been full of zeal for building a new nation by feeding its citizens. But inevitably, his enthusiasm and popularity had threatened someone with a higher rank — the bully party leader who controlled local matters. Her father's ideas for improving crop yield were twisted into evidence of corruption and individualism, which everyone in the village knew could not possibly be true, but no one dared to contradict. Then came the sham of the "trial," and the sentence: five years in a reeducation camp. The one thing her father's strength of character won was protection for his family; the official was shrewd enough to calculate that there was a limit to what the villagers would go along with, and sent her father off alone. Two years after his departure, Soon-ok still did not know whether this was a piece of fortune or not.

She felt the pull in her calves as the path steepened, the growing lightness in her spirit as she got farther from the village, where her father's tormentor still presided. She gazed about at the thickening trees. The forest was the school where her father had been the wise teacher, she the eager pupil, absorbing his instructions of when to gather and how to prepare that fern, that wild green, the new shoots of bamboo. Much of the wild harvest happened in the spring, but as he had taught her, there was always something to be foraged. The roots she sought now were still abundant in autumn.

They were fortunate to live here. The hilly contours and often poor soil made farming much more difficult than in the wide plains, but those places suffered more when drought or floods or lack of fertilizer caused crops to fail. Here they could always turn to the forest for sustenance. Though there were difficult years, there had never been a time when her father had not been able to produce something he'd grown or foraged to feed his family.

As she crowned the rise, she reached a sheltering high canopy of bright foliage. The rain barely reached her now that she was under tree cover. She felt her face relaxing, releasing the careful mask. Since her father was a convicted criminal, their whole family was suspect. And she had something to hide: her knowledge that an innocent and upright man could be unjustly accused. That all his devotion to and good deeds for the cause meant nothing. That the gap between what her country preached and what it practiced was wide.

She knew her duty. She was her father's daughter, loyal and true. Despite what had been done to him, it was not in her nature to take vengeance or become subversive. For her father's sake, she did what was expected. But she had taken her heart back from her country. Her allegiance now was only to her family.

CHAPTER 16

OCTOBER 7

The rain had come just after dawn. Through the hole in the roof, the sky lightened, then darkened again as storm clouds thickened. It started sprinkling, then increased to a steady drizzle, as if someone was gradually turning on a faucet. The floor beneath Mia was cold.

"Yuck." She sat up and wrapped her arms around herself, looking over at her brother. Simon was still sleeping. His color was better, less flushed. His breathing sounded normal.

Mia got up and went out to the porch, watching the rain dripping from the roof. She needed to make another fire, but she'd used up all the kindling she'd gathered the night before. She shook her head. Nothing to do but get wet.

By the time she got back to the lean-to with armloads of damp brush and branches, her back and shoulders were soaked. She knelt to build the fire, crumpling a few of Simon's magazine pages into balls. She'd burned up all of *Sports Illustrated* and was halfway through *Car and Driver*, but she figured he'd think it was worth it. Even with the dry paper, it took three matches to light the kindling. Only ten left.

She huddled, shivering, close to the firepit, feeding bits of grass into the tiny fire, willing it to spread. When the flames were finally strong enough to generate warmth, she turned her back to it. Dodging the little waterfalls streaming through the leaky roof, she gradually dried off her jacket.

She and Simon weren't going anywhere today. They could get hypothermia in no time. Simon probably needed another day to rest anyway. She sighed. She could feel the weight of the need to hurry, but they'd never be able to survive, much less help Dad, if Simon couldn't finish the journey.

She pulled the pot of leftover snake meat over the fire to heat, then climbed back into the room to sit on the gradually warming floor. Her jeans still felt clammy, but at least she'd stopped shivering. She pulled her knees to her chest and rested her head against the wall. The rain fell through the open roof and pooled in little streams on the broken floor, spilling through the cracks. All the impossibilities and uncertainties of the journey ahead crowded around her, like a pack of hungry wolves.

After a while Simon woke up. They ate some snake meat and shared a persimmon. Three left. She scooped the leftover meat onto a stone and the broth into one of their water bottles and ran back out into the rain to rinse the jar in the stream and fill it with water. When the water was warm, she showed Simon how he could take a bath too.

The drizzle continued through the long hours of the morning, trapping them in the corner.

"Remember when Dad used to read us those books?

About the Boxcar Children?" Mia asked. "This keeps reminding me of them." They sat side by side, backs against the wall of the room.

"Yeah, except they lived in a make-believe sunshine world where all people were good and loving. While we're lost in the middle of a country that starves its people, has arrested our father, and is hunting us down this very minute!"

"Yeah, well, there's that." She turned to Simon, raising an eyebrow. "I still loved the stories. All the details of how they did everything for themselves. That's what this reminds me of."

"*The Boxcar Children, North Korea.*" Simon's voice was deep and dramatic, like a TV announcer's. Mia laughed. They were joking with each other. She couldn't remember the last time they'd done that.

Who changed?

"Simon?"

"Yeah?"

"I just wanted to tell you . . . I'm sorry."

"Sorry? For what?" He sounded genuinely surprised. Given all that she'd been doing for him, that was appropriate. But she still needed to say it.

"The other night, when you were sick, I woke up from a nightmare. I thought about all the horrible things that had happened. And I realized, this is really all my fault." It was easier to say it not looking at him, just staring into the misty rain.

"Your fault? Squeak, we already talked about this. Sure, you opened the phone, but if you hadn't, we wouldn't have run away with the photos, and someone could have found them. That would have been much worse for Dad. And for us."

"That's not what I mean. I'm talking about back in August." She still didn't look at him. She just needed to blurt this all out. "You know how I always said I didn't tell on you? Because I didn't know anything? Well, that's not really true. I mean, I didn't know where you had gone, what you were doing. But I heard Mom on the phone telling Dad you were at Nathan's. I'd seen Nathan around town that afternoon. So later I asked Mom where you were, just so I could tell her you weren't with Nathan. I did that on purpose. So it's my fault you got caught. And we came on this trip because of all the difficulty we were having getting along. So whatever happens, I just wanted to say that I'm sorry for getting us into this whole mess."

There was a pause.

"You didn't get me into this mess, Squeak."

"Yeah, I did."

"No way. You may have done that one sneaky little thing, but if we're playing a blame game, I win, hands down. There was no way I would've gotten away with all that stuff in August, whether you said anything or not. Going to New York even though Mom and Dad told me I couldn't, lying, stealing a car —"

"*Stealing a car?*" Now she turned to him, wide-eyed.

"Told you; I win."

"What happened? I mean, I knew you went to New York. But stealing a car?"

Simon sighed.

"You don't have to tell me if you don't want to," she added quickly.

"No, it's fine. It just seems so ridiculous now, with everything that's happened." He took a breath. "It starts way back in the spring, I guess, when things were really going south with Randi. Most of the time I couldn't get her to even talk to me. She wouldn't respond to my texts or return my phone calls. It was like she was disappearing, erasing herself." He lifted his hurt leg and adjusted it on the floor. "That felt like my fault. I was her boyfriend, I was supposed to make her happy, and I couldn't." His voice sounded bleak.

Mia murmured a protest, but Simon raised a hand, cutting her off. "I know, I know. Depression. We had a whole assembly on it at the beginning of the year. But knowing there was nothing I could do to fix it didn't make me feel better. It was worse — I just felt helpless." He blew out a breath and let his head fall back against the wall, fiddling with the woven cord on his wrist.

Mia was listening so intently, she was practically not breathing. Simon never told her stuff like this. She didn't dare look directly at him, in case he stopped, but she leaned closer, wanting to catch every word.

"It was the crappiest feeling. Everything about the situation made me angry. That Randi hadn't trusted me to stick around when things were hard for her, that I hadn't been able to figure out any way to help her. Maybe that I was even a little bit relieved when she broke up with me, because it felt kind of like getting out of prison."

There was a long pause. Mia didn't make a sound.

Simon sat forward, wrapping his arms around his bent leg, the good one. "So fast-forward to late August. The deal was I wanted to go to this concert in New York that Jen and Rusty and I had bought tickets for. But then Mom and Dad decided they didn't want us driving back in the middle of the night. We didn't have a place to stay in the city, and Dad was going to be gone, and they just thought it didn't seem safe. Or 'wise,' as Mom put it."

Mia gave a half-grin. That sounded exactly like their mother.

"Thing was, I was kind of into Jen. She'd been flirting with me a little, and it was a great distraction from all the bad stuff with Randi. So I argued and argued with Mom and Dad, but it was no good. I thought I was going to have to miss the concert." Simon reached down and adjusted the cloth on his leg.

"Then Mrs. Fasulo called. Could I feed her cats while she was gone for the weekend, and could I pick up her lawn mower at the shop on Saturday morning? She'd leave the car keys on the counter. Saturday morning I did all that stuff for her. Rusty and Jen had already left. And I thought, why not? So I just . . . took the car, drove to Stamford, left the car in the parking lot, and took the train into New York."

"You stole Mrs. Fasulo's car?!" She faced him, mouth wide. "I never heard that!"

"It seemed like a fine plan at the time." He turned and gave her a wry grin. "She wasn't coming back until Sunday, I'd leave a message with Mom saying I'd be at Nathan's, I'd catch a ride back to the train station with Jen and Rusty. Nobody would even know."

"Until I told." It really was her fault. "But wait a minute, you didn't come back Sunday. You were gone for three days!"

"Yeah, well, stuff happened. For one thing, my phone died. That made it that much easier not to call home. And the whole experience, it just blew me away."

"Good concert?"

"Yeah, but what happened after was even better." He leaned back against the wall, looking up through the hole in the roof. "There were booths from all these different organizations, and one that was working on climate change asked us to help hand out brochures, and then they said could we join this big protest the next day. They thought we were college students. So we said, why not, we could still get home on time. We slept in the office, they fed us breakfast, then we helped pack the van with boxes for the event. The people were amazing, and they were telling us these incredible stories of how things had changed through mobilizing people all around the globe. Best of all, I have to admit, was that things were getting pretty sweet with Jen. She is so into that whole change-the-world thing; she couldn't have been happier. After Randi, that was different too."

Simon turned to her, his mouth in a twist.

"Of course, we didn't mention that we were high school students and our parents didn't know where we were. It was so great — everything — and there was more and more to do, so we just kept not going home."

Mia remembered what it had been like at home.

"Mom and Dad were pretty scared."

"I know. I just . . . I dunno, I just put all that out of my mind. It seemed like it was such a small thing compared to the big things I was involved in down there. But the truth was, I just didn't want to deal with that problem."

"I was scared too. Scared that you'd never come back."

"No such luck, Squeak. You're stuck with me." He reached over and bumped her lightly on the arm with his fist. "Especially now that you've apparently brought me back from the dead."

"Were you in humongous trouble?"

Simon smiled and shook his head. "No, Mrs. Fasulo refused to press charges, even though Mom wanted her to.

'He only borrowed the car. . . .' But I have to mow her lawn and paint her fence and all that for like the rest of my life, or at least until I leave for college."

"What about her cats?"

"Her cats?"

"You were supposed to feed them! Weren't they hungry?"

He groaned. "Squeak. You are too much. All this, and you're worried about the cats?! They're fine. I gave them lots of extra food on Saturday and Mrs. Fasulo was home Sunday." He stretched his leg again. It must have still been bothering him.

"Now, back to that part about this being all your fault. Sure, you opened the gift, started using the phone. But I don't think you really get how big it is that we have the phone, not the North Korean government. They may accuse Dad of collaborating or spying or something, but they can't prove anything if they don't have any evidence. If you hadn't found the photos, we wouldn't have been hiding when Dad got arrested. They'd probably have taken us too. And if you hadn't had the phone with you, it would've been in the hotel room and someone would have gotten ahold of those photos. Dad could've ended up in one of those prison camps. So there are things that are your responsibility, yes, and there are things that are mine, and overall, I think we should be pretty damn proud, not sorry."

She cocked her head, looking at him. "Okay. I'll think about that."

She was quiet for a bit, until she remembered something else she wanted to know. "So what's going on with you and Randi now?"

"What do you mean?"

She felt emboldened to say what had really been on her

mind, things she would never have dared ask him a week ago. "Well, weren't you supposed to be seeing her? And you couldn't because of the trip? And you're still wearing her bracelet. Do you think you guys will get back together?"

He shook his head. "Nah. It's not about that. We're just friends. But she'll always be important to me." His smile was wistful. "She's been at this place, a special school with counseling and a lot of art, and I think she's doing okay. We were gonna go out and get a chance to talk. I wanted to support her, and to clear stuff out from the mess in the spring. So I was not happy about missing that." He sighed. "But now . . . stuff I thought was so important? It all seems okay, nothing to get so riled up about. As long as we can stay alive, it will work out. Everything looks different, you know?"

Mia nodded. She did know.

They leaned against the wall of the farmhouse room, side by side, watching the rain fall through the roof.

"So what was your nightmare about?" Simon asked.

"What?"

"You said you had a nightmare, and that's when you realized this was all your fault."

"Oh, it was about Dad. I couldn't get to him. Only —" She realized the truth of what she was about to say, unknown till this moment. "Only then it wasn't Dad anymore, it was a woman. Maybe . . . it might have been my birth mother. She was this shadowy figure. It was like I would die if I couldn't get to her. But she was always just out of reach." Her voice came out soft, hushed.

She put her hand up to touch her locket, then smiled as she remembered. She rested her hand over her heart.

"Hey, where's your necklace?"

"I lost it. Probably when the rocks fell on me."

"Wow. Aren't you bummed about it?"

"I was at first. But . . . it's okay now." She realized it was.

"Do you think about her much, your birth mother?" Simon asked after a while.

She was quiet, considering.

"Not so much. I mean, not so much *consciously*. But there's some way, I can't explain it, some way that I'm always missing her, kind of. Not really thinking about it. More like feeling it."

"Hmm."

"Maybe she's coming into my dreams because of being out here like this. Without Dad and Mom. Being hungry. Wondering if we'll get home or not . . . Maybe it's 'cause I feel so vulnerable. Like I felt when I was a baby — abandoned?"

She couldn't remember ever having shared such things with Simon. Such close-to-the-heart things. But enclosed together in their tiny bit of shelter, looking out at the rain, it felt safe.

"And being in Korea . . . I mean, I know my birth mother isn't here. She's in South Korea. If she's still alive, that is. But being on the same peninsula, I wonder . . . where she is, what she's doing." She hadn't known that was what she had been thinking. But as she spoke the thought, she could tell it had been there all along. "Like if she has other kids. Why she couldn't keep me. If she thinks about me. That kind of thing."

"I never really thought about that. I mean, of course we talked about your adoption and your birth parents. But I thought of them as where you came from, in the past. I never really imagined what it might be like to have another set of parents somewhere, wondering about them." Simon's voice was soft too. After a moment, he went on. "So maybe all this is worse for you than it is for me."

"How?"

"Being separated from Mom and Dad, not knowing if we'll ever see them again. Because you've already lost one mother and father."

Mia slid over a little on the wall. She rested her head on her brother's shoulder. Together, they watched the rain stream down.

. . .

In the late morning, it started to clear. Mia and Simon moved to sit out on the porch. After a while, Mia's stomach started squawking. She sighed and stood up.

"We need more food. There's only enough for tonight — a little meat and broth and three persimmons."

Simon nodded.

"I think I should go down the hill a little, see what's down there." She pointed toward the valley. "It looks like there might have been a path. Maybe we should go that way instead of along the tracks."

"That's south, Mia. We want to go northwest."

"Yeah, but what if it's the quickest way to civilization? You know — people, food? And maybe roads and vehicles that will take us northwest."

He was shaking his head. "I don't want you going off alone. Someone might see you."

"Okay, how about this: I'll just follow the stream for a little ways. See if it goes anywhere. If there's a real path, I'll follow that. I'll leave things on the way, rocks or bent branches. Like Hansel and Gretel. That way I can't get lost. We'll do the time thing, an hour like last time." She watched his face carefully. "If I don't find anything, we'll keep following the railroad tracks tomorrow."

They stared at each other, eyes locked.

"You've got to admit, it turned out pretty well last time." Mia grinned at him.

When Simon gave in, he shook his head like he couldn't believe what a pain she was. He stood in the yard, exercising his leg, watching her go.

She followed the stream down the hill, weaving her way among the dripping foliage, trying to avoid getting soaked. She broke a few branches and stacked some stones to mark her way. But she'd be able to follow the stream back to the farmhouse.

In the valley the stream widened and split, a thin fork winding off to the left into the woods. The branch to the right was wider — heading west, she calculated, checking the sun and shadows — and the undergrowth along it was less dense. If there had once been a path, this was it.

Twenty minutes left before she had to start back. She turned right. The stream began to wander, crossing the trail to curve away, then return. Large stones made stepping paths across the shallow water.

Her heart fluttered. Every step she took away from Simon and the farmhouse felt dangerous. It was hard to imagine that she would find anything they could eat. More likely that she'd stumble upon a village, or another farmhouse. Maybe she could find a road sign or town name without anyone seeing her. Or steal a bit of some late crop growing in a garden. She had to do something.

Then a voice spoke. "Ah-nee, noo-goo-shim-ni-ka?"

CHAPTER 17

Mia whirled around to see a girl squatting on the ground among the trees a little way off to her left. She looked older than Mia, and she was staring at her.

Mia stood frozen, poised to run.

The girl's hands were full of roots she had been digging. She placed them in a shallow basket beside her, picked it up, and took a few steps forward, moving carefully, as if Mia were a wild forest creature that might bolt. Mia glanced around quickly, but there didn't seem to be anyone else nearby.

The girl's black hair was pulled back into a short braid. She was slim, but she seemed healthy enough. Not like she was starving. She wore a padded navy jacket.

She spoke again.

Mia tipped her head and opened her hands. *I don't understand.* Then she put her hand on her chest and said the first phrase of Korean that popped into her mind.

"*Han-gook-mal chal mot-ham-ni-da.*" *I can't speak Korean well.*

"Unh?" The girl started and swiveled her head, eyes narrowed. She'd probably never met someone who looked Korean but couldn't speak the language.

Then Mia remembered. South Koreans called their country *Hangook*, but North Koreans called it *Chosun*. "I mean, *Cho-sun-mal chal mot-ham-ni-da*," she corrected herself.

The older girl moved her head slightly. Maybe she'd understood.

Mia touched her chest again. "Mia." Then she shook her head. "I mean, Sung-Mi. Han Sung-Mi." She pronounced the syllables slowly and precisely.

The girl nodded, then indicated herself. "Kang Soon-ok."

"*An-nyung ha-shim-ni-ka.*" *Hello.* Mia bobbed her head in a little bow.

The girl bowed back. They looked at each other. Six years of Saturday language school, but the moment Mia needed it, everything she'd learned seemed to have flown out of her head.

The girl — Soon-ok — was very pretty. Long eyes set at an angle under perfect bow-shaped eyebrows, a clear, smooth forehead, red lips. She reminded Mia of the revolutionary heroines in the paintings they'd seen in the subway in Pyongyang. Was she the kind of person who would turn in two Americans?

Soon-ok's eyes had gone to Mia's jacket, and her forehead creased, staring at her badge. A wary, measuring look crossed her face.

Mia made an instant decision. Wondering if it was the stupidest thing she'd done since they got to North Korea, she undid the clasp of the badge and took it off.

"*Ah-ni-yo.*" *No.* Mia shook her head. She put the badge in her pocket. "*Mi-gook sa-ram.*" *American.*

Soon-ok's eyes widened. She probably couldn't imagine how in the world an American had ended up in the middle of this forest. Then her expression shifted. Lightened. It was barely perceptible, but Mia felt as if she'd been given a signal. Maybe the girl wouldn't report the presence of two Americans to the authorities.

Two Americans. Simon.

Oh no, what time was it? Mia checked her watch. Twenty-four minutes to get back to the farmhouse! She glanced back up the path, then pointed in the direction she'd come from.

"*Oh-bba.*" *Older brother.* That was one word she knew. Mia motioned with her hand up above her head, trying to indicate someone taller. She pointed at her watch. "*Bbal-li, bbal-li.*" That meant "quickly." It was the only thing she could think of. The expression on Soon-ok's face was puzzled but also amused. Mia's Korean must sound really funny. She needed her dictionary, but it was back at the farmhouse.

"*Oh-bba,*" Mia repeated. "*Bbal-li, bbal-li.*"

Maybe she could get Soon-ok to go back to the farmhouse with her. Once she saw Simon, maybe the Korean girl would understand that they were lost. Maybe she could help them find their way.

Ka. That meant "to go." *Ka-ja* meant "Let's go" in the lowest form, the one used to speak to children. It wasn't the polite form used for someone older, someone Mia had just met, but it was the only thing she knew how to say.

"*Ka-ja?*" She tried making it a question so it wouldn't seem rude. She gestured in the direction of the hill, took a few steps, gave Soon-ok an encouraging look. "Come with me?"

Soon-ok nodded uncertainly, her brow creased, and followed.

When they reached the top of the path, Simon was sitting on the porch. He started, then slowly rose to standing. On alert.

"Mia?" he said, low and slow. His eyes were narrowed, his body tense. His eyes flicked to the room. The phone.

"This is Soon-ok. I met her on the path."

"And you brought her here?"

"I think she's safe. I think she's . . . not a friend of the government."

"How can you possibly know that?" Simon was keeping his voice calm, but Mia could hear the tension beneath it.

"I just think. . . . It's her reactions. Anyway, what was I going to do? She saw me." Mia stopped, realizing they were talking in English, leaving their guest just standing there. Soon-ok was staring at Simon in astonishment. Probably she'd never seen a white person before.

"*Oh-bba*," Mia said to her. "Si-mon." She gestured toward him with her hand open, remembering that Koreans don't point directly at people.

Soon-ok looked from one of them to the other. "Oh-bba?" The term was used for a girl's older male acquaintances too. Mia wanted Soon-ok to understand that Simon really was her brother.

There was one more phrase she knew. She touched her chest again. "*Ee-byang-ah.*" *Adopted child.* Most of the time at Korean school, she'd been the only adopted one, so she'd heard the phrase a lot.

Soon-ok's eyes went from Mia to Simon again. She nodded. Mia wondered if Soon-ok could imagine their family. She gestured to the porch, inviting the other girl to sit.

"Koreans always serve things to guests," she said to Simon. "We should give her something. I'm going to share the last persimmons with her, okay?"

He shrugged, still tense.

Soon-ok's eyes widened when she saw the persimmons. "Kam!"

Mia beckoned, guided her to the side of the farmhouse, and pointed to the tree. Maybe Soon-ok would come back and get the last few after they left.

Mia brought the bottles with fresh water from the stream. Soon-ok ate and drank gravely, giving her whole attention to the persimmon.

When they'd finished eating, Mia got her dictionary. "She can tell us where we are. We just have to figure out how to communicate." She riffled through the pages, looking up words.

"Ki-cha . . . Choon-gook . . . ka. Ki-cha uh-di-eh-yo?" Train China go. Where train? She knew she was mangling the Korean, but she hoped Soon-ok would understand. She showed her a map in the guidebook, but there was no close-up of the northwest corner. They already knew where they were in the big picture. It was the small details they needed.

Soon-ok said something in Korean, gesturing into the distance. Mia shook her head. They needed to find a common language.

Mia looked up one more word. Then she got off the porch, squatted on the ground, and cleared a small area of earth. She reached for a small stone and placed it in one corner.

"Jip." House. "Yo-gi." Here. Mia pointed at the farmhouse, then at the stone. Then she indicated the rest of the patch of earth. *"Choon-gook uh-di-eh-yo?" Where is China?*

Soon-ok squatted beside her, gazing at the stone. Then she stood, walked around the overgrown yard, found two long strips of straw, and placed them beside the stone. She pointed north, behind the farmhouse. Mia nodded. The old train tracks.

Soon-ok picked up a twig and scratched a wavy line in the dirt, from the straw, past the stone. "Shi-neh."

"Must be the stream," Simon said from the porch, watching intently.

Soon-ok added more stones, bits of grass, strands of straw, some weeds. The questions and simple words went back and forth. *Tree. Mountain. Road.*

"Ma-ul," Soon-ok said, placing a group of stones together. A village or a town. A cluster of green leaves, the forest. Gradually, a colorful design of natural textures appeared on the ground, like a woven rug.

"Nice," Simon said. Despite his wariness, he was getting drawn in. Maybe because they were getting so much information.

Soon-ok took the stick and drew lots wavy lines at the very edge of the patch of dirt. "Ba-da."

"Must be the ocean," Simon said. "So we're pretty close to the coast. That's good news."

She placed a handful of pebbles in one heap. "Sonchon."

"A town? Or a city? Maybe it's a proper name," Simon said, reaching over to pick up the guidebook. "Here it is. The town of Sonchon. And it's only about forty or fifty miles from the border! We're not far off course at all."

"*Choon-gook?*" Mia asked.

Soon-ok cocked her head, studying the design. She took a few steps backward, then a few more. With the stick she drew a long wavy line in front of her. Then she pointed to where her feet were, on the far side of the river border. "Choon-gook."

"She says that's where China is," Mia told Simon.

"Awesome."

Soon-ok looked up and her eyes met Mia's. *I wonder,* thought Mia. *Has she ever imagined crossing the river?*

The other girl moved back toward the porch, motioning to the path. She picked up her basket, plucked a small bunch of dirty brown roots from the top of the pile, and held it out. "Oo-ung."

"*Oo-ung?*" Mia repeated.

Soon-ok nodded. She held the plants up to her open mouth. The roots must be vegetables of some kind. She handed the bunch to Mia, who bowed her thanks.

Mia checked the dictionary for a final word. *Nae-il.* Tomorrow. Mia gestured to Simon and herself, made walking motions with her fingers, and pointed to the map. "Sung-mi, Simon. *Nae-il ka. Choon-gook.*" Soon-ok nodded her understanding.

They exchanged good-byes with many bows. Simon even remembered how to say thank you. Soon-ok moved off down the hill, along the side of the stream and out of sight.

Simon was shaking his head. "I sure hope she's not running straight to the nearest police station." He turned to Mia. "I knew I shouldn't have let you go off on your own. Now someone knows where we are."

"I couldn't help it, Simon. She saw me."

"That's just what I was afraid of. This is so messed up." He was running one hand through his hair, still looking down the path.

"She's not going to turn us in. I just know she's not."

He turned back to her, scowling. "You don't know anything, Mia. There may be a reward, she might get brownie points from her local Workers' party leader, she might hate Americans. There could be all kinds of reasons, things we can't imagine."

Simon must really be better. He was back to being a jerk. Mia shook her head. "I don't think so. I think she really wants to help us. And I think we have to accept help, or we're not going to make it."

He blew out a breath. "Guess we'll find out soon enough." He turned to the plants Mia held in her hand. They looked like dry brown carrots, with long roots and hairy tendrils, covered in dirt. "What is that? Looks like a pile of dirty sticks."

"I have no idea."

"If it's a vegetable, it's just what we need. What did she call it?"

"*Oo-ung*, I think. I wonder what we do with it."

"Try washing it first. And it wouldn't hurt to boil it." Now he was ordering her around again. She reminded herself that she had wanted her brother back, just the way he was.

She searched the dictionary until she found what she thought was the right spelling. "It says 'burdock.' That doesn't tell us anything. Where's Google when we need it?"

She washed the vegetable, whatever it was, in the stream, then cut it up with the knife and boiled it with the bits of remaining snake meat and a little more fresh water.

"Soup!" she called, when the vegetable pieces seemed soft enough. They took turns spearing the chunks of vegetable and meat with Simon's knife. The roots had a strong earthy taste.

"Sort of like medicine," Simon said, "but could be worse."

OCTOBER 8

"Yuh-bo-say-yo!"

Mia woke up with a start, her heart leaping into her throat. Simon was crouched on the floor beside her. She scooted back against the wall of the room. There was nowhere to hide. They were trapped.

Simon eased over to the wall by the door opening and peered around the corner. The tension in his body slackened. "It's only the girl."

Mia let out her breath and joined him at the door.

Soon-ok was standing in the yard a few feet from the porch, carrying a bundle wrapped in a blue cloth. Setting it on the porch, she uncovered a basket holding several covered bowls. The big one held something that looked like porridge. Two smaller ones were vegetables, one a kimchi with a red pepper sauce. Soon-ok held out two pairs of metal chopsticks.

"We can't take her food. Her family might not have enough," Simon said.

"We have to. It's really impolite to refuse hospitality."

They tried to get Soon-ok to join them, but she shook her head, saying something and pointing down the hill. She'd already eaten — or would eat — at home. Mia hoped it was true.

"I think it might be potatoes," she said, sampling the porridge. The vegetables were seasoned with soy sauce, wonderful on her tongue. It was the first salt they'd had since the peanuts.

"Shouldn't we leave some for her?"

"No, it's good manners to eat it all, to show you like it." They cleaned each bowl. Soon-ok smiled with pleasure. She wrapped up the dishes, then sat on the porch, waiting. Apparently, she intended to lead them out of the woods herself.

It was time to go.

"You need to get all those wrappers and bury that bowl," Simon said. As they took a last walk around the little house and the yard around it, covering up any evidence that they'd been here, Mia felt a tug of sadness. The farmhouse had been a safe island in a dangerous sea. Everything ahead seemed uncertain and uncomfortable, if not impossible and life-threatening.

Soon-ok led them down the hill in single file.

"How's your leg?" Mia turned to ask Simon, bringing up the rear.

"It's okay. The heat really did the trick."

The day was cloudy with gusts of wind. Mia shivered in her thin jacket, stamping her feet to warm up as they walked. After the flat patch along the stream where she'd met Soon-ok, the trail dropped steeply, zigzagging down the mountain.

Simon was the first to notice the cluster of roofs through a gap in the curtain of trees.

"Hang on a sec," he said. They were on a curve of the path, looking across toward another ridge. The village lay in the valley below.

"Soon-ok?" Mia touched her shoulder, pointed at the roofs. She held up her hand while she slipped off her pack to pull out the dictionary.

Danger. "*Wi-hum?*" Mia pointed again at the village. Soon-ok's expression was puzzled.

"Simon, she doesn't know anything. That Dad was arrested, that the authorities are after us, that we're in danger . . ."

Simon was sitting on the ground, stretching out his leg. "Yeah, it probably hasn't been broadcast. It would only embarrass the regime. Though you gotta know they'll publicize the hell out of it if they catch us!"

Mia shivered. She ripped a page out of her journal and tore three pieces into rough human shapes, one small, two taller. Mia. Simon. Dad. "Sung-mi. *Oh-bba. Ah-buh-ji.* Pyongyang."

They acted out Dad's arrest, running away, the officials chasing them. Then walking, hiding, the mountain, the house.

Soon-ok was nodding. Her eyes were shining with tears. She gestured to herself. "Oo-ri ah-buh-ji."

"Something about her father."

Soon-ok began to speak, punctuating her words with actions. She showed hands being bound, stern-faced people issuing orders, someone being taken away.

"I think her dad got arrested too. What do you think happened?"

"Maybe jail. Maybe a labor camp. Although I thought they usually sent the whole family to the labor camps," Simon said. "Maybe it was one of the reeducation camps. People can survive those."

Mia had to focus on what they needed to do now. She

pointed to herself and Simon, then toward the village, and shook her head.

"*Mi-gook sa-ram.*" *Americans.* "*Wi-hum.*" *Danger.*

Soon-ok nodded, her face serious. She signaled for them to wait, turned down the path, and disappeared around the bend.

"You don't think she went to tell somebody about us?"

"I don't think she would turn us in, Simon. Not after whatever happened to her father. Anyway, if she was going to, wouldn't she have brought someone to the farmhouse last night?"

"You better be right on this one," he said, frowning.

Yes, I certainly better be right. As the minutes went by, Mia pulled on her lower lip, watching the path for any sign of people. Simon paced up and down.

Then, there was Soon-ok. Alone, coming back up the trail, carrying something black in her hand. As she reached them, she stretched out her hand toward Simon.

"Mo-ja."

It was a black cap with a short brim, the kind that schoolboys wore. Simon placed it on his head, then pulled his hood up over the back.

"That helps a lot, especially with the profile. And the blond hair," Mia said. "From a distance no one will be able to tell you're a foreigner."

"*Kam-sa-ham-ni-da.*" Simon ducked his head to Soon-ok in appreciation.

They resumed their trek, Soon-ok leading them on a path winding around the village and on down the mountain. An hour or so later they came out onto grassy hills, fields stacked like a staircase for giants. In the distance a man moved through a dry field with an ox and plow. A little later a woman crossed a far hill, carrying a large bundle on her head. Then another turn, and below, between tall bushes, they could see a stretch of paved highway.

Simon stopped. "She should go back. It's not safe for her to be seen with us."

Mia pointed at the road. "*Wi-hum*." She gestured to Soon-ok that she should return up the path. Then she took out the package of Starbursts and offered Soon-ok one of the last pieces. Strawberry.

"She's got to eat it now. It could be dangerous to her."

Mia used her awkward basic vocabulary again. *Danger. Americans. Eat.* Then she unwrapped a lemon Starburst and put it in her mouth, gesturing to Soon-ok to do the same.

The two girls gazed at each other as they chewed.

"Get —" Simon began.

"The wrapper. I know." Mia held up her own wrapper and held out her hand, feeling foolish. Soon-ok nodded and put the pink wrapper in Mia's hand.

Then it was time to let her go. Mia felt her throat tighten. She took both of Soon-ok's hands in her own.

"*Kam-sa-ham-ni-da*," she said. "*Man-hi, man-hi kam-sa-ham-ni-da.*" *Lots and lots thank you.* It wasn't the correct way to say it, but she knew Soon-ok understood. Tears stood in her eyes, mirroring the ones in Mia's own. They bowed to each other.

Mia and Simon watched Soon-ok move back up the path. Then it was just the two of them.

CHAPTER 18

After Soon-ok left, they settled in a small grove of trees on the hillside above the highway to wait for dark. They'd been mostly under cover as they descended the path with Soon-ok, but now, near the road, there was almost nowhere to hide. The light and open space all around them were disorienting after so many days in the forest.

Lying back on the scrubby tan grass, Simon propped his leg up on a slender trunk.

"How's it doing?" Mia asked.

"If I keep it up for a while, I'll be good to go."

Mia nodded and lay down under a nearby tree. Maybe she could doze for a bit.

"So, Squeak, do you think about being Korean a lot?" Simon's voice surprised her. "I mean, are you kind of conscious all the time that you're, I guess, not white?"

Mia opened her eyes to look at him. Where had this come from?

He was gazing up at the sky, not at her. "I've just been noticing how, since we got here, I think about being white — or really, being *not* Korean — all the time. Because everyone keeps staring at me. Or like now, it's so much harder for me to hide than it is for you." His face was turning a little red. "It makes me realize how, at home, I never think about it much. I guess I don't have to think about it. So I'm wondering . . . what it's like for you."

Mia considered his question, mostly feeling the strangeness of talking about race at all with Simon. Her family acknowledged her Koreanness through their actions — taking her to Korean school all those years, to the Korean grocery store, to restaurants — but they didn't talk about it much. And she couldn't remember ever discussing *their* being white.

"Daniel and I talked about that," she said, "how different it was — how good it felt — to not stand out here. But yeah, back home I pretty much never get to forget that I'm Korean. Every time I stop noticing, someone does something to bring it to my attention. Even in our family," she went on. "I'm not saying I don't want to be Korean, or I don't want to think about it. But the way our family handles it, especially Mom, it's like something *extra* I have that no one else has. Like the rest of you guys are normal, but I'm *special*. I mean, you never got special foods or, I dunno, tiny German or English things in your Christmas stocking to remind you of your heritage. Even when I was little, I didn't want to be special, I just wanted to be 'normal' — like everyone else."

He nodded, looking as if he was mulling it all over.

"So . . ." he began, then stopped. This was different, seeing him off-balance, unsure of himself. It struck her that this was a subject she actually knew more about than her brother did. "So — I don't know how to say this — is there something I should be doing? To, you know, help you or something. Be on your side."

Now she was really surprised. She rolled over on her side

to face him. "I don't need *help*. But it's nice to not be the only one seeing it."

"Okay," Simon said, looking at her now. "I'll keep that in mind. It's just kind of weird that I never noticed any of this before."

"Yeah. Yeah, it is weird," Mia said, smiling a little to herself as she turned onto her back. She tried to relax and doze, but the sense of being exposed kept jolting her awake. After a while she sat up and checked her watch. 11:16.

"It's not even twelve yet. Doesn't it feel as if it should at least be afternoon? As in, I'm starting to get hungry again."

"We ate early, before seven, and we just walked down a mountain. That's a good reason to be hungry."

"But it's not good. We don't have any more food."

"We had a real breakfast this morning, that'll hold us."

"Tell my stomach that."

They each took a stick from the last package of gum, just to have something to chew on. Three left. And six Starbursts. Mia took a swig from her water bottle. They'd have to be careful about that now too. How easy it had been at the farmhouse, living next to the stream.

Her skin felt crawly, like she wanted to jump out of it. The border was maybe only fifty miles away. But they had to just sit there on the hillside, doing nothing. She was going to go crazy before it got dark.

Propping herself against a tree, she took out her colored pens and journal. She wrote down everything she could remember about the last two days, using just Soon-ok's initials.

Afterward she lay on her belly in the grass and read through her journal from the beginning, slowly. It was a complete record of their entire trip, except the details about the phone. That had seemed too dangerous to include, even if no one else might ever see it. And she didn't want to think about the pictures from the prison camp any more than she had to.

It made her tired, just reading it all. They'd been through so much. But then, some of the hard stuff had led to discoveries. It was like those steel wool pot scrubbers Mom used: The experience scraped off the surface to reveal what was really underneath.

Some of what was there wasn't easy to accept. Stone Warrior was scared. Squeak was angry. But that same Squeak had found the strength to save herself, then save her brother. The scouring made the metal shine, like a star.

Mia turned back to the page where Daniel had written her name. Sung-mi, Beautiful Star. Underneath she wrote her other name. Mia. That meant "mine" in Italian. Like she was becoming her own self. Maybe she was growing into both her names.

Mia wrote her Korean name in *han-gul* over and over, practicing shaping the letters as neatly as she could. She tried to copy the Chinese characters Daniel had written.

She flipped to the map she'd drawn based on Soon-ok's picture of stones and grass. She looked at the guidebook map of the northwest section, trying to compare the two maps to see where they were on the road. It was impossible to know their exact location, but she figured she had it within ten or fifteen miles. *You are here.* For some reason, that made her feel better. A little more in control of what happened to them.

"Simon?"

He grunted. He was lying on the ground, arms behind his head, foot braced on the tree. His MP3 player wires ran from his sweatshirt pouch up to his ears. His battery must still be working. Mia scooted closer to him on the grass, holding out the guidebook map.

"It looks like the train tracks are on the other side of the road, closer to the ocean. But really close. Maybe within a mile. So it might be safer to go along the tracks, like we did before."

"No, the road's our best bet. It's right here, and much easier to walk on. There's hardly any traffic, even in daylight; I've only heard one car pass since we got here." He didn't even look at the map.

The Decider had spoken. Mia considered reminding him that they were a team, that she had a say in their route as well. But it did sound better, traveling on a smooth road they didn't have to search for.

12:37. All that activity and not even two hours had passed. Five or six hours left before dark. It had been easier in the forest when they were free to move around and do things. When they hadn't been scared they'd get caught.

Being busy had also given her something to think about other than how hungry she was. She couldn't even imagine where food would come from now.

She sat up and pulled out the guidebook. She read a few passages in the section on Sinuiju and the area north of it.

"Hey, listen to this. There's a section of the river that's so narrow and shallow that you can actually walk across the border. It's called 'One-Step Crossing.'" Dad had said the guidebook was maybe ten years old, but rivers didn't change that much. "Nearby, there's a part of the actual Great Wall of China. It's called Tiger Mountain. Maybe we should try going that way, instead of across the bridge in Sinuiju. It might be easier."

Mia pointed to the spot on the map. Simon barely glanced at it.

"I still say we go for the bridge," he said. "It's a direct route, the road goes there, the train goes across it. If there's a way to get across the bridge, it will be the easiest way by far, and we'll be safer there because they're used to seeing tourists. If we get there and see it isn't going to work, we can maybe try this other place."

Mia put the guidebook away. She sighed. "Simon, I can't stand it anymore. We still have at least five hours till it's dark enough to start walking!"

"Squeak, just chill. There's nothing we can do till then."

"I'm trying! But I can't wait five more hours, I just can't!" She knew she sounded like a pouting, whining six-year-old. *Simon, play with me.*

"It's not that hard. Just . . . I dunno, write in your journal or something."

"I already did that."

"Well, write some more, then." He turned on his side away from her. As if she was a pest he wanted to shoo away.

"Simon." She made her voice strong. Mia, not Squeak.

"What?"

"This is not working. I'm just trying to get you to help me. But you're using that tone. Like I'm bothering you. I just spent the last three days working my butt off for you. So could you give me a little hand here?"

He rolled onto his other side, facing her. He looked surprised. Mia was kind of surprised too. It sounded like the voice of a girl who could lift rocks. Treat wounds. Kill snakes.

Simon pulled the buds out of his ears and sat up. "So, teach me something."

"What?"

"Like something you learned in Korean school, something that might come in handy."

Mia stared at him. "Seriously?" She couldn't remember ever having taught Simon anything.

"Sure. What else are we going to do for five or so hours?"

"Okaaay . . ." She thought. What had she learned at Korean school that she could remember well enough to teach? "The alphabet. I'll teach you *han-gul*. Then you'll be able to read the signs."

"Cool. You're on."

"You won't know what they mean. But you'll be able to sound them out."

"So let's do it."

"Okay." Mia picked up a colored pen and opened to a blank page in her journal. She drew an upside-down L. "Start with the consonants. That's the first one. It's a *k*, but softer, like between a *k* and a *g*."

She drew a right-side-up L shape next. "This is the second one. It's an *n* sound." She wrote all fourteen consonants in a row.

"They're so simple."

"It's the most scientific alphabet in the world." Mia smiled. "I sound like my teacher. But it is pretty amazing. Mrs. Ahn said that to invent the alphabet, King Sejong and his scholars studied the way the tongue is placed in the mouth for each sound. They designed the letter based on that."

"Really cool."

"Now the vowels. The first one is *ah*." She wrote all ten. Simon repeated the sounds after her.

"Okay, now here's how to put them together. First consonant, plus the first vowel." She drew them beside each other. "So what's that say?"

Simon studied the rows of letters and sounds. "*Ka?*"

"Yeah! See, you can do it!" She felt like a real teacher, with a prize student. She showed him a few other combinations. "If the vowel has a vertical line, it goes to the side of the consonant. If it has a horizontal line, it goes underneath. Now you have to memorize them. I'll make flash cards."

After a half hour or so of practice, Simon could recognize most of the letters.

"So now, if there's a sign for a town, you'll be able to read it."

"Awesome. I'll practice more later, but right now my brain is stuffed. Anyway, we should get some sleep. It's gonna be a long night."

Mia dutifully lay back in the grass and closed her eyes. She lay there for a long time, but she didn't get sleepy. There was too much tension running through her body, waiting for dark so they could move.

Opening her eyes, she couldn't believe how light it still was. 3:28. At least another couple of hours to go, she figured. Her stomach was getting more insistent, demanding food.

Time crawled by.

"Simon? What do you think is happening to Dad?"

He was lying flat on his back in the grass. She might have woken him up. Too bad. He'd slept for most of three days, while she had been working.

"I dunno, Squeak. Since we don't know why they arrested him in the first place, whether or not someone knew about his secret meeting, it's kind of hard to guess."

"I keep wondering if he's getting treated okay. If he's getting enough to eat. They wouldn't *hurt* him, would they?"

"Mia, I don't know, okay? There isn't anything else to say. Let it be. I don't want to talk about it anymore. Get some sleep." He turned on his side, his back to her.

And here we go again. Well, he could shut the door all he liked. But that didn't mean she couldn't keep knocking till he opened it.

"How come you're getting angry just because I want to talk about Dad? Don't you even care what's happening to him?"

"What kind of crazy question is that? Of course I care."

"Then how come you don't want to talk about it? C'mon, Simon. If we're going to survive this whole thing together, we can't shut down like this. We have to share stuff."

He sat up quickly, crossed his legs, and faced her. His expression was fierce. "You really want to know what's going on for me? I'll tell you. The last couple of years, I've had this whole list of stuff about Dad that bugs me: He's never around. He's missed most of my games and my debates. Starving kids seem to come first, before us. But then he comes home from North Korea and other places where terrible things are happening and he just gets on with everyday life in suburban Connecticut, as if what he saw in those places doesn't even affect him. He pretends that stuff is okay when it's not. He keeps on giving food aid to the North Korean government, making it possible for them to stay in power, starving and torturing their own people. Here on the trip, he was just going along with the program." He took a breath, huffed it out. "I was so superior about it, throwing that stuff at him."

He paused and raised his eyes to the sky. "Of course, now it looks as if he wasn't just going along with things. Maybe that was his cover, and in reality he was supporting people who are trying to change the government, to keep people from going hungry. Who knows how deeply he's involved and how long this has been going on?" He met her eyes.

"So now you keep pestering me, 'Where is Dad?'" He

pitched his voice higher, mimicking her. "'What's happening to him?' It just reminds me that the last days I spent with Dad I was mad at him the whole time. What if that's it? What if I never see him again?" Simon's voice cracked and he turned his face away. But not before Mia saw his eyes glistening.

She waited, holding her breath. He cleared his throat.

"So, I'm incredibly angry at myself for being so, so . . . *stupid*. Thinking I knew so much. It just makes me *sick*." He spit the word out. "And it reminds me that Dad's probably still in a North Korean prison and I can't figure out any way to help him, except maybe getting those photos — and you — out of this country."

He turned to her. There was pain in his eyes. "But it's even more complicated than that. Because I'm still mad at Dad too. For taking such risks, for involving his own kids, for endangering us. 'Cause it feels as if I got one thing right about Dad: He seems a lot more concerned about starving North Koreans than about us." He looked away, then let himself back down on the grass and stretched out.

Mia stared at Simon, speechless. Everything in her wanted to protest: *Nooo, Dad loved his kids! He would never —*

But a door was opening in her mind. If Dad had been sneaking out to meet someone that night, it seemed almost as if he had been using them as cover. They would never be in this desperate situation if he hadn't decided to bring them on this trip.

One thing Simon said was right: It was really complicated. In a way, they were all to blame for something. What about Mom? It was hard to imagine her knowing what Dad was up to and letting him risk their lives. She wouldn't have allowed them to come along on the trip. But Mom was always looking for things to fix. Maybe she was in on the secret with Dad.

Mia wished she had a map showing the path for their family to find their way. Like a Parcheesi board, with Mom and Dad and Simon and herself as game pieces, and all they had to do was eventually roll the right numbers and all of them would end up back home, together again.

She turned away and closed her eyes.

. . .

"Ready or not, here we go," Simon said a few hours later.

They moved down the hill in the cover of dark, through the tall grass to the road. No lights anywhere. The half moon dimly lit the pavement. They slipped through the night like shadows.

We're on our way, Dad.

It felt so good to be moving, as if she could walk all the way to the border in one night. The quiet and the rhythmic movement calmed her mind.

"Simon?"

"Yeah?"

"Do you really think Dad cares more about starving people than he does about us?"

There was a long silence, the only sound their feet scuffing on the road. Simon sighed.

"No, of course not, not really. I guess . . . well, I think Dad thinks we're fine, you know, that we don't really need him? But the starving North Korean kids aren't okay at all. They need him desperately.

"The thing is," Simon continued, "I just would've liked it if Dad had talked to me about it. Like, acknowledged that missing my games and my debates and all mattered — to me, maybe to him too. But instead, it was always clear that when it came to needs, starving children in other countries were always going to win."

She held that idea, turning it over and examining it. She knew the story of her adoption so well, she could practically recite it: how Dad and Mom had always planned to adopt their second child, how they'd wanted a daughter after Simon was born, how they'd chosen Korea because of Jae Kim — a Korean exchange student who'd been one of Dad's best friends in college, how long they'd waited for her, how excited they'd been when they got the referral photo. . . . But she didn't know how all that connected with Dad getting so passionate about the North Korean situation. Had that happened before or after her adoption? If it was before, then maybe adopting her was part of his wanting to save the world. Like Mia sometimes felt she was for Mom: a fix-it project. But if it was after her adoption, maybe he felt this emotional bond to all Korean children. *Because* of Mia. Or maybe all of it was about a father wanting the world to be a better place for his children, or all children. So maybe caring about North Koreans wasn't separate from caring about her and Simon. Maybe it was all connected.

That was a conversation to have with Dad. When — if — she ever got to talk to him again.

She followed Simon's silhouette along the road. The world around them was dark against darker against darkest. The dim moon dropped slowly toward the line of hills to their left. Her nose was cold.

"You know, Dad's grandparents — Nona's parents — left Germany because they didn't like what was happening as Hitler was coming into power." Simon was talking again. She thought he'd shared more with her since he'd recovered than in their whole life together up to this point. "Even though they weren't Jewish, when they got to America, they started sponsoring Jewish families, helping them to escape. So that save-the-world thing is sort of in our blood" — Simon caught himself — "well, our heritage. Definitely not blood; you've got it worse than I do." In the dark, Mia could hear the smile in his voice.

"When you were little you were always wanting to save the whales," he went on, "or the dolphins . . . or the polar bears. Remember that birthday when you said you didn't want presents, you just wanted pet food to give to the animal shelter?"

"Uh-huh."

"You always were the good kid. Me, not so much. There was always this pressure that I was supposed to care. It's not that I don't care, but that I don't want to *have* to. I want to decide myself what I want to care about. A lot of the time I feel like, do I have to want to change the world all the time? What if I like it the way it is?"

Mia noticed that Simon's anger and criticism of Dad, of their family, wasn't freaking her out the way she knew it would have just a week ago. Before, watching Simon and Dad fighting, she couldn't bear it. Like something terrible would happen if they didn't stop. Maybe Simon was right that the fear came from having already lost one set of parents. From knowing that families could break.

Now, it didn't bother her that Simon was mad at their parents. In fact, she was discovering she might be mad at them too. The way they handled her being Korean, for instance. Mom especially had always done a lot to bring Korean stuff into Mia's life, but there was something about it that didn't feel right. Mia couldn't quite figure it out yet — this was all so new, even admitting she had these feelings. But somehow the way her family acknowledged her Koreanness had always focused on the *outside*, the surface, in a way that made Korea seem like a foreign culture, and made Mia feel different from her family. It always drew attention to the fact that Korea was hers and not theirs.

There was so much here she wanted to keep thinking about, like a complex puzzle to solve. In a peculiar way, this journey was freeing her up to see her family as they really were. It no longer felt dangerous to notice that they messed up.

They had fights. They kept secrets from each other. They could make bad choices. None of it had to mean they were losing each other. Or that they had stopped loving each other. It was nothing compared to someone really getting taken away. Like Dad getting arrested. Or Simon getting sick. Being afraid one of them would die.

Then you saw that all you wanted was to get them back, exactly as they were. So you could go on loving them. No matter how much they annoyed you.

So maybe they could all find their way back to each other, if only they could all get out of North Korea alive.

The night got darker and colder. Mia's legs grew heavy. She put one foot in front of the other, endlessly. After a while she moved into a trance state. The fatigue and cold were just how things were. She had no energy left for thinking.

Every two hours, Simon called a rest break. They crawled into the tall grass by the side of the road to sleep. Each time he set his alarm to wake them after just half an hour.

"That gives us five or ten minutes to fall asleep, twenty minutes to sleep. I learned about this at wilderness camp. It's been scientifically proven that you get the most benefit and remain the most alert from twenty-minute naps." He seemed energized by the exercise and the cold. "If you sleep longer, unless you can get at least ninety minutes, you actually feel more tired."

It was all she could do to just follow Simon's lead. Each time she got pulled from sleep, she felt more and more disoriented. She trudged along the road in the pitch black. When they stopped she fell instantly into a dream state, in which she was also walking endlessly in the dark. Time disappeared.

Somewhere in the endless night they came to a signpost with white letters. Ahead was a cluster of dark shapes.

"Hey," Simon said. "That's the *s* sound, like a roof? *So — Son.* Then *ch —* right? *Sonchon!* We made it to Sonchon. And I can read the sign!"

Mia nodded. She felt as if she were wrapped in a gauzy web. They walked through silent streets. The outlines of the town were black against the dark sky. Tall blocks of apartment buildings. Low tile roofs and walls of single homes. Some of them had small garden patches surrounded by wooden screen fencing, but it was too late in the year for any vegetables to be left for her and Simon to steal. They must have stores here, with food for sale, but she and Simon couldn't risk being seen in the daytime in an off-the-beaten-path town where a foreigner would never be expected to visit.

They trudged on, back out into the countryside. By the time the sky started lightening toward dawn, Mia no longer had the energy to lift her feet. She shuffled along, following Simon.

Endless hours later, he turned off the pavement, along a path beside dry rice paddies and up a rise into a thicket of bushes and small trees.

"Wait here." Mia slumped to the ground as Simon pushed through the brush. Twigs snapped and branches rustled. Then he was beside her again.

"Okay, c'mon. There's a patch of grass."

She felt the ground, hard beneath her body, then sleep taking her as if she were drowning.

OCTOBER 9

When she woke, Mia's belly screamed: *Food!*

The next thing she noticed was how cold she was. Limb-shaking, teeth-chattering cold. Like she couldn't ever get warm again.

It was light. She gazed up at scraps of clouds against a deep blue sky, covering the sun, then revealing it. The grass-covered patch was surrounded by a thick tangle of bushes, small trees, and brush. Mia examined them, wondering if any parts of the plants were edible. She thought she could eat bark if it would quiet the gnawing in her stomach.

Where was Simon? He must be nearby, scouting. He wouldn't have left her.

She pushed herself to her feet. She felt sore all over, like she'd been hit by a truck. She couldn't imagine walking another half mile, much less the miles and miles they'd walked the night before.

Where was Simon?

Her teeth were chattering hard enough to hear. She tried jumping up and down a little to get her circulation going, but it jarred her aching body. She began circling the little enclosure. She twisted slowly from side to side and bent over to try to touch her toes, stiff muscles resisting.

Where was Simon?

Panic surged through her. She'd been awake more than ten minutes. Maybe he lost his way back to their spot. She had no idea how long he'd been gone. Maybe she should go looking for him. But if she left this spot, he might come back. They could lose each other completely.

She pounded the ground around the circle. Breathing, breathing to keep her fear down. Twenty minutes, then twenty-five. Where could he be?

Sticks cracked as something made its way through the brush toward her. She started to call out, then stopped. It might not be Simon.

But over the top of the thicket, there was the black cap, bobbing. When Simon pushed through the bushes into the circle, Mia threw her arms around him and burst into tears. He stiffened and stepped back a little. She clung to him.

"You were gone so long! I thought something had happened to you!" Sobs racked her body, feeling as if they were cracking her back. She was crying like a little kid, even though there wasn't anything to cry about.

Simon stood still. He was probably hating this, but she couldn't stop. Then she felt her brother's arms come around her.

"Sorry, Squeak. I didn't mean to scare you. I didn't think you'd wake up for ages." He patted her back. "It's okay, it's okay."

Gradually, the storm passed. She kept her head on Simon's chest. Then she pulled away, looking down at the ground.

"Sorry," she mumbled. "I don't know. . . . I didn't mean. . . ."

"Don't sweat it. It's one of the symptoms of not having had anything to eat in twenty-four hours."

"Where were you?"

"I was scouting around, trying to get a sense of where we were. And see if I could find any food. No luck. But there's no sign of any people, so I think we can risk a small fire to get warm."

He made her take a swig of water so she wouldn't get dehydrated, and eat two of the six remaining Starbursts, to get a little sugar into her system. Mia squatted by the fire he was building, chewing slowly, feeling the sweetness fill her mouth and trickle down her throat. As the flames flickered, catching on the pile of dry leaves and twigs, she held her hands over them. The warmth began to thaw her fingers.

"Now we wait until it's dark," he said. "We need a distraction. Let's work on my Korean."

Concentrating actually helped a little. The voice in her brain screaming *Food!* quieted a bit when she thought about something else.

She turned her left side to the fire as she held up the flash cards for Simon. Bit by bit her clenched muscles relaxed in the warmth. She curled as close to the flames as she could without burning herself.

Through the afternoon she dozed by the fire, eyes flickering open to see Simon napping, then tending the fire, then napping some more.

She woke again near dusk. Her brother's dark form was bent over, smothering the smoldering ashes.

The bushes rustled, the unmistakable sound of something moving toward them. They froze. The sound came closer.

"Simon?" Mia whispered. He put a finger to his mouth, then signaled with his hand for her to stay put. The curl of smoke rose into the air. A signal announcing their location.

A figure — a man in dark clothing — broke through the brush into the circle and halted. He saw them.

CHAPTER 19

In the half-light the man's face registered astonishment. His eyes ping-ponged back and forth from Simon's face to Mia's. The three of them stared at one another, an image frozen by the pause button.

A giant alarm was blaring in Mia's brain. The phone. They needed to hide the phone.

The man was thin and wiry, his hair in a buzz cut. He wore a padded jacket made of coarse brown fabric. Not a smooth city guy. Not a government agent.

Mia pulled herself up and gave a polite bow.

"*An-nyung ha-shim-ni-ka.*" She gestured to herself and Simon. "Mia. Simon."

The man put out his hand, vigorously shaking each of theirs. "Ah, hallo, hallo. Mis-tah Shin." He gestured to himself. He seemed completely delighted to have discovered them, as if having foreigners turn up like aliens from outer space was something he'd been hoping for. He clearly knew a little English.

Mia said, "*Sinuiju ka-yo. Ki-cha-yuk ka-yo.*"

"Ahh. You go Sinuiju, you go train station. Very good." His English was strongly accented, but she could understand him. And he'd understood her. Nothing about the encounter seemed to puzzle or distress him. He spoke some rapid phrases and beckoned, motioning back in the direction from which he'd appeared.

"You come. Come my house."

Mia looked at Simon.

"What else are we gonna do?" he said. "Run? The happier he is with us, the less likely he is to turn us in."

Mia picked up her pack. She was too tired and hungry to care whether or not it was safe. "I just hope he takes us somewhere with food."

Simon finished stomping out the fire.

They followed Mr. Shin through the twilight, on hard-packed dirt paths running along the ridges of a range of hills. Mia saw Simon looking around, probably keeping track of where they were in relation to the road, just as she was doing.

It was completely dark by the time they came to a wall and a cluster of roofs, barely visible in the gloom. Mr. Shin led them through a gate into a courtyard ringed by several buildings with white walls and tile roofs. The light spilling from the house fell on a large motor scooter standing in a corner against one wall.

The man called out. Mia flinched. But it was a gray-haired woman in an apron who appeared in the lit doorway. The man spoke to her, gesturing at his surprise guests. The one phrase Mia understood was "weh-gook sa-ram." Foreigners.

The grandmother's face registered amazed delight as she took in Simon's face and, as he pulled off his hat, his blond hair. She motioned with her hands and made coaxing sounds, beckoning them to enter the home.

"Take your shoes off," Mia whispered to Simon. They stepped up into a concrete entryway, following the woman down a hallway to a room with a floor covered in oiled yellow paper. The usual portraits of Kim Il-sung and Kim Jong-il hung high on one wall.

The floor was warm under their sock feet. The grandmother pulled out large square cushions in a bright orange print and patted them, smiling at Mia and Simon. They sank to the floor on the cushions. The woman left, closing the sliding door behind her.

Mia and Simon turned to each other.

"Where did Mr. Shin go?" Mia asked warily.

"It could be a trap." Simon shrugged. "But I don't know what choice we have."

Dishes clinked in the next room. Then the door slid open and the grandmother carried in a little wooden table, placing it on the floor in front of them. Mia's mouth dropped open.

"There's so much food!" Large metal bowls of rice and soup and small ones of side dishes. Everything was colorful and fragrant and fresh.

"Amazing." Simon spoke in an undertone. They both continued to smile and nod at the woman.

At that moment, their host entered the room. "Okay, okay! You eat! Very good!"

He sat down to share the meal. The grandmother — his mother, Mia guessed — sat a little ways away, watching. It felt weird, but she beamed and nodded at them, clearly expecting them to eat without her. Mia hoped she'd eat later.

The food tasted even better than it looked. The rice — a mixture of white grains and barley, studded with black beans — was steaming and moist, clinging in clumps that made it easy to lift with chopsticks. Pieces of tofu and vegetables floated in the soup's deeply flavored broth. The small bowls held chunks of potatoes seasoned with soy sauce, two kinds of kimchi, and tiny hard brown beans with a sweet coating — soybeans, Mia thought. It was really just a simple vegetarian meal. But to her eyes, tongue, and belly it was a feast out of a dream. She almost didn't care if someone was coming to take them away, as long as they could finish eating first.

When they'd eaten all they could hold, the woman cleared the table. Mr. Shin left the room behind her.

Simon leaned back against the wall. "I'm trying to figure out if we should get him to take us back to the road now, so we can cover some distance while it's still dark. Problem is, we can't walk all the way to the border before light, and then where would we hide till dark?"

"We might be safer here. Maybe Mr. Shin can help us get to Sinuiju. If we're with him, we might not stand out as much. And once we get to the city, we'll look like a tourist and a guide. Tourists come over from Dandong all the time."

Simon nodded. "We also don't want to seem too eager to leave, as if we have something to hide." Footsteps sounded in the hallway. He opened his hands as if he was resigned to whatever happened.

Now that Mia was full, she could feel all her muscles on alert, tuning in to the slightest sound and movement. They were so vulnerable here. If their hosts knew what was hidden on the phone, how would they react?

Mr. Shin moved through the doorway to a tall wooden cabinet standing in one corner. Inside, folded bedding was stacked, white covers bordering bright blue, yellow, and green quilts. Reaching to a high shelf, he pulled down a small black television, set it on the floor, and plugged it into a wall socket.

As they watched, wide-eyed, he took out a DVD player and attached all the wires. He turned, smiling.

"Okay, okay, we see video. Very good!" He held out a DVD. Mia and Simon exchanged looks.

The final surprise came when Mr. Shin fiddled with the remote until he produced English subtitles. He beamed at them. "English! Very good!" The grandmother joined them as the movie began.

"It's a South Korean movie!" Mia tried to keep the astonishment out of her voice. "I thought everything like that was forbidden here."

"Maybe, this close to the border, with black markets and all, it's hard to control."

They were sitting in a North Korean home with North Korean citizens, watching a DVD of a romance set in South Korea, under the watchful eyes of the Great Leader and the Dear Leader. All of them — Mr. Shin and his mother included — could be arrested for this. Mia's eyes were fastened to the images and words on the TV screen. But her ears scanned for any sounds from the courtyard. From time to time Simon glanced toward the door.

"Doesn't seem likely that he'd report us," Mia whispered. "Not while he's playing a South Korean DVD."

When she could concentrate on it, Mia found herself loving the movie, the wonderful novelty of having all the parts — heroine, hero, antagonists, background characters — played by actors whose faces had features like hers. A whole world of Koreanness.

It wasn't that she didn't know about Korean dramas; at Korean school, the other kids — those *real* Korean kids who had matching parents and already knew how to speak the language — gossiped about K-drama actors and K-pop stars as if they were friends of theirs. Mia had always felt impossibly out of it. She'd tried to look some stuff up online, to watch some dramas and music videos, but she couldn't figure out where to start. Watching this film, she realized how much she'd been missing. When she got home, she resolved that she'd ask someone at Korean school for a recommendation. There should definitely be more K-drama in her future.

When the movie ended, the man gestured to the bedding in the cabinet.

"You sleep. Tomorrow we go Sinuiju. I drive." He jiggled his hands and made a thrumming noise. "Very good!"

"He's going to *drive* us." Mia felt a fierce longing to just be comfortable for a little while. A warm, soft place to sleep. Maybe another hot meal. Imagine not having to walk the last twenty-five or thirty miles.

"I don't know what else we can do," Simon whispered. "It's not as if we'd be safer if we left. If someone's coming, they'd still be able to find us. We just have to hope this guy means well."

Just as they got the quilts laid out on the floor, the lightbulb hanging from the ceiling went out. Mia jumped.

"Probably a power outage," Simon said. "It's like an enforced 'lights out.'"

After a moment, the darkness actually felt like a relief. If someone came, they might have a tiny chance of escaping.

The grandmother brought a candle and directed Mia to the bathroom, handing her some folded clothes. She pointed to a yellow metal basin of warm water next to a drain in the tile floor. Then she slid the door closed behind her, leaving Mia alone in the flickering light.

The entire room was tiled. Mia squatted by the basin to wash and shampoo her hair. A thin little striped towel hung on a hook on the wall, the only thing she could find for drying herself off. She dressed in the grandmother's baggy, quilted gray cotton top and pants, like a pair of long underwear.

Standing to replace the towel, she caught her reflection in a square frame of mirror. The face that gazed back at her in the candlelight belonged to a stranger. Mia pulled her wet hair behind her ears and studied herself. There were smudges under her eyes and hollows in her cheekbones. Behind the shelf of her eyelids, back in the shadows, she saw something. There was someone there. Someone alive and vivid and free. A creature who wasn't contained by any of the ways she thought of herself. Not Korean or American. Not nice or self-centered. Not a sister or a daughter. Just . . . more. It was her, but bigger. Peering out through the mask of her face.

Hi, there. I see you.

The moment passed, and it was just herself, Mia, looking back.

. . .

Back in the single room, all four of them lay down on the thick cotton mats on the warm floor, heavy quilts over them. It felt weird to be lying in bed next to strangers. Mia wondered if she'd make funny noises in her sleep. But it was sublime to be lying on a soft padded surface. To be warm. To have a full belly.

If she'd been born in a Korean village way out in the country, to parents who could care for her, maybe this is what her life might have been like.

But no Dad. No Mom. No Simon.

Without them, she wouldn't be who she was.

OCTOBER 10

A rooster crowed in the still-dark morning. Next to the quilts, their clothes lay neatly folded, clean and stiff. The grandmother must have washed them in the night and dried them on the heated floor. Or else she had North Korean elves as helpers.

By the time Simon and Mia had each dressed in the bathroom, she was carrying in another meal. Rice with a fried egg on top. Soup and side dishes. *Heaven*.

Out in the courtyard, they found Mr. Shin attaching a sidecar to his motorcycle. He pointed to Mia, then to the sidecar.

"You sit!"

The air was brisk, an inky-blue sky overhead, pinpricked by stars. As they climbed aboard, the grandmother carried out a blue plastic sheet. She chattered animatedly to Mr. Shin, gesturing as if she were berating him. He motioned for Mia to wrap the plastic around herself. She pulled it over her shoulders like a shawl. The grandmother tucked the sheet around her.

Mia smiled and nodded. "Why is she covering me with a plastic sheet?"

"'Cause it's probably in the mid-forties," Simon said. "As soon as this thing gets going, we're going to freeze our butts off!"

"What about you?"

"I'm sitting behind the guy. He'll be my wind block."

Mr. Shin was pulling on gloves and a hat, zipping up the collar of his jacket. At that moment there was a ringing sound. Mia froze. Mr. Shin put a hand in his pocket and pulled out a cell phone. Mia and Simon exchanged glances as their host put the phone up to his ear and began to talk.

"I just hope the call isn't about us," Simon said under his breath.

As Mr. Shin returned the phone to his pocket, his mother called and gestured for him to wait. She came back with her arms full: a black fake leather jacket that she insisted Simon put on, and packages of snacks and bottles of water she pressed into the corners of the sidecar. They bowed their thanks over and over.

As the motorbike putted out the gate, the grandmother followed them to the edge of the courtyard, waving. Mia kept her eyes on her until they turned the corner.

The beam of the bike headlight on the hard-packed dirt was the only light in the black landscape. They turned onto a wider alley that ran between other walled homes, then onto a paved street. The engine revved louder and settled to a hum.

As they picked up speed, the wind rose, cutting like a knife. Mia shivered and pulled the plastic sheet closer. The wind kept finding holes to sneak into with its freezing fingers. Finally, she pulled the sheet up over her head and wrapped it tightly around herself, with only her eyes exposed. She was cold, but at least the plastic cut the wind's bite.

She focused on how much ground they were covering. Imagined having to walk it, step by tired step.

To their right, the deep navy of the sky was lightening to blue. Dawn coming on. Soon they were passing silhouettes of houses. Then big blocky towers, the buildings closer and closer together.

The highway sign said Tongrim. Mia tried to picture the

map. If she remembered right, Tongrim was only about twenty miles from Sinuiju. They were so close. They could soon be in China, calling Mom. Possibly even this very day. But first they had to get through Sinuiju, and somehow, across the border.

Then they were speeding past rice paddies and fields of corn stretching out on both sides of the highway. Brown hills rose from the fields. No trees or bushes, just dry grass. They passed through more towns. Brick homes with tile roofs. Tall, concrete apartment buildings painted turquoise, pink, and blue. Everything looked worn down, edges pockmarked, painted surfaces streaked with rust and age.

There were a few people on the roads now. Some walking, some riding bicycles. No one glanced at the three of them on the motorbike. With Simon's face hidden under his cap and sweatshirt hood, his head in close to Mr. Shin's back, they could pass for ordinary North Koreans. For the moment, they were safe. Mia wished Mr. Shin could just keep driving. Right through Sinuiju. Across the bridge into China.

They drove through two more heavily settled areas — "Yomju," Mr. Shin called out, then "Ryongchon," over the roar of the engine. It must be working hard, carrying such a heavy load.

A band of lemon yellow widened on the horizon. The promise of a clear day. Mia felt a tremor of anticipation. Maybe their way was clear as well. Maybe today . . .

Sinuiju, a highway sign proclaimed in Korean. *5 km*. Five kilometers was . . . around three miles. Really close. And on the far side of Sinuiju, the river. The bridge. The border. Mia's heart beat faster. They'd almost made it. How crazy amazing was that?

But she knew this could be the most dangerous section of

the trip. The place they were most likely to be stopped. After everything they had survived to get this far, it could all be for nothing.

They reached the city limits. As if she'd had a premonition, at that moment she caught sight of a grouping of men in uniforms — police? — at an intersection four or five blocks ahead. They were waving at the few vehicles to slow down so they could peer in at the drivers and passengers. A checkpoint. Mia's heart sped up. She grabbed Simon's knee.

"Uh-oh," he said.

But Mr. Shin turned right at the next street as if he was taking his usual route with nothing to hide. Mia let her breath out and tried to relax her body.

Gray buildings crowded together, many of them topped with political slogans. Sinuiju was sootier and more run-down than Pyongyang. Less ordered, less prosperous, less scoured clean, more like a random collection of shops and factories, jumbled together every which way.

Mia scanned the surroundings for any sign of the river, trying to place them on the map in her mind. As they slowed to drive through the city, the wind dropped. She poked her head out from the sheet and rubbed her nose to warm it. The sky was growing light overhead. The motorbike slowed, turned, purred down a city street. They made a sharp right into a long, narrow alleyway between two- and three-story industrial buildings with tin sides. The packed dirt was black with oil and soot. Mr. Shin maneuvered between parked bicycles and scooters and small trucks jutting out from open shed doors.

After several blocks, they pulled up beside a rusty tin warehouse. A row of horizontal windows faced the alley, the panes of glass smudged and dirty. Mr. Shin turned the key and the engine shuddered and died.

"Okay, okay. Sinuiju! Very good!" Mr. Shin beamed. His arms were extended as if presenting the city to them as a gift.

Mia stood up slowly, dropping the plastic and unwinding her cramped limbs. Mr. Shin pointed to a metal door into the warehouse.

"One minute," he said, holding up a finger. He disappeared into the warehouse, leaving the door open behind him. Piles of crates and stacks of cardboard boxes filled the concrete floor. Behind him, Simon gave a low whistle.

"Cell phones. Chinese cell phones," he said quietly. "They can be used to call internationally. I remember Dad saying that's how defectors can talk to family left behind in North Korea. Strictly against the rules. Looks like our guy has got himself a nice little share of the black market. So he probably won't call the local party official to come pick us up here. Question is, what do we do now?"

"Maybe we can get him to drop us off at the train station," Mia said. "When we met yesterday, I told him that's where we were going. It seemed like the least suspicious place. The guidebook says that foreigners can travel back and forth between Sinuiju and Dandong on the train. It also says Americans can't take the train, but Mr. Shin might not know that. I thought the station would be good, because on the map it looked like it was pretty close to the bridge."

"Good thinking, Squeak." He was still calling her by that silly nickname, but she found she didn't mind it. There was history there, and connection, reminding her of where she'd come from.

Mia smiled and pulled out her dictionary. When Mr. Shin returned, she asked, *"Ki-cha-yok uh-di-eh-yo?" Where is the train station?*

Mr. Shin nodded with enthusiasm. "Yes, yes. Very good. I drive."

In the dawn light, the town had a dingy, gritty look. It was the first time they'd been out in public since the train station in Pyongyang. Simon pulled the brim of his cap low on his forehead and tugged the sides of his hood close.

Mr. Shin took them through a maze of narrow streets and down another alley. The streets got wider and cleaner, the buildings more imposing, business offices and hotels instead of run-down factories and warehouses.

The motorbike turned onto a broad street, the morning sun bright on Mia's right side. They were headed north. Railroad tracks on their right. Coming up, a massive building with banners. The station. Directly ahead was the huge square with the statue of Kim Il-sung that was described in the guidebook. With its open spaces and broad empty streets, this section of Sinuiju looked like Pyongyang.

Mr. Shin sped right by the train station. Mia's heart skipped. She and Simon exchanged alarmed looks. The bike slowed, leaned left in front of the square, and turned onto another wide street. They passed the station hotel, then on the next block, a multistory building with clothing in the windows. A department store. Where was he taking them? Mia wondered if they'd need to jump off the speeding bike.

Two more turns. Mr. Shin pulled up along the curb in a narrow side street with walled houses crowded in close, several blocks from the main thoroughfare. As she climbed out of the sidecar, she tried to steady her breath.

"Guess he's being careful too," Simon remarked, glancing around. No one was in sight.

"You see train?" Mr. Shin asked. Mia nodded.

"We need to give him some money," she said to Simon. "Everything he did for us, all that driving. Hang on, let me look up the word for gasoline."

Simon reached for his backpack and held out several euros.

"*Hwee-bal-yoo,*" Mia read from the dictionary. Mr. Shin looked surprised, then shook his head.

"No, no. Too much-ee." He held up his hands, shaking them from side to side.

"People always refuse at first. You're supposed to offer three times. With two hands, not one. And bow."

Simon followed her instructions. Again Mr. Shin refused. But on the third try, he glanced up and down the street, then took the money from Simon. *Whew.* It must have been the right thing to do or he wouldn't have accepted.

They bowed their thanks again and again, Simon following Mia's lead. Mr. Shin turned the motorbike around and started back down the street. He turned once and waved before disappearing around the corner.

They were alone, out in the open.

"We need to get out of sight," Mia said.

"Absolutely. Mr. Shin doesn't seem to have reported us yet, and maybe he won't, but it would be awfully tempting. And it's a little early for a tourist and a guide to be walking around."

"The bridge should be just a couple of blocks north."

"Let's get near enough to examine it and find a place under cover."

SHIN HYUN-TAE

⋆ ⋆ ⋆

"Come this way, Comrade Shin." His Chinese contact beckoned, shepherding him down the warehouse aisles between towering stacks of boxed goods. "You may be interested in this, just came in. Swiss."

It was not yet mid-morning. After the drop-off downtown, Hyun-tae had returned to his office, picked up his mini-truck, and driven across the bridge to Dandong.

What an intriguing week this was turning out to be. Yesterday he'd run into two foreigners in the middle of a field and brought them to his own house. Who knows what they were doing there or where they were going, but he knew not to implicate himself in something that could only bring trouble. If he turned them in, there would be questions and investigations, which he certainly did not need. Besides, they had paid him handsomely for the gas, and he and his mother had a fantastic memory to share with each other for years to come.

And now, he knew by his Chinese contact's expression, he had something special to sell.

The top carton was already opened. Hyun-tae lifted out a tall, elegant, apricot-colored bottle with gold lettering, then another. Silky body lotion, bath foam, facial care products. He nodded and smiled. The village im-min-ban-jang — the minder who reported to the authorities everything that went on in their neighborhood — would be thrilled. She was quite vain about her skin. His record book held an extensive inventory of her appetites: DVDs of recent American blockbusters, Japanese pearls, European liquors, Chinese cell phones. He was happy to provide these gifts, as he did for the Chinese merchants with whom he traded the border guards he interacted with daily, the party worker responsible for his section of the city, and the inspectors who visited his small warehouse in Sinuiju. When everyone was satisfied, everything ran smoothly.

The Chinese warehouse workers had already loaded his other merchandise onto the flatbed of his mini-truck, covered with a layer of identical boxes of tools and machine parts — the products his company was licensed to import from China. He took a box of cosmetics and carried it to the truck. Opening the passenger-side door, he lifted the seat cushion and carefully fit the box in the cavity, then covered the precious cargo.

He pulled out of the warehouse yard and onto the airport road, heading east toward downtown Dandong. Traffic thickened as he neared the city center: taxis, vans, buses, and private cars clogging the arteries among tall department stores, banks, and office buildings. Along the riverside boulevard, apartment complexes rose in silver towers to the sky.

Pulling the truck into the queue for the bridge, he parked, then stepped out to light a cigarette while he waited. The smoke billowed, then dissipated in the crisp, cool air. He glanced toward the cab of the truck, then gazed across the river at the low, sooty skyline of Sinuiju. As he drew in the tobacco, he smiled again, thinking not of the neighborhood busybody, but of his elderly mother, imagining her pleasure when he presented her with a tall, elegant, apricot-colored bottle of scented cream from Switzerland.

CHAPTER 20

The sky brightened as they walked. Then the sun was up, a radiant white glow behind the dingy buildings to the east. To the west, a large park stretched along the riverbank, with the top of a Ferris wheel visible over the tree line. A grove of trees provided cover from which they could watch the bridge. Beyond it, the morning light sparkled on a broad brown river.

"Wow, the Yalu River!" Mia said. "That's China, right over there! That's Dandong!" It was amazing to see all the points she'd studied on the map come to life before them. They were really here, on the border.

Across the span of the water, skyscrapers stood bright in the early morning light. They glimmered like a mirage in a desert. Escape. Safety. The way home. Incredible to think they were so close. They just didn't know how to get from here to there.

Simon stood, peering through the screen of trunks and leaves to study the bridge. Suddenly, he dropped to sit on the ground. He was shaking his head, scowling.

"No way can we get across there." He pointed at the bridge. "Those posts are too high to climb. There's a guard box just ahead. There's plenty of traffic, but I don't know how we could possibly sneak onto a vehicle without somebody seeing us. I'm betting the search is pretty thorough on both sides. There's no pedestrian walkway and no way to make it over underneath." He sighed and lay back, one arm thrown over his eyes.

Mia sat down next to him. "So we'll have to go north to that place near the Great Wall." Lucky she'd done her research, she thought.

"What?"

"The place I showed you a couple of days ago. When we were waiting at the bottom of the mountain. The 'One-Step Crossing' place. It's shallow there. On the Chinese side, there's part of the Great Wall." She pulled out the guidebook and paged through to find the section. But Simon still had his arm over his eyes. He wasn't even bothering to look at her.

"We should stay here, at least one night, see if something happens."

He hadn't heard what she'd said. She shut the book with a snap. "Simon, you're not the boss here."

That brought his arm down. He turned his head and frowned at her.

Better.

"Look, you know a lot," she began. "But I've got stuff to offer too. We need to be a team. You're taking over again, like you're the only one in charge."

Simon sat up.

"Look yourself." He sounded annoyed. "I'm trying to figure out how we can get across the border. Maybe you don't like how I'm doing it, but there are way more important things at stake. I don't need a guilt trip."

"Then don't take one."

They stared at each other, both a little startled by her response.

There was a pause. Then one side of Simon's mouth turned up.

"Squeak, you used to be such a nice girl."

"Not really. I just didn't say what I was thinking."

He closed his eyes, opened them.

"And you have some thoughts you'd like to share?" His tone was just shy of sarcastic. Mia would take it.

"I have what I think is some very valuable information about how we might get out of here."

"And that is?"

"Just read this section." She opened the book and held it out to him, meeting his eyes like a challenge. He took the book.

"Okay . . . pardner," he said using a voice like the cowboys in the old movies they watched with Poppy. Mia squinched up her face at him. He studied the guidebook.

"Okay. This sounds like a good Plan B," he said. She couldn't help smiling. "But — we still have to wait for nightfall again. No way a tourist would be walking along the river going north." She raised her eyebrows at him, expecting more. He rolled his eyes. "Do you agree?"

Mia's smile widened. She nodded.

"So, how about this: We wait till dark, look around and see if we have any inspiration or opportunity here, then if not, we try your way. Plan B."

She nodded again and slumped back against one of the trees, feeling the momentary satisfaction of getting Simon to listen to her slipping away. What she'd just convinced him of meant that they still had a long way to go. They were going to have to sit here for another twelve hours or so. They were hidden in the shadows of the trees, but the longer they stayed, the more likely somebody might see them. And it was so hard to sit there, seeing their destination, just out of reach.

A hawk glided on the air currents over the river. It was free to fly back and forth between the two banks, oblivious to the barriers people had made. Boats could navigate the span of water. Trucks could drive back and forth on the bridge. But she and Simon were trapped there, unable to cross.

Only two weeks ago she'd been hanging out with Jess and Alicia, with nothing to worry about except getting their homework done. They'd sat on another bridge, the one over the stream by the Citgo station, dangling their legs over the edge. Hours and hours on a lazy Sunday afternoon, just talking and watching the light reflecting on the water. Bright leaves floated along like boats. They'd been a little bored, wishing something would happen. Strange to remember how much time they'd spent discussing how cute Johnny Shales was. Whether the grin on his face as he passed Alicia at her locker on Friday had been meant for her.

Mia couldn't recognize that person she'd been, with such small and inconsequential concerns. Not a single thing that was a real problem. And not a clue of what she was capable of enduring, capable of doing.

She thought about what she'd said to Simon, how she just didn't say what she was thinking. Maybe her whole life, she'd been trying to be nice, to be good, to not be a problem to Mom and Dad. Like Simon had suggested once, it probably had to do with being adopted — some idea that her birth family hadn't wanted her, so she had to be good so this one would keep her.

But she was seeing now that her mom and dad had been kind of clueless about her Korean background, like her culture was this thing she could visit like a tourist, or put on like a costume. Mom used to drive her all that way to Korean school every Saturday, but she'd drop Mia off and then go sit in a coffee shop and work on her To Do lists. In the car afterward, she would ask what Mia learned, but Mia had no way to explain it to her. To her mom, Korea remained something foreign.

And Dad? He *appreciated* her Koreanness, the way he was proud of Simon being good at sports. But maybe she was so much his *daughter* that he didn't want to focus on any way she was different from him. As if that would put distance between them, or he'd be losing her somehow. So Mom kept focusing on Mia's difference in a because-she's-supposed-to way, while Dad didn't really want to deal with it at all.

And neither one of those was what Mia wanted. She leaned back against the tree trunk. There was so much to think about. When — if — they all were back together again, she was going to speak up. She wanted some things to change. She was going to get serious about learning to speak Korean, get tapes, really study. Maybe Simon would want to learn too. She was going to learn about K-dramas and K-pop. Maybe they could even get a Korean exchange student, like Dad's friend Jae, who could live with their family. She could have a real Korean friend, someone to practice with, someone to teach her to make Korean food, someone with whom she could really dig into the culture. Then, after she'd learned more, she wanted to take a trip to *South* Korea with her whole family. . . .

She lay there, imagining, distracting herself from the fear that she might never get home to make these dreams come true.

. . .

Mia and Simon were sharing a snack of peanuts Mr. Shin's mother had given them when, through the trees, they caught glimpses of people. At first there were just a few individuals, then some family groups. Soon a growing crowd.

"What's going on?" Simon asked. Mia shrugged and shook her head. They lay on the ground, watching.

The park kept filling. Mia paged through the guidebook, looking for clues.

"What's today?"

"I dunno, the ninth or tenth?"

"Our first day here was October first," she began. They calculated together, counting the places they'd stayed — the shed, the hillside, the boxcar, three nights at the farm, one at Mr. Shin's.

"The tenth," Simon concluded.

"October tenth. 'Korean Workers' Party Foundation Day,'" Mia read. "That's what this must be about."

"And there are boats," Simon said, pointing. Down the river, a line of people was forming at a dock, boarding a small ferry. "I wonder. . . ."

"What?"

"Well, if we got close enough to the Chinese side, we could jump ship."

"Simon, no way. We could drown, or get hypothermia! Or they'd just haul us back in. Or shoot us, right there in the water!"

"They probably wouldn't shoot us. On the other hand,

you're right, we really can't pull off a border crossing with all these people watching. But somehow — I can't see how yet, but somehow — this may be the opportunity we're waiting for. As long as nobody sees us hiding."

The park was now full of people on holiday. Fathers and mothers held the hands of toddlers. Students in blue uniforms and white shirts with jaunty red scarves waved their red flags. Young couples walked together, the men in dark suits, the women in brilliantly colored *han-bok*.

The lines for the boats lengthened. Vendors sold snacks from carts. In the background, military-sounding music blared from tinny speakers. Soon, large numbers of people began assembling into lines by groups — soldiers, students, maybe factory workers. Some held banners. An official shouted orders over a megaphone. Spectators lined the riverbank.

"Looks like a parade." Mia had seen lots of photographs of North Koreans marching. Any special occasion seemed to be an excuse for a parade.

The music crackled more loudly, a vigorous marching tune. Soldiers kicked their legs high with each step. Children marched in perfectly formed lines. Everyone chanted slogans in unison.

Mia gazed out through the screen of leaves, north across the river. West to the park beyond the parade. South toward the city.

Then her eye noticed movement in the trees and bushes above them. A cluster of soldiers was moving downhill.

"Simon! Soldiers! They're moving in our direction!"

He was beside her in a moment. He groaned.

"I don't know what they're doing, but if we stay here, they'll find us. We're going to have to go out there, hope we can get lost in the crowd. Get to the other side of the park before they catch up with us." He pulled the brim of his cap down, his hood up. They grabbed their packs and started down through the trees, toward the river, trying to stay out of sight of the soldiers.

"We'll walk along the bank," Simon whispered, "behind the crowd. They're watching the parade; maybe we can get through without anyone noticing."

They slipped out of the grove of trees into the open. Mia's heart raced. *Stand up straight. Don't look back. We're just a tourist and a guide, here to see the sights.* Simon kept his head down. A few people glanced at him, but most of the bystanders were turned toward the parade.

Halfway across. On the far side of the park, Mia could see a good patch of brush. Cover. If only they could get there without being caught.

"Hello, Americans!" Their heads jerked involuntarily toward the sound.

Behind them, a military officer was approaching from the river walkway. He wore a uniform with red flaps on the shoulders and a brimmed cap. Several soldiers followed behind him. Mia and Simon froze. She clutched his arm. The man's eyes were fixed on them, and the corners of his mouth were turned up in a smile.

"Simon and Mia Andrews, I believe. I am Colonel Pak. You have been causing us quite a bit of trouble."

CHAPTER 21

Mia felt the breath leave her body.

"It is no use trying to run," the colonel called out. "I have soldiers everywhere. You would not get one block before you would be caught." He continued strolling toward them, in no hurry.

Simon was tearing off his backpack, opening a side pocket.

"Stop there!" he shouted. He raised his arm, a black rectangle in his hand. For a crazy instant, Mia thought he was holding a gun. Then she realized — the phone.

The colonel and soldiers halted, their gaze on Simon's hand.

"Don't come any closer! We have pictures on this phone — of the labor camps!" He was waving his hand. "I'll throw it into the crowd — anyone could get it!"

Mia's insides clutched at Simon's bravado. Scared for him, scared for both of them. He was only postponing the inevitable. They couldn't possibly get away.

"When I throw it, turn and run like hell," Simon said under his breath. His arm went back, the pitcher winding up. The colonel saw the movement and started toward them, signaling to the soldiers. Simon's arm came forward and the missile flew from his hand in a long arc, over the heads of the colonel and the soldiers, out over the water.

Mia put her hand to her mouth. The phone would land in the river.

The colonel barked an order. Mia felt Simon move beside her and followed. One step backward, then another. Watching as the colonel and his men turned to trace the path of the phone. A few soldiers started down the bank as it descended.

"Run!"

Mia whirled and plunged after Simon through the onlookers, into the sea of marchers.

She wove and dodged in and out of the parade lines, trying to stay close to her brother. Terror coursed through her body like molten lead. At any moment she expected to feel a soldier's heavy hand grasping her arm or shoulder. Astonished faces flashed by as they hurtled past. But no one reached out to grab them or block their path.

Simon's charge took them diagonally through the marchers, away from the river, toward the sidewalk on the far side of the boulevard. Mia glimpsed an intersection ahead, then a cross street running up through the park. Empty of traffic and people. Nowhere to hide. No place safe for them now.

Simon had pulled ahead of her. She couldn't keep up. Her heart thudded. Breath seared her throat. She propelled herself forward, desperate.

Simon had broken out of the parade and was heading for the trees, picking up speed on the open ground. He turned, looking for Mia. She fluttered her hand, too spent to even lift an arm. He registered her location, then scanned the parade. She willed herself to keep moving.

Then, finally, she was through the crowd, onto the street, the way clear before her. She tried to move her legs faster, tried to catch up with Simon, but he was hopelessly far ahead. She had no more strength.

Two cars came then, black sedans moving fast. Simon whirled around toward the whine of the engines. Then he took off sprinting. He was leaving her. Mia's panic surged.

The black cars roared toward her and stopped in a cloud of dust. The doors swung open. Before she could take another step, three men in dark suits had surrounded her. They had her by the arms, lifting her toward the open door of one of the cars. She had no energy to resist.

"Simon!" she screamed.

Across the lawn, Simon froze, looking back. The men holding her, the drivers beside their doors, all halted for a moment. They watched Simon. He watched them. Part of her wanted to wail, *Simon! Help!* The other part wanted to yell, *Run!*

Simon's shoulders slumped, then straightened. His head came up. Then he began to jog back toward the cars. Mia's heart swelled with love and grief. It was over. They were caught.

But he had come back for her.

The men put Simon and Mia in the back of one of the cars, just like they had with Dad. Two of them climbed into the front. The doors slammed shut. They sped off, following the first car. From behind the passenger's seat, Mia watched all this from a distance, as if it were a movie. Her chest hurt, her lungs felt squeezed, still demanding air. She turned to Simon and locked eyes with him. His jaw was clenched, his eyes steely. There was nothing to say.

Mia let herself go limp against the seat. She tried to catch her breath, to slow the pounding of her heart. The cars raced along deserted streets through Sinuiju. Within minutes, they were on the highway. Going south.

It hit her then. The hopeless waste of all of it. The planning, the hiding, the hardships. The phone was gone. With it, the terrible evidence of the prison camps. Of course Simon had had to get rid of the phone. They couldn't be caught with those photographs. He was only protecting them — and Dad. But no one outside would ever know the fate of those people. She and Simon could tell their story, but who would listen to two teenagers with no proof?

They had failed. They were caught. They would be held. They might be tried. Dad might spend the rest of his life in a North Korean prison.

All of it had been for nothing.

The misery and terror and defeat filled her. Tears ran down her cheeks. She didn't bother to wipe them away.

The cars sped along the empty highway. In the front seat, the two men talked in low tones. Through the tinted windows, the countryside flew by. In minutes they were covering distance it had taken Mia and Simon days to travel.

A green sign announced an upcoming exit. Mia was too exhausted to try to make out the *han-gul*. The car slowed and pulled onto the shoulder. It came to a stop behind the other car. The driver and passenger from their car got out. The doors clicked shut behind them.

Mia and Simon exchanged glances, his forehead drawn into a puzzled frown. She looked ahead between the seats. Outside, five men stood talking, occasionally gesturing down the road.

Then the men headed back to the cars. The locks clicked again, the doors opened. The driver and passenger slid back in. Their car started up and pulled out onto the highway, into the left lane. The other car pulled up on the right side beside them, then pulled away, bearing right down the exit ramp. They were splitting up.

Mia dropped her head back against the seat. She had no energy to even hold it up. She stared out the window. Brown fields, barren hills. She listlessly noted the road sign for Tongrim as they entered the outskirts of the city. This was the same route that Mr. Shin had driven them on his motorbike, just that morning at daybreak.

Ten minutes or so later, they passed through Sonchon, which they had walked through two whole nights ago. The car purred through the nearly empty streets. Everyone must be off for the holiday. The car continued south on the deserted road beyond the city.

"Roadblock."

Simon whispered so low Mia barely heard him. She looked up. Far ahead, a knot of black cars and Army jeeps blocked the road.

The two men talked in short phrases, the tone of their voices urgent. Their car slowed as it approached, then it came to a stop, right in the middle of the empty highway lane, still quite a distance from the line of vehicles. The driver sat for a moment, looking at the roadblock. Mia noticed a thick raised scar across the back of his right hand. After a moment, he spoke to the man in the passenger seat. Then he turned and directed a look at Mia, diagonally behind him. Holding her eyes, he twisted the key in the lock with his scarred hand, back and forth.

Mystified, Mia turned to look at Simon. What was going on?

Once again, the two men got out of the car. The driver

called a question to the soldiers standing at the roadblock. They signaled to the men to drive the car forward. But instead of returning to the car, the driver and his companion began to walk down the road toward the soldiers, fifty or so feet away.

Mia and Simon were sitting forward now, alert, peering out from behind the front seats.

The men were strolling, taking their time, calling out to the soldiers. One pulled a package of cigarettes out of his jacket.

"I don't think," Mia said slowly, "that the soldiers know we're in the car."

"And it looks as if our guys don't want them to know either. Stay out of sight." The men had reached the roadblock now. They were approaching the soldiers, offering them cigarettes.

"What the hell is going on?" Simon said. They exchanged a look, then turned back to peer down the road. Mia noticed something.

"Simon!"

He started. "What?!"

Mia pointed, barely able to speak. "The key! The car key!"

The key was in the ignition.

CHAPTER 22

"The driver was giving us a signal!" Mia said. "Do they want us to escape?"

At the roadblock, their guys stood with the soldiers, smoking. They had positioned themselves facing the car, so that the soldiers faced south, away from Mia and Simon.

"It could be a trap," Simon said.

"Yeah . . ."

"But it's not like they're going to *shoot* us — they can't afford an international incident like that."

Their eyes widened as the idea bloomed between them.

"How could we be in any worse trouble than we already are?" Mia shrugged, then nodded. "Let's do it."

Then Simon was wedging himself through the gap between the seats, unwinding behind the wheel. Suddenly, the engine roared to life and they were hurtling forward into a steep U-turn, tires screeching, across the highway and into the northbound lanes. Mia was thrown across the backseat.

She twisted to peer out the back window. The line of men was frozen in place, staring after them, rapidly shrinking into the distance as they sped away.

"They're not after us yet!" She grabbed her pack and clambered through to the front seat, fumbling to find the seat belt. She fished in her pack with her hand to get out the guidebook.

"Okay, we probably have a minute on them, if we're lucky," Simon yelled over the noise of the whining engine. "So we need to find another route, fast!"

Mia frantically flipped pages to the map. "The road split just before Sonchon, just a couple minutes ago!" She tried to focus on the page as the force of their speed plastered her to the back of the seat. "Yeah, here it is, a right turn, east to Chonma."

Moments later they were speeding back through the empty main thoroughfare of the town, between tall gray buildings. Mia scanned the streets for the turn.

"The turn-off was a couple of miles north of the city, I think." The countryside flew by. Her eyes bored into the map, frantically checking their location.

"*Chuh — Chon —* Chonma!" Simon sang out.

Suddenly, the car was turning, the driver's side tires nearly lifting off the pavement, and Mia was grabbing the edge of the seat and the door handle and hanging on for her life.

The car rocked as it hit the straightaway, Simon gripping the wheel to keep from spinning out of control. Where had he learned to drive like this? Maybe hundreds of hours of Grand Theft Auto were good for something after all.

Soon they were through the settled area, out in the countryside, the road climbing into the surrounding hills, running alongside a broad stream with wide sandy banks. Mia craned her head to scan the road behind them.

"Nothing yet."

Simon was gunning the gas, pushing the car to accelerate. Mia didn't want to know how fast they were going. The sides of the roadway blurred into stripes of gray, gold, brown. She yanked her eyes forward and took a deep breath to push down her nausea.

The car raced past rice fields, past farmhouses with red tile roofs, past barren brown hills. They came to a valley snaking between tree-covered foothills when Simon shouted out, "Uh-oh, we got company!" He sounded almost cheerful.

Mia sat up, turned. A military jeep was visible in the distance. A chill went up her back. Despite their speed, it was gaining.

Within minutes, the jeep had pulled up behind them, horn blaring.

"I'm going to pull over!"

"Simon, what?!"

"It's the only way to get them off our tail! Trust me, it'll be okay! Lock your door!"

Mia reached over to push the lock down. The turn signal clicked and the car began to slow, shuddering as it returned to normal speed. They gradually slid over to the shoulder and came to a stop, the engine still idling. The jeep did the same, fifty feet back. Mia's heart pounded.

"Okay, guys, what are you waiting for?" Simon was watching his side mirror. Mia glanced over to her mirror. The jeep sat behind them, still. Then the doors opened. Two men in olive green uniforms emerged from the car. Mia wanted to cover her eyes with her hands, to disappear.

"C'mon, c'mon, that's right." Simon's hands tightened on the steering wheel. The two men approached, one on either side of the car. Mia kept her eyes on the floor. She was shivering now, the fear coursing through her.

"And . . . *good-bye!*" Simon stomped his foot on the accelerator, flooring it. Mia was thrown back against the seat. The tires skidded on the pavement, shrieking, as the car shot forward.

"Yee-*HA!*" Simon was chortling now, sounding like the star of an action flick, his favorite kind of movie.

As exciting as that was, it didn't take their pursuers long to catch up.

"They're trying to pass us!" Mia yelled. The jeep was moving into the southbound lane, pulling even with them. The two vehicles raced side by side. She turned her head forward. There was something really frightening about looking into the soldiers' faces.

"Where are we? What can you see on the map?" Simon yelled over the straining engine.

She held the map up in front of her so she wouldn't have to glance down, trying to hold her hands steady. "It looks like . . . about twenty miles to Chonma from that exit we took. The last part before Chonma looks sort of twisty, like a backward S curve. At Chonma we run into a route that goes . . . um, northwest to the border, or southeast."

"That road to the border, it goes through the town?"

"It looks like it, yes!"

"We gotta lose these guys before then!"

The two-lane road was rising now, following the path of the river winding through the hills. Ahead were low mountains. The jeep kept pace beside them, as if the two vehicles were attached.

Up ahead was a truck, moving south down the slope. "Simon!"

"That's their problem!" He stomped on the gas pedal. The truck's horn blared. The jeep slowed and backed off, then pulled in behind them just as they hurtled past the truck.

Simon negotiated a twisting turn, a dip, another climb. Their pursuers clung to their tail. Around a curve, a long stretch of road climbed the hill, straight and empty. The jeep pulled alongside the trunk of their car, then moved closer.

"They're going to ram us!" Mia yelled.

"Hang on!"

The whole car jolted as the jeep knocked into their back panel on the driver's side. Mia screamed, gripping the edges of the seat. The car spun counterclockwise, rotating in a circle. Then they were straight again, still heading north. Her body was plastered to her seat, every muscle tense. Simon gunned the engine and they shot ahead.

"Yes!" He was leaning forward, his knuckles white from gripping the wheel. The jeep pulled alongside them again.

"Okay, their turn." He turned to look at the men in the jeep and raised his left shoulder, as if he were moving to ram the jeep. The driver reacted, jerking the wheel and swerving left onto the shoulder of the other lane. Mia's head swiveled to watch the jeep as Simon surged ahead.

"They're coming back across the road — they can't stop — they hit the guard rail!" she called. "They're not moving!"

She saw the men get out and stand by the hood of the jeep, examining it. The scene retreated, growing smaller and smaller as they sped ahead. Then the road turned again, blocking the view.

"*Omigod*, Simon! You *did* it!" Mia flopped back against the seat, totally spent, grinning. "I can't believe you did it!"

"I saw that move on a cop reality show," Simon called over the noise of the engine and the shaking car. He was grinning too, his eyes focused on the road, holding their speed. "We're not out of the woods yet. They may fix it, and they've probably got a radio or cell phone or something. So we don't have long. We've gotta get as close to the border as we can and find a place to ditch this car. How far is — what was it, Chonma? — from the border?"

She held up a bent index finger, measuring the map. "Twenty, maybe twenty-five miles or so."

"Are we near that place you showed me in the guidebook?"

"Uiju? Where One-Step Crossing is? I think we're just about due south of it."

"Plan B it is. We'll get as close as we can, then ditch the car someplace hidden." He paused, then glanced over at her. "That okay with you, pardner?"

She met his teasing smile with a grin. "Great plan, pardner!"

The road twisted and turned alongside the mountain brook. Water spilled in falls between large, dark boulders, gathered in pools, then spread out between banks of gray stone. Mia kept glancing at the side mirror, watching the road they were leaving behind. Every falling leaf, every branch shifting in the wind, set her heart racing.

She had seen no sign of their pursuers, in fact no sign of anyone at all, by the time they reached the outskirts of what must be Chonma. A strip of rice fields ran along the riverbed. The car slowed as they came to a split in the road. The main route turned to the right alongside a schoolyard. To the left was an unpaved turnoff. No road signs.

Mia looked again at the map. She checked the position of the sun, low in the sky, the lengthening shadows.

"Turn left," she said. "I don't know if it's the right road or not, but it goes north."

Simon glanced over at her with a half smile. Despite the anxiety that filled her, she felt warm.

Through the dimming light they sped along a valley road following another riverbed, foothills and mountains crowding in on either side. They passed isolated rural dwellings and small villages, an occasional lone farmer in a field or someone riding a bicycle along a path. Mia kept glancing back, searching for headlights.

Simon had slowed to a normal pace so as to not attract more attention. But vehicles must appear so infrequently on these remote rural roads, especially government cars. Any person they passed would remember the black car that had gone by late in the afternoon on National Workers' Party Foundation Day. They were leaving a trace, a trail of crumbs, marking their escape route. Their only hope was that the holiday would slow the processing of information. Then it might take until tomorrow for the soldiers to come this way, asking questions.

Several times they came to a crossroads where Mia had to guess which route would take them north — left, right, or straight. Every time they approached a town, she took a breath. Simon had his black cap on, hiding his hair, but anyone who got a good look at him would be able to see that he wasn't Korean. But each time, mercifully, the streets were deserted.

The road, now unpaved, began to rise, winding and

twisting around in switchbacks up a bald mountain. Though the sky above was still bright, the southern slope they were climbing was shadowed in dusk. The road got steeper, and then they were atop the crest.

"Wait, Simon, slow down. I need to see where we are."

He pulled the car to a stop. The mountain they had just climbed was the slope of a much taller peak to the west. Beyond, in a line of bright light, the sea reflected the just-setting sun.

"Look! That's Dandong!" Mia cried, pointing at the shining skyline, tiny in the distance. With her finger, she followed the narrow curving thread of the river to the east, to what looked like a concentration of buildings directly ahead. "So that must be Uiju. One-Step Crossing has to be nearby. Tiger Mountain in China should be right across the river, about there." She turned to her brother, grinning. "We did it! We got the right road!"

"Problem is, it's all open now. And we've got to get rid of the car before we need headlights," Simon said as they started forward again. "Given that we've been the only car on this entire road, it would be easy for them to spot us. Someone could see the light, even from the air."

They wound slowly down the mountainside as the sky turned orange, the landscape silhouetted in black against the dying light. The river plain spread out in a nearly flat expanse of terraced rice fields. Spindly trees lined the road at regular intervals. There was no place to hide.

Pinpricks of light ahead marked Uiju, but all around them it was darkening into twilight. Once again Mia thanked their lucky stars that North Korea wasn't brightly lit at night.

They came to a T in the road.

"Okay, gotta find a place to hide this soon," Simon said. "Like now."

"Let's go right, away from the town."

"And here's our best shot," Simon said a few moments later, slowing and pulling off the road onto a dirt path just wide enough for the car, in a gully twisting between two low hills. A few moments later, he slid the car into a patch of dirt under some scraggly overhanging trees and stopped.

He got out of the car and stood on the path, looking back in the direction of the road.

"Can't see the road, at least not much, so I don't think anyone will find the car till morning."

Mia opened the car door and stretched her legs, feeling the tightness in her muscles.

"Let's search the car before we leave, see if there's anything we can use," Simon said.

They found nothing but papers in the glove compartment. But the trunk held two bottles of water, a rope, and a sack.

"Think they were going to use this to tie us up?" Simon asked, holding up the rope, then coiling it and stuffing it into his pack.

"Not the guys who caught us. Maybe the ones at the roadblock, though."

Simon opened the sack. He pulled out a screwdriver, passing it to Mia to put in her pack. He added a pair of pliers, a utility knife, and a roll of tape to his. Then a flashlight. He switched it on and lifted the sack, shining the light into the trunk.

Mia gasped and started back, her hand to her mouth. There, lying on the floor of the trunk, was a rifle. Simon gave a low whistle, handed the flashlight to Mia, and leaned in, reaching his hand toward the weapon.

"Simon, careful." Mia's voice wavered. She wanted to slam the trunk lid down, locking the gun out of sight. She backed a few steps away.

Simon lifted the rifle out of the trunk. Then he turned to the hillside and with a forceful motion, jammed the barrel deep into the soft dirt. He pulled it out again and examined the muzzle. "It'll be a while before that works properly," he announced, tossing it back into the trunk and closing the lid.

In the dusk, they started off along the gully, then up a hill to a cluster of trees, black against the dark sky, where Simon stopped. "Let's wait until it's really dark," he said.

Mia settled on the ground next to him. The evening was still and quiet. A light breeze picked up. She pulled the collar of her jacket snug around her neck. Long minutes passed. She felt her body relax as the extraordinary tension of the day fell away. For the first time since their capture, she had time to think about what had happened.

"Simon, I'm confused." She kept her voice low, nearly a whisper. "Those guys in the black cars had a gun, but they made it so easy for us to escape. And why are soldiers chasing us now?"

"I've been trying to work it out," Simon said. He was quiet for a moment. "Maybe we did get caught between two groups, like the regular police and the secret police, like we were talking about earlier. Maybe Colonel Pak is leading one faction — if so, I'm guessing it would be the secret police, the SSD."

"So the guys who caught us might be with the regular police? The MPS?"

"It seems likely, if the two groups are working against each other, with conflicting ideas about how things should be done."

"That's what Daniel told me."

"Yeah, well, Dad said it was one of the most difficult things about his work — one ministry would say yes to something and another one would say no, just to contradict the other," Simon said. "Then there's the soldiers at the roadblock, but they'd just be following orders from Colonel Pak's side, I'm guessing."

Mia shivered, remembering the standoff with Colonel Pak. The phone flying into the air with the prison camp photos. It had all been brushed out of her mind by their escape and flight. But it hurt to think about the loss now, about all the ways they weren't going to be able to help anyone else.

"You're positive the phone landed in the water, right? That the soldiers couldn't have gotten ahold of it?"

"I'm absolutely positive that the soldiers didn't get ahold of it," Simon said. The tone of his voice said he didn't want to talk about it. It must be bothering him too. Everything they'd tried to do had failed. In fact, people might have been beaten or tortured or sent to labor camps because of them. Mr. Shin, if anyone had seen him drop them off. Soon-ok. The man with the scarred hand and his partner who let them escape, whose car they stole. The soldiers whose jeep got wrecked in the chase. The tour guides — Mr. Lee, Miss Cho, Mr. Kim. She and Simon were like a contagious virus. They endangered everyone they met.

Someone must have risked their life to take those photos. Now they were gone. At least they were at the bottom of the river, not in the hands of officials who could use them as an excuse to hurt more people.

Now she and Simon were only trying to save themselves. Mia hoped they didn't meet anyone else between here and the border.

When the sky had turned midnight blue, they started across the spine of the hill, keeping the city lights of Dandong to their left. The clusters of houses and factory buildings were all on level ground, so staying on the crest was a good way to avoid any people who might be out at night. At the edge of the ridge, they climbed down, crossed a stream, and picked up a path that passed through wide fields, then over railroad tracks.

Mia gazed up at the stars. She traced the line from the Big Dipper to the bright North Star, their guide. In the west, a half moon was high in the sky.

The path ended at the road, at a large boulder. Ahead, the land dropped to the river basin. To their right, the tall smokestack of a factory made a black pencil stroke against the sky.

Then they came to the river.

They both stood and stared.

The stretch of water before them was wide, gleaming in the moonlight. Not as wide as the section between Sinuiju and Dandong, but five or six house lengths across. It was far too deep to wade across, and way too cold to swim.

So much for Plan B.

CHAPTER 23

"Mia . . . I thought you said that the river was shallow near Uiju." Simon spoke slowly and deliberately. "That we could walk across?"

"The guidebook said —" Her brain felt numb. Simon swore.

"Could we have made a wrong turn?" Mia felt panic rising. Simon had trusted her. He'd gone this way because of the information she'd given him.

"No way. As you pointed out, we can see Dandong right there. Just where it should be."

"But there's a river in the way." How could this be? Mia closed her eyes and opened them, as if she could blink the river away. Nothing in the guidebook had warned them that a lot of water might block the route to One-Step Crossing and Tiger Mountain on the other side of the border.

"Lemme see the guidebook." Simon's voice sounded compressed.

"It won't do any good. The map of this area isn't that detailed." Mia looked up and down the river, studying the lay of the land, trying to understand what she was seeing. Dad had said the guidebook was ten years old — but a stream you could step over didn't become a wide river in just a decade. *Don't panic; figure it out.*

"I think that might be an island" — Mia pointed to the dark shape on the far side of the river — "that's still part of North Korea. There are hardly any lights, not like China. So maybe One-Step Crossing is on the other side of the island?"

They stood and stared some more. To their left was a wide sandbar. To the right, the water lapped against the bank.

Mia reached out and grabbed Simon's arm. Even though she appeared to have totally screwed up, he wasn't blaming her. At least not out loud.

He let out a sigh.

"So what do we do now?" He sounded like he was asking himself the question.

"Find a boat?" It was a joke. The awful kind of joke you make when you feel like you're about to start screaming.

But Simon responded seriously. "Yeah. That's it. C'mon."

They moved west along the shore of the river, toward the lights of Dandong on the far side, away from the factory and houses. Mia kept turning to look behind them. At any moment the jeeps and black cars could come roaring up. They had to find a way across.

They came to a small wooden dock. There in the moonlight was their miracle: a wooden boat, tied with a single length of rope. Mia stared, feeling as if she were in a fairy tale, as if she could make something appear simply by wishing it.

"It's a ferry landing. Look." Simon was pointing across the river. Mia could just make out another dock on the far shore.

The boat was old and worn, but it looked as if it would survive a river crossing. Simon shoved the boat into deeper water at the end of the dock, then lowered himself into it.

Mia clambered in after him. A long pole lay in the bottom of the boat. He picked it up and stuck it into the water, pushing against the sandy bottom to propel them out into the river.

The stretch of inky water lengthened between them and the dock. Mia wished the boat would go faster. At any moment she expected shouts and running feet as someone discovered the theft, or the whine of a police boat speeding toward them. She shivered as the wind rose off the water.

Out in the center, the current caught the boat. Simon had to work to keep them on course. At another time Mia would have laughed to see her brother struggling with the pole. But every piece of their journey had taken on a desperate urgency. Colonel Pak and his soldiers could be right behind them.

And everyone — even the guys who might be trying to help them — had guns.

Overhead, the blue-black expanse seemed endless, shimmering with tiny crystals, the half moon tiny in the hugeness. Compared to all that, Mia thought, they were like specks of dust. Tiny people. Tiny problems.

All they needed was a few more tiny miracles.

She focused on one of the pricks of light among the thousands in the glittering dome. Stars were made to light the darkness; that was their job. They did it not just one by one, but together with millions and billions of others.

Yet in its own galaxy, each star could be a sun. And each star mattered to the place where it was planted. *Beautiful Star.*

Then they were across the river, pulling up to the dock on the far shore. The boat thunked against the planks at the base of a small hill. Mia flinched; in the distance to their right she could see the dark outline of tiled roofs on top of the rise. She hoped that everyone was shut in for the night.

Simon jumped out and tied up. Mia stepped onto the dock, trying not to topple into the water as the boat rocked beneath her.

They crept to the top of the riverbank. In the light of the moon, they could see a line of houses to the east, a stretch of fields to the west. Straight ahead, a double-humped shape rose in the distance, dark against a glow in the sky. It must be the lights of the town behind the mountain. In *China*.

"Aim for that tall hill. I think — I hope — that's Tiger Mountain," Mia said. "We still have to cross the river — the shallow part — at the border."

They followed a path going north across stubbly fields. Moonlight caught on patches at the edge of the fields — the plastic covers of a line of greenhouses, low to the ground. Mia's heart was drumming again.

As they drew closer, the black silhouette of the hill seemed to rise and become more defined, a small mountain range. A square tower sat like a crown on the crest of the eastern peak.

"That's it — the Great Wall! Tiger Mountain! We must be really, really near the border!"

She hadn't messed up after all.

"If we're that close, we better be on the lookout for soldiers," Simon said. "I'm sure they patrol the border constantly, especially if it's an easy crossing. We gotta get out of sight."

In the dark, they crept along the dirt path between paddies. Then, on the raised ground ahead, movement.

Mia grabbed Simon's arm and pointed. They dove down into the ditch along the field. The soldier, a black figure against the dark sky, walked the short ridge. Back and forth, three times. Then he disappeared from view.

"I'm gonna crawl up there, see where he's gone," Simon whispered.

Mia waited while he crept forward. She couldn't see anything. There was no way to tell if Simon was safe. Time passed. She tried to stay calm. Then the grass rustled nearby and he was beside her again.

"There's a guard tower up ahead. He walks up and down on the ridge, then goes back to the tower for a while. He's in there now. The next time he does his rounds, then starts toward the tower, that's when we'll move."

They waited what seemed like hours until the guard returned. Again he walked back and forth on the ridge. Once, twice, three times.

"Okay, now." They crouched low and crawled along the ditch as silently as they could. When they reached the end of the field, Simon crept up the slope, then pointed to the right. Mia climbed the slope to see the soldier moving away in the distance. Beyond him, the square silhouette of the guard tower rose above the field.

Mia touched Simon's back and pointed straight ahead. Below them in the blackness was a liquid gleam. Light on water — the river!

They dashed toward a cluster of brush and trees on the ridge above the water. Then Mia almost ran into Simon, who had stopped short. He swore.

Mia stood and stared, not able to believe her eyes. Stretching out in either direction through the tangle of foliage was a tall fence. Strands of barbed wire were strung along an endless line of white concrete posts shaped like Ts. An impenetrable barrier, invisible in the darkness until they were nearly on top of it.

They crept to the fence to examine the heavy wire. A

dozen strands stacked up from the ground to higher than Simon's head, each a handspan apart. You could get an arm through the space between the strands, but not even a small child's body.

They had made it to the border. The fence was proof. But they were still on the wrong side, with no way to get through.

It couldn't be.

"It ain't over . . ." Simon was ruffling through his pack.

". . . till it's over," Mia responded automatically, but her voice lacked conviction. Her heart was sinking. It was all her fault; she's the one who'd made a plan based on a ten-year-old guidebook. Impenetrable barriers were exactly the kind of change that could happen in a decade. They'd need more than a miracle to get through this fence.

"Remember?" Simon's head came up. In the darkness she could just make out his face. He was actually smiling. He held up the pliers he'd taken from the trunk of the car.

"Wait! What if it's electric?"

He stopped and let his eyes follow the fence. "Look, there are plants touching it. If it was electrified, there'd be nothing but bare ground."

Mia held her breath as Simon reached out and touched the pliers to the wire. No zap.

"It'll take a while, but I'll be able to twist the wire to make an opening," he whispered. "But I think it's actually lucky we ran into the fence. It made me realize we need to wait a few hours."

"*Wait?* There may be soldiers coming after us!"

"Yeah, but we need to cross over just before daylight."

"Why?" Mia forced her voice low, though she wanted to scream at him.

"Because once we get into China, we may need help. And

we're not going to get any in the middle of the night, when everyone's sleeping. It's just after ten now; I think we should cross between four and five in the morning."

"So we're supposed to wait for *six hours*?"

"It won't hurt us to get some rest." He turned to scan the foliage along the fence. "How about there?" He pointed toward a clump of tall bushes. "That should be enough cover."

They wriggled behind the bushes and settled as well as they could on the rocky ground among the branches. They could hear the river trickling in the gully below them. Half of that water was in China. To be so close, yet held back . . .

Mia's exhausted brain began to run a horror video, on replay: Images of soldiers bursting in on their hiding place. Dragging them away. Being thrown into prison. Being blindfolded and shot.

She didn't want to die. She wanted to go home.

"Simon?" Mia whispered, when she couldn't stand it any longer.

"What?"

"Are you asleep?"

"Not anymore." He must have been awake, if he could razz her.

She couldn't think of anything to say. There was a long silence.

"You rang?" he prompted.

"I'm glad you're my brother."

"You woke me up to say that?" She could hear the tease, even in his whisper. "Me too, Squeak. Now get some rest. Tomorrow we're getting out of here."

CHAPTER 24

OCTOBER 11

Simon was nudging her.

"The guard seems to be gone for the night."

She must have slept a little after all. It was time to go.

It was still as dark as ink. The moon was down and the only light came from the faint stars and the glow in the sky behind Tiger Mountain. In China, where they had electricity at night.

They crawled through the bushes to the fence, finding a spot near one of the concrete posts where foliage provided a bit of cover.

"You keep watch," Simon said, taking out the pliers.

As he worked, the sky began to lighten in the east. Mia knelt with her back to Simon, shivering in the early morning cold. She wrapped her arms around herself. Soon, soon, they'd be warm, she told herself.

She scanned the area on both sides of the fence for any sign of guards. More and more of Tiger Mountain emerged in the growing light. The slopes were covered in foliage, broken by the snaking line of the Great Wall as it climbed to the peak. So ancient, so majestic. For a moment it took her mind off the discomfort and danger.

"Yes! We're through!"

Along the base of the post, Simon had bent back the strands of wire, opening a gap big enough to crawl through.

"Simon! You did it!"

"Any sign of anybody?"

Mia took a last look. No movement, no sound. "All clear."

"You go first; I'll hold it for you."

Mia slipped one leg through the narrow gap and placed her foot down, anchoring herself. Then she slid her body through, pressing against the concrete post to avoid catching her clothes on the barbs. Simon handed his pack to her, then crawled through.

He squatted on the ground, bending the wire back so that the hole was still there, but not immediately visible.

"Hope it helps someone else someday," he said.

The water in front of them was wide and flowing.

"It's too deep to cross here," Simon whispered. "Let's go downstream, see if there's a place that's shallower."

They inched westward, keeping close to the slope of the bank. Mia pointed to a curve of gravel stretched out into the river, nearly touching a sandbar on the opposite shore. The water narrowed to a channel between the spits of land.

They crept down to kneel beside the water, gazing at the black gap between the two spits of land. The channel was perhaps fifteen feet across. Not exactly one step, and too far to jump. The current was flowing swiftly. It looked deep. So close, yet so far.

"Can we make a bridge?"

"We don't have time," Simon said. "We'd need to find a huge log — and anyway, we couldn't lift anything that big."

"Maybe there's another way to cross." Mia stared at the flowing water. Dread was spreading through her gut, making her feel nauseous.

"If there is, we don't have time to find it. The next guard shift could arrive any moment. I think we'll have to risk it. I'll go first and take the end of the rope, then you can hang on. I'll pull you over."

"We're gonna freeze."

"Yup. I still think it's our best chance."

"Won't we get hypothermia? I'm so cold already!"

"I know. But I can't think of anything else, can you? I just hope to hell we're in the right place, that we can get across fast and find a place to warm up."

Mia raised her eyes to Tiger Mountain, right there, just across what was really only a stream. Just when their goal was within reach, just when she needed it most, all of her courage seemed to have evaporated.

"I don't think I can do it."

"I'm scared too, Squeak. But we can do this. We have to."

She blew out her breath. "Okay," she said in a small voice, not feeling that it was okay at all.

Simon pulled the rope out of his backpack, uncoiled it, and tied one end around her waist, the other around his. He held his pack over his head and stepped into the blackness. The water covered his feet, his shins, his thighs. He cursed.

He gasped as he slipped in, submerged to his neck, with only his head and his arms holding the pack visible above the water. Mia shivered violently. A moment passed, and Simon was rising out of the water, climbing up the bank on the other side, pulling the rope taut.

"Okay," he called, just loud enough for her to hear. "C'mon, I'll pull you over."

Mia stood. Behind them, a border guard might have already caught sight of them. There were other soldiers searching. There was Colonel Pak. Ahead was a stretch of cold black water. The nausea deepened.

"Squeak, you can do this. Just like you've done everything else." Simon's voice floated across the chasm between them.

She took a step closer to the water. She slipped out of her backpack shoulder straps and held it overhead, just as Simon had done, to protect her books and phone from the water.

"Just get in. I'll pull you across."

She took a shuddering breath, then stepped into the river. The cold, the freezing cold, hit like an electrical shock as the water flooded her shoes. She started, felt her footing give, felt herself falling forward. She threw her arms out to catch herself. Her backpack flew out of her hands, landing with a splash. The black water seized her and swallowed her up.

She felt the tug of the rope around her waist.

"Keep your head up. I've got you," Simon called.

Her body glided through the water, pulled by the rope. Then she felt Simon's hands under her arms, lifting her. Her feet touched solid ground, but she couldn't seem to move them, couldn't stand. Simon picked her up and pulled her out of the water.

He crouched on the ground and she collapsed against him. She turned her eyes back to the river. No sign of her backpack. Everything was gone. Snacks. Water. Phone. Wallet. Dictionary. The guidebook. Her *journal*. She was naked, a turtle without her shell.

Gradually, she began to feel Simon's body heat thawing her. She took a deep breath. What came bubbling up from somewhere inside her was . . . a laugh. She stifled the sound, but the giggles rippled through her. She felt Simon catch them. The two of them crouched there on the border, soaking wet, shaking with cold and silent laughter.

"Nice job, Squeak." Mia could hear the smile in Simon's voice.

"We did it!" she finally managed to whisper. "We're in China!"

"Yeah. Let's get going."

She found she could stand then. She managed to trudge after Simon, clothes dripping, feet squelching in water-logged sneakers. Nothing could stop them now.

They crossed the sandbar to the northern slope of the riverbank, then up to a grassy area dotted with bushes and trees. Once again, there was a fence, but it was made of thinner wire, easily bent.

As Simon worked on the fence, Mia raised her eyes to Tiger Mountain. She grabbed Simon's shoulder and pointed. Pink light flooded the leafy slopes. They turned to the east where the edge of the sun showed, a brilliant red crescent along the horizon.

Mia passed through the gap Simon created in the fence and turned back to watch him. He stepped through, then paused. They exchanged a look, their eyes lit with the sunrise and the bigness of the moment. Mia couldn't help grinning. They were over the border, through the barriers, in China!

Suddenly, she didn't feel cold or hungry or tired. She didn't mind that she'd lost her backpack and everything in it. Excitement sizzled through her like a warm electric current. She turned to look back at North Korea, across the stream, the fields, the river, beyond to the mountains. They had made it out.

"Okay, I've got something for you," Simon said. "I want you to hide it, just in case." He had his pack off, one arm reaching into it.

Mia watched, puzzled, as he pulled out a black rectangular device. Why would he want her to hide his music player?

He placed it in her hands.

The *phone*.

Mia stared at it, then looked sideways at him. How in the world — ?

"But — I saw you throw it —"

"It was my MP3 player. They look so similar, I thought it might fool them."

Her mouth dropped open. "Simon!" She looked down at her hands again. "So we . . . we still have them? The photos?!"

He nodded, eyes shining. A smile played at the corners of his mouth.

"You — But —" To Mia's surprise, what came blazing through was — anger. "Why didn't you tell me?"

"I couldn't, once they'd caught us; they would've heard. After that, I thought it was safer if you didn't know."

"So you were still thinking for me. Thinking I needed protecting."

"Squeak, give me a break. I'm your big brother; it kind of comes with the territory. But I'm giving it to you now. Just in case something happens. They'll search me first." He reached back into his pack. "And here's the battery."

"But —" She was still trying to get her brain around this

astonishment. The photos, the images of the prison camps — they still had them. She zipped the phone and the battery into the front pocket of her jacket, patting the nylon to feel them secure against her belly. To think that the images were right there . . .

"Do they know? That it was your player that you threw?"

"If they fished it out of the water, which they probably managed to do, they know."

"That was pretty quick thinking on your feet." She gave him a twisted smile. "You're a hot ticket."

He grinned back at her. "C'mon, let's get to the Wall," he said as he slipped his arms through the straps of his pack.

They started down the path that led to Tiger Mountain.

Then someone shouted from behind them. Mia whirled. Figures in uniforms were running down the embankment on the North Korean side, barreling toward the river. *Soldiers!*

"Run!" Simon yelled as he took off. "We're in China — I don't think they can do anything!" he called over his shoulder. "But let's get to the Wall!"

They sprinted along a grassy ridge beside a pond, weaving through a grove of skinny trees. Mia struggled to keep up with Simon. Ahead was a wooden hut. Beyond that, on the far side of a gully, a fortress-like gate with battlements on top guarded the base of the mountain. That must be the entrance to the Wall.

Simon passed the hut and plunged down into the gully, then up a leafy slope, Mia clambering after him. Next to the fortress gate was a paved area, deserted. No one to help them. Daybreak was too early for tourists. They could still hear the faint shouts of the soldiers, but no one was in sight. Yet.

"I don't know what they're gonna do," Simon said, panting. He circled, scanning the empty road to their left, the borderlands behind them, the mountain to their right.

"The guidebook said —" Mia gasped, "sometimes the Chinese help — to catch people escaping — so the North Koreans might be able to come in!"

There was the sound of an engine, growing closer. Down the road, a jeep appeared in the distance.

"It's military!" Simon shouted. They wheeled and ran toward the only place they could see that a vehicle couldn't reach.

The Great Wall.

CHAPTER 25

On the front of the fortress, a huge block of black stone was covered with worn carving in Korean, Chinese characters, and English. Beneath the stone was a door, a museum or gift shop. Closed. No shelter there. They ran along the north side of the fortress to the entrance stairway. Wide stone stairs led up to the top of the Wall. Mia was breathing hard as she pounded up the stairs, a few steps behind Simon.

On top, the broad walkway ran straight for a short section, then rose, a zigzag pathway scaling the mountain, all the way to the top of the cliff high above them. Many, many more stairs. From this point, some of it looked like a straight vertical ascent.

How in the world was she going to run all the way up the side of a mountain?

She caught up with Simon at the first landing, where he'd paused to look. Far below, the jeep pulled into the parking lot and soldiers jumped out. Mia and Simon couldn't stop to find out if they were Chinese or North Korean. They took off again.

Mia put one foot down, mounted a step, then the other. Simon was always ahead, just out of reach. She longed to catch him, hold on to him, use his momentum to pull herself up. Through the vertical gaps in the side walls, she caught glimpses of the river and fields. The early sun cast long shadows and bathed the countryside in brilliant light. She pushed herself on up the slope.

They reached another flight of stairs. On the first step, she paused to catch her breath, her heart pounding against the walls of her chest. Her legs, encased in waterlogged denim, felt as if they couldn't take another step.

"More jeeps! And the first soldiers are on top of the Wall!" Simon yelled from the top of the flight.

The fear inside Mia roared, breathing fire. Somehow her legs found the strength to scramble up the stairs after Simon. Her feet flew over the gray stones. There were short sloped sections where she could run, then more stairs to climb. Parts of the staircase had walls on both sides with regularly spaced gaps, like the top of a castle. Other sections were solid brick with small holes cut out, for shooting weapons.

Her heart lurched at the reminder: The soldiers chasing them probably had guns.

She grasped the metal railing with her right hand, using the strength of her arm to pull herself up, up, up. She was on a vertical section now, more like a ladder than a stairway. It was scary to be moving so fast. If she slipped, she might tumble back down the steep path.

The higher she climbed, the more the wind picked up. Inside, she was overheated, but on the outside she was freezing in her wet clothes. The wet ends of her hair dripped icy water down the back of her neck.

Shouts behind her. It sounded as if the soldiers were

gaining on them. Her breath came in loud gasps, scraping her throat. Every step felt like the last she could take.

Mia came to the top of another flight of stairs. The Wall turned slightly, and there, at the top of the next long flight, was the summit of the mountain. Simon was halfway up. One more set of steps. She had to make it.

Then she was there. Simon reached out a hand to pull her up. Mia stumbled between the walls into the landing on top of the cliff. She bent nearly double, hands on her knees, heart hammering, throat searing. She felt like she was going to throw up. She'd made it all this way only to die from exertion.

"They're still coming, maybe a dozen of them. I can't tell if they're Chinese or North Korean." Simon was peering down the mountain. "But they're taking their time, not running like we did." He crossed to the other side of the platform now, looking north. Mia tried to get a breath out of her squeezed lungs.

"The main entrance is down there. There's a big gate and a town." He had turned, pointing with one arm, but Mia couldn't see over the wall from where she was, and she couldn't move yet. "The whole thing looks like about a half or three-quarters of a mile."

She bobbed her head again, still gasping.

"So we have maybe half a mile to the other end, but this is the highest point. It's all downhill from here. If we can get to the main entrance, there might be some people there. Or maybe we can find a place to hide along the way until tourists come up here."

Mia slowly began to straighten. Her heart was still pounding, her face burning with heat. But she might, possibly, live. And taking their time or not, the soldiers were climbing after them. She waved a hand to indicate that she could move again.

"Okay, let's go," Simon said.

The view from the top of the Wall stretched for miles in every direction. North Korea to the south, China to the north, east, and west. Mia traced the bright line of the river to the west. Far in the distance, the early light reflected white on the sea.

They started down the snaking walkway, following the backbone of the mountaintop, then dropping sharply as the Wall began its descent down the north cliffside. There was the town far below — there could be help there. Mia pushed to keep up with Simon. It was such a relief to be moving downhill, though her knees wobbled with the exertion. She still felt nauseated, but no longer as if she was going to vomit.

Around the next curve, she was surprised to see Simon waiting. His expression was grim.

"Might as well slow down," he called out. "I just realized . . . they're certain to have soldiers coming up from the other direction too. That's why they weren't hurrying. They know we're trapped up here."

"But —"

He shook his head. "They've got us. We can't get away."

CHAPTER 26

The knowledge hit her like a physical blow. Of course they'd sent troops to the other end, the minute they saw them climbing.

"Simon, we can't let them — have the pictures — It will get Dad in trouble." She gasped out the words, her breath still coming hard. "Not after all this —" There had to be a way.

Her mind worked furiously, refusing to acknowledge the terrible facts. She raked her eyes over the Wall, the surrounding hills, looking for a hiding place. The town down there in the distance. Where she could blend in.

"I can — get away — somehow — with the phone."

"What are you talking about? I told you, soldiers will be coming from both ends. There's no way to outrun them. And when they catch us, they'll search us. First me, then you. What are we going to do, throw the phone over the wall?"

Over the wall.

Mia straightened. "*I* can go over the side."

"What?!" His brow creased.

"The rope — you can lower me. I can get to the town."

His eyes lit up as he understood, began to calculate. They ran to the west side of the Wall, peering over the edge.

"No way, not here. It's sheer cliffs, way too steep to climb," Simon said.

"But if we get down to the flatter section . . ." She pointed ahead. "Look, down there." Far below them, the Wall straightened out on more level ground, then widened into a square like a small room, before snaking its way down to the base and the tower gate entrance.

They ran again, moving down the nearly vertical staircase as quickly as they could without falling. At the square where the Wall widened, a gap cut in the stone was wide enough for her to slip through. She glanced up, scanning the tower on top of the mountain. No sign of the soldiers yet.

"Come help me." Quickly, before she lost her nerve.

"You really think you can do this? Get down there by yourself?"

"I can do this." Her heart was hammering again. "I have to do this. It's the only way."

She reached out a hand for him to boost her up. Her legs trembled as she clung to the sides of the opening.

"Get down to the town and try to get a call out," Simon said, "to the American embassy or something. But whatever you do, hide the phone, until this is all sorted out."

"Wait, Simon, I need money! My wallet fell in the river."

He huffed out a breath, took off his pack, grabbed his wallet, and jammed it into her hand. Shaking, she unzipped her jacket pocket and slipped the wallet in beside the phone.

"Okay, here you go."

"Wait, aren't we gonna use the rope?"

"No time — it's not that far, maybe fifteen feet — I'll lower you partway. C'mon!"

Before she had time to reconsider, she was through the gap, facing the wall, walking her feet down the side, holding tight to Simon's hands.

"Okay, just hang there, I'm gonna let you down."

She went limp, her body dangling in the air. The ground below seemed very far away, rocky and uneven. She clamped her lips shut to keep from screaming.

Simon leaned over as far as he could and straightened his arms. "It's only about a six- or seven-feet drop now. Okay?" Mia managed to nod. "Now let go."

Quickly, before the fear grabbed hold, she inhaled and released her grip on his hands. She felt herself falling, then hitting the hard ground, rolling over with the impact, bouncing a bit between sharp branches and brush before she caught herself.

Simon was leaning through the gap, peering down. Mia jumped up, brushed off her damp jeans, and gave him a thumbs-up. She was scratched and bumped, but nothing hurt too much.

"Run, Mia!" he called in a whisper. He pulled himself up and disappeared.

Mia swallowed the panic that rose as she lost sight of him. She turned to examine the area where she had landed and saw a path running right along the base of the Wall. A few plastic wrappers, tissues, and an empty bottle littered the ground, evidence that many people had come this way. But today it felt like a gift, a magic path just for her.

She began jogging downhill along the path. Trees and shrubs covered the slope to her left, the thick screen of leaves allowing only brief glimpses of the landscape below, but she knew if she followed the twisting Wall, it would lead her to the town. She kept glancing up, but the high sides of the Wall blocked her view of the top. At least if she couldn't see anyone, they couldn't see her either.

Once, she thought she heard shouts in the distance. The soldiers might have caught Simon. Her anxiety pushed her to move faster. Through gaps in the trees, she saw a few village houses along a road, a pond, and beyond, the high gates of the main entrance, the crossroads at the town's center, fields and mountains in the distance. She couldn't see well enough to discover what — or *who* — might be waiting for her there at the base.

The path rose up for a final time, then dropped to a set of stone steps leading down to a paved road. She'd made it to the bottom of the Wall. At the top of the stairway, she stopped for a moment to catch her breath. She peered through the leaves toward the entrance gate, but a line of cone-shaped fir trees planted along the road hid the parking lot from sight.

She brushed off her damp jeans and jacket, combed the stringy ends of her hair. She probably looked a mess, but maybe from a distance it wouldn't be that noticeable. At least the Chinese couldn't immediately tell that she was American. And no one was expecting her down here at the entrance to the Wall.

Her heart pounding, she descended the steps, trying to walk normally. To her right, an archway led beneath the Wall. She turned left. Two billboards with images of cloud-wrapped mountains marked the lower edge of the parking lot. Broad steps led up to the massive gray stone tower with a red-pillared pavilion on top, the entrance to the Great Wall.

Mia tensed. There at the top of the parking lot, right next to the steps, were two military jeeps. To get to the town — and maybe, somehow, a phone — she'd have to cross the parking lot. There was no way to avoid going past the jeeps.

She forced herself to slow down, breathe. Look like an ordinary Chinese villager on an early morning errand. The soldiers would be keeping watch on the Wall, not looking away from it.

She kept to the edge of the wide parking lot, close to the billboards. Her heart pounded so violently in her chest that she thought the soldiers at the gate must be able to hear it. She faced forward, walking as casually as she could force herself to, when all she wanted to do was run screaming for help. No movement around the military vehicles. From this distance, she couldn't tell if any soldiers were even sitting in the jeeps.

Then she was past the parking lot, walking along the entrance road toward a small gatehouse. Her back felt exposed. Fields to her left, garden plots and a few houses to her right. She searched desperately for someone who might help, someone who wasn't a soldier. But this was China — her few Korean words wouldn't do any good. She needed a phone.

She was carrying the North Korean smartphone, but it probably only worked on the DPRK network. Even if the battery was still good, she didn't want to chance sending out a signal that could be traced.

Ahead, the access road joined the main highway at a crossroads with a cluster of houses and shops. At the junction on the right was a building with a broad, flat concrete roof, painted red with white Chinese characters, held up by pillars. A gas station.

She ran then.

She scanned the gas station lot for a phone booth. She pushed her way into the station.

"I need a telephone!" she burst out to the smiling young woman behind the counter. "Teh-leh-fone." She held up her hand to her ear, thumb and pinky extended, cocking her head.

"Teh-leh-fone." The clerk pointed down the aisle. There, mounted on the wall, was a public phone. Mia sprinted to it.

Then she ran back to the clerk.

"Card? Phone card?" She sketched a small rectangle in the air with her fingers, then pointed back at the phone. It took several tries. Finally, the young woman nodded and gestured at the wall behind her to a display of phone cards. Mia grabbed one with a picture of the planet, held up euros from Simon's wallet with a questioning face. The clerk nodded again and took some bills.

Mia ran back to the phone and picked up the receiver. Her hand trembling, she peered at the back of the phone card and frantically punched in the code numbers. Halfway through, she hit a wrong digit. She bit her lip to keep from letting out a whimper. She closed her eyes and took a breath. If she didn't stop panicking, she'd never be able to make a call.

She forced herself to move deliberately, checking each number as she punched it in. A recorded voice said something in Chinese. The prompt for the pin number? She peered at the card, entered each digit. The Chinese voice again. Was this where she put in the number she was calling? Who should she call?

Holding her breath, she punched in Mom's cell phone number. Her finger moved with ease through the familiar digits. Nothing happened. Then the Chinese voice came on again. Mia thought she would explode. She probably needed some overseas area code.

The recording played again, sounding like musical tones. She slammed the receiver down and checked her watch. Nearly thirty minutes had passed since she left Simon on top of the Wall. The panic in her chest threatened to burst out in a scream.

She had to figure this out.

She had no idea how to find the number of the American Embassy. There must be another number she could call. She made fists, chewed on her knuckles, then, when she realized what she was doing, jammed her hands into her jeans pockets.

At the bottom of her pocket, her fingers found a piece of paper. She pulled it out. It was the business card Daniel had given her.

Daniel! He might be able to get help. At least he could tell Mia what to do. How to get in touch with the US Embassy. How to call Mom. The card hadn't been under water long; it was hardly damp. Mia's hand shook as she peered at it.

Simon had said that Daniel couldn't be their friend. That he was working with the North Koreans. Mia had to figure out what she believed. She closed her eyes and took another breath.

She believed that Daniel could be trusted. Nothing Simon said could change that. She would trust herself. Until she was proven wrong.

Daniel had four phone numbers listed — home, work, cell, and next to the fourth, "in China." The tour was supposed to be five days. Anything could have happened after Dad had been arrested. Daniel could be anywhere.

In Beijing. Back in the US. Or possibly still in North Korea.

But one of the numbers was in China. Could it still reach Daniel? She didn't know if she had to dial anything first. Were there area codes? Mia ran back to the young woman, showed her the card and pointed to the number she wanted to call, then gestured back to the phone. "Can you help me?"

The clerk smiled and followed Mia down the aisle. She picked up the receiver and punched in the phone card codes. Looking at Daniel's card, she pressed each digit of the Chinese phone number, then handed the receiver to Mia with a smile and nod.

Mia pressed it to her ear. It was ringing! Every bit of her being concentrated in a prayer. *Daniel. Please pick up, please pick up.*

A voice answered in Chinese.

Mia's eyes swam with tears. It was a moment before she could speak.

"Hello? Is Mr. Moon there?" she said.

"Who is this?"

"Daniel? It's Mia. Mia Andrews."

"Holy God in heaven." Then, *"Mia?!* Mia, where the hell are you?"

"I'm in China. At Tiger Mountain. At the Great Wall." A sharp exhalation. "Daniel, they caught him! They caught Simon! Soldiers chased us up the Wall. I got away, but I'm sure they caught Simon. I don't know what to do." She was crying now.

"Okay, Mia, it's okay. I'm going to help you. But first you've got to tell me where you are."

"At the Tiger Mountain Great Wall."

"Yes, I know. But where exactly?"

"There's a gas station, in the town, at the crossroads by the entrance to the Wall. It has a red roof."

"Okay, stay there. Stay inside. Don't move. I'll come get you."

"But how — where are you?"

"I'm in Dandong. I'll be there in twenty minutes."

CHAPTER 27

Twenty minutes wasn't long enough for Mia's stunned and exhausted mind to calculate how in the world Daniel Moon could be in Dandong, China. Yet with Simon in the hands of the North Koreans, or their Chinese allies, twenty minutes was far too long to wait. She paced the aisle of the gas station and peered out the windows, her eyes glued to the highway. She had no idea which direction Daniel would be coming from. Or if the soldiers trying to catch them would get there first.

A bell jangled as the front door opened. Mia tensed. Then there was Daniel, coming down the aisle toward her. Mia ran to him, threw her arms around him, and buried her head in his chest.

She could feel Daniel shaking his head as his arms went around her. "I never — how in God's name did you — you amazing girl . . ." he kept exclaiming, without ever finishing a sentence.

Mia just wanted to rest there, with someone to lean on. But Simon needed her.

"Daniel, we have to hurry, we have to help Simon!"

They rushed outside, and Mia's heart jolted at the sight of

two black cars with soldiers standing on alert. Then her frayed mind processed the uniforms. Not North Korean. *Chinese.* Daniel had brought backup. The soldiers, including one who looked like an officer, acted as if Daniel was in charge. And Daniel seemed to be speaking Chinese. Mia felt more confused than ever, but there was no time to ask questions. The only thing that mattered was rescuing Simon. Daniel opened the back door of one of the vehicles, motioned for Mia to get in, and climbed in after her.

"Okay, tell me where you were, where you left Simon, what happened," he said.

As quickly as she could, Mia told him about climbing the Wall, the soldiers chasing them, her escape over the side. After that, Daniel and the Chinese officer talked a lot in urgent tones on cell phones.

"They've got Simon, they're on the bridge in Dandong," Daniel said. At her look of panic, he added, "Don't worry, the Chinese will hold them. We'll be able to get there in time."

Mia started to breathe.

"Daniel, what about Dad? Do the North Koreans still have him?"

His face sobered. "Yes, he's still being held. But he's in good health and being treated well, and we're doing everything we can to arrange his release."

Then they were driving away from the Wall. Mia collapsed against the seat. A tidal wave of disappointment flooded over her. She hadn't realized until that moment, when she heard the hard truth, how much she'd been holding on to the impossible hope that Dad would have already been freed. That somehow he'd be waiting for them in China.

They sped along a country highway by the river, a siren blaring from the roof. Everything seemed to be out of Mia's hands now. She was completely wrung out, a leaf being carried along on a strong current.

She tried to sort out the tangled maze of thoughts and impressions in her brain. One question was on top. She took a breath to gather her courage.

"Daniel — what's going on? How come you're here, in China?"

"I'm an aide for Senator Ashton, Mia. The chair of the committee overseeing North Korean affairs. I was there to meet with MPS officials, to see how the DPRK was doing with food distribution."

So Simon had been right. Daniel wasn't just some ordinary tourist. Daniel's eyes were on the road. Mia concentrated on hearing him over the noise of the siren. "I have some contacts . . . on the inside. One of them is someone who arranged to let you escape, at the roadblock. He's part of a faction that's opposing hard-liners like Colonel Pak."

"That's what Simon and I guessed! You mentioned them, at the Mass Games."

He nodded. "When those people got information about you, they passed it along to me."

Mia sat up. "Information about us?"

"You were seen, and reported, several times in Pyongyang, the last time at the West Pyongyang train station. There were some confusing reports after that. My contacts sometimes got leaks from Colonel Pak's side as well. Then I received word of your capture — that was MPS, extracting you from the clutches of Colonel Pak — and your convenient 'escape.'" He made quotation marks with his fingers. "That roadblock was a showdown between the two factions."

Another point for their detective work; she and Simon had guessed that part correctly.

"Colonel Pak must have had other reports of your whereabouts, which is how those soldiers managed to be so close behind you. But I didn't get any of that information, so I had no idea where you were. We didn't expect that there was any way you could possibly make it across the border. But you'd gotten to Sinuiju, so it made sense to stay nearby, waiting until we heard more."

It was chilling to think how often they'd been seen and reported. But not because of Soon-ok, not because of Mr. Shin, or they would've been caught much sooner. Mia hugged the knowledge to herself. Despite the danger she and Simon had exposed them to, their friends had not betrayed them.

They were careening through busy city streets now. Traffic scattered to let them through. The car screeched to a stop at a tall, official-looking building with Chinese flags on either side of a wide stairway. Daniel dashed out of the car, calling to Mia to stay put.

She waited in the car with the driver for a long time. Too tired to move, too anxious to breathe.

Then there was Daniel, walking out of the building.

Beside him was Simon.

Mia jumped out of the car and ran to her brother. They grabbed each other, laughing and whooping and jumping around. Daniel and the soldiers stood grinning at them.

"You've got it, the phone?" Simon asked into Mia's ear. She smiled up at him, patting the pocket where it lay against her stomach. He raised both hands and she slapped them.

"We *did* it! I can't believe we did it!" Simon kept exulting, with a little exuberant swearing on the side.

Then Daniel was dialing his cell phone and saying, "I've got them both, Kay, they're safe."

"Mom!" Mia screeched. Daniel handed her the phone, and she was crying again, "Mom, Mom! It's me! We're okay! We're in China, we're with Daniel!" and she heard, "Oh, Mia!" and then Simon took the phone, his voice cracking, not even bothering to wipe the tears on his cheeks.

✶ ✶ ✶

NBA ALL-STARS ARRIVE IN NORTH KOREA

NOVEMBER 15

Six former All-Star members of the National Basketball Association arrived in Pyongyang today for a series of exhibition games.

Leader Kim Jong-un's well-known fondness for basketball has led to an ongoing international exchange that many observers call "sports diplomacy." In the past, individual celebrities who traveled to the authoritarian country were criticized for propping up the dictatorship and ignoring human rights abuses. Recent sports delegations have included some State Department officials, however, who have been able to use the opportunity to hold informal talks with their North Korean counterparts, aimed at lowering tensions between the DPRK and the US.

This basketball delegation is likewise thought to include some diplomats, raising speculation that any talks might include the status of detained American aid worker Mark Andrews, who has been held in the DPRK since October 2.

✪ ✪ ✪

NORTH KOREA RELEASES US AID WORKER

NOVEMBER 24

In a surprise development, American aid worker Mark Andrews of Food for the World was released from detention and allowed to return to the US with the NBA All-Stars delegation.

Andrews was arrested in October while touring North Korea and accused of "hostile acts against the republic," allegedly for meeting with members of opposition groups. North Korean officials had previously threatened to put Andrews on trial with the likelihood that he would receive a lengthy prison sentence, but he was unexpectedly released during the visit of the basketball stars. Sources attributed the sudden move to informal talks held between unidentified US and North Korean government officials.

Andrews's wife, Kay Andrews, and his teenage son and daughter, who accompanied him to Pyongyang in October but were not detained with their father, met him at John F. Kennedy Airport in New York City.

EPILOGUE

NOVEMBER 30

"Hey, Dad."

Mia placed a glass of tomato juice and a bag of tortilla chips on her father's desk and slung her backpack off her shoulder onto the floor of the den.

Dad pulled his eyes from his laptop and swiveled in his big chair to envelop her in a hug.

When he'd gotten home six days before, he'd seemed tired but unhurt. He said he'd been treated well enough, kept in a couple of rooms that were more like a hotel suite than a prison. Plenty of food, even exercise breaks. Round-the-clock minders. The hardest part had been the endless interrogations and the demand that he write long confessions of crimes he hadn't committed. His biggest fear had been that something he said might get one of his North Korean colleagues in trouble. He'd assumed all along that Mia and Simon were safe in Daniel's care and back home in Connecticut within a few days. Mia was glad to hear he hadn't been worried about them too.

For the past week, he'd been mostly resting and

recovering, when he wasn't meeting State Department officials for debriefing.

Mia and Simon had had a few days home with Dad, over the Thanksgiving break, but now they were back in school. In the hallway between classes, Mia texted — "Hi, Dad," "xoxox," "<3," any silly thing — just for the relief of seeing his response come back. He really was home. *Safe.*

Dad turned to the screen and Mia draped herself over his back, her arms folded over his shoulders.

"How was your day?" he asked.

"Okay. We're reading this book set in Cambodia in English Lit, about somebody who survived the genocide. Some of the kids were saying it was too disturbing."

The first objection had come from Kyle Herland. "Do we really have to read this stuff?"

Then the girls started chiming in. "It's really upsetting," Oakley James said.

"I'm getting nightmares," Amanda Turner whined.

Ms. Tapley let them go on awhile. Mia sat there until she couldn't stand it anymore. Until listening without saying anything felt like agreeing, which felt like some kind of betrayal.

She raised her hand.

"Mia?" She saw surprise in the tilt of her teacher's head as Ms. T turned to her.

"We need to know about it," Mia said. "Even if it's upsetting. Especially if it's upsetting. Because it really happened. Avoiding it is like pretending it didn't happen."

And it's still happening, she thought. *If not in Cambodia, in North Korea.* No, that might open a dangerous door. She was still figuring out what was safe to say.

"Thank you, Mia," Ms. T said, a weight in the phrase

that showed she really meant it. She held her eyes for a moment.

"I agree with Mia." That was T.J. Now Mia was the one who was surprised. "We should pay attention when bad things happen, even if we don't feel like it. If we don't, then people keep making the same stupid mistakes over and over."

"That reminds me of a line from the play *Death of a Salesman*," Ms. T said. "Terrible things happen to one of the characters, ruining his life. One of the other characters speaks out, saying his tragedy can't be ignored: 'Attention, attention must finally be paid to such a person.'

"'Attention must be paid.'" She let the line hang in the air for a moment. "Here's the reason I think it's important to read books like the one I've assigned: If other people had to suffer through something so horrific, the least we can do is listen when they tell their stories. To pay attention. To bear witness."

Mia had been holding those phrases in her head all day. *Attention must be paid. To bear witness.*

It was like what she and Dad did together now. After school — and sometimes in the middle of the night, when she woke to the sound of him moving around downstairs — they read everything they could find online that might give them a clue about what was happening in North Korea.

"Anything new?" Mia asked.

"No sign of personnel shifts in the ministries."

They especially watched for any news about the State Security Department, SSD, which Mia thought of as Colonel Pak's group, and the Ministry of People's Security, MPS, which she thought of as the scarred man's group. They were the ones who gave Mia and Simon the phone and let them steal their car.

Dad scrolled through blogs, analyses, and news stories. Mia read with her chin on his shoulder.

The front door opened, then banged shut.

"Hey, Squeak. Hey, Dad." Simon passed the door of the den and headed for the stairs.

"How was debate practice?" Dad called, but Simon was already out of range.

Since they got back, Simon had thrown himself into getting caught up with his schoolwork, his debate team, soccer. He didn't talk a lot about what had happened to them, but Mia didn't need him to say anything. Sitting across from each other at the dinner table or passing in the hall on the way to their rooms, their eyes would meet. So much in one look.

"The story of your disappearance," Daniel had told Mia and Simon while they were still in China together, "is that when your father was detained for questioning, the two of you were taken to a safe location, then flown home. No one knows that you made it out by yourselves — no one except me, several other US government officials, your mom, and certain DPRK officials."

Outside of their family, their experiences had to remain completely confidential. People's lives could be at stake.

She and Simon walked around all day, every day, with all that inside, not being able to talk about it. They were, for each other, the only other person in the world who understood what they'd been through. And what they were still going through.

At first Mia had felt weird around Alicia and Jess, keeping all those secrets. Simon had lent Mia his phone for a day so she could show them photos of the monuments and talk about the first two days of the tour. But she couldn't share anything real about the biggest thing that had ever happened to her. It created a distance between her and her friends, but only Mia knew it was there.

In a strange way, it had helped when Dad was still being held in North Korea. Mia didn't have to pretend then that she was fine. She could be worried or distracted or frustrated — all of which she was, a lot — and they thought they understood why.

Then one afternoon, the third week after she and Simon got back, Mia and Alicia and Jess were crammed into their usual seat in the back of the school bus.

"Okay, Mia, spill," Jess said.

Mia stared. How had Jess figured out that she wasn't telling the truth about the trip?

Then she realized that Jess was just referring to their old game, what her friends called the "Weirdest Thing Mia Observed Today." Jess often said when she opened her detective agency, she was going to hire Mia to collect evidence.

"Okay," Mia said, keeping her voice low. "Jacob Weintraub never has anything to write with. He's always borrowing other people's pens or pencils. He chews on the ends as he uses them, then he gives them back. So if he borrows a pen from you, tell him to keep it."

Alicia, who had a huge crush on Jacob, burst into laughter. Mia couldn't help laughing too.

In that moment, somehow, it got okay. Mia could hold the weight of everything she had experienced in North Korea. And at the same time, she could be there on the bus, being silly with Alicia and Jess.

Korean school had been different as well. She'd needed time at first, just to adjust to being at home, but by early November, she told Mom she wanted to go back. She felt awkward walking in, but it turned out she was the only person there who'd ever been to North Korea. Her teachers and classmates were fascinated by every detail she shared, and asked a lot of questions. Despite all the things Mia had to keep secret, she found a lot to say, and everyone expressed concern about Dad, who was still being held in the DPRK. It seemed so strange, so upside-down, being the one at language school who knew the most about something Korean.

In class, new Korean phrases took on greater meaning when Mia imagined speaking them to Mr. Lee, or Soon-ok, or Mr. Shin's mother. She was still working at a beginning level while the others were advanced, but now she didn't mind asking a couple of the girls — Hannah Lee and Grace Jung — for help understanding something. She thought someday she'd invite them to a sleepover at her house and they could watch K-dramas and K-pop videos together.

On her third Saturday back at school, she came out of the building and found her mother waiting in the car as usual. Mia slipped into the passenger seat but left the door open to hold her mother's attention. She had something she was determined to say.

"Mom, next week I want you to come inside," she said, facing her. "There's a nice area with a couch where you can sit and work while I'm in class."

"Oh, I don't want to bother anyone," her mother said. "Can you close the door? We need to get going."

"Just a second. I'm trying to tell you something. You wouldn't be bothering anybody. I just want you to be there. I don't want Korean school to be some strange thing I go off and do all by myself."

Her mother put one hand to her forehead. "I've got so much on my mind, with your father —"

"Mom, I know," Mia said. "But I'm not asking a lot. Just

do your phone calls or whatever, but stay here at the church. Meet these people. Okay?"

Her mother sighed. Her hand came down. "Okay, I'll try."

The next week Dad had come home, and of course there'd been no trip to Stamford. But Mia could tell that things were going to be different. Because *she* was different.

The first few days after Dad had gotten home, they'd had so much to talk over. Mia and Simon wanted to know all about what had happened to Dad, and he wanted to know all about what had happened to them. Daniel visited once, and Mia and Simon had a long list of questions to ask.

"Why did the guys who caught us want us to escape? And why didn't they just drive us to the border?" Simon had demanded. "Why did we have to go through the whole charade of stealing the car?"

Daniel had explained that the Ministry of People's Security agents understood just how disastrous holding not just an American aid worker but his *kids* would be for North Korea's image. But helping them too directly would have been treason, and no one could have protected his contacts from the consequences.

More questions: Why did the Ministry of People's Security give them the phone? Who put the pictures on it? Did they really think it would work to get the pictures out? Mr. Lee had told Mia not to open the package until they got out of the country. Was he part of the plot?

Dad and Daniel speculated that it was a plan by the MPS to embarrass the SSD, just as Mia and Simon had guessed. On the other hand, Dad's arrest might have been a setup by SSD to expose MPS. There could be moles and double agents in both ministries. Neither Dad or Daniel had any knowledge of Mr. Lee's role.

Everyone agreed that there was appearance and there was reality, and they'd almost certainly never know exactly what the truth was. Lots of questions, most without answers.

But gradually, Mia realized, she could get an answer to *the* question, the one that had been on her mind throughout the whole trip.

On a Sunday night, when Dad had been home four days, she'd finally gotten the courage to ask. The entire family had gathered in the living room, talking events over.

"Dad. I saw you. The first night. You sneaked out of your hotel room, down to the first floor, where you met with someone. And what I want to know is, what was really going on? Why did we go to North Korea? For real?"

Dad sighed, like someone putting down a heavy load. He told them he'd gotten messages from North Korean colleagues that this would be a good time to visit. It had seemed like a perfect opportunity to accomplish two things: to be in North Korea when he might be able to make a crucial connection, or support some small shift to get more food to the people who needed it, and to bring his children on the tour.

"When we got to the hotel," Dad said, "there was a message asking me to be in the lobby at twelve thirty a.m. It wasn't that unusual. I've sometimes met agency contacts in the middle of the night, when they wanted to say something off the record. But when I got downstairs, the person waiting was someone I'd never met. He introduced himself as an official from MPS. He suggested we go for a walk along the river. We talked about music, of all things. He was an admirer of Beethoven and Mahler. I kept waiting for something to happen, but nothing did. Maybe he had something he wanted to tell me, or give me. Maybe it was some sort of test. I never found out."

So Dad really was a kind of a spy. But not really. Not intentionally.

"Whatever it was," Dad went on, "the whole thing was ill-advised. As soon as I was arrested, I suspected that meeting was the reason. The whole time I was being held, all I could think of was how foolish I'd been, and how I put you and Simon in danger. I owe an apology to both of you — and to you, Kay. I put my own children at risk."

Mia took a deep breath.

"Okay," she said. "We did some things too. We decided to keep the phone and try to get it out of the country. Probably not the safest choice. There was one time I was thinking of deleting the photos. That would have made things less dangerous for us. Maybe for you too, Dad. But I thought about the people in the pictures and I couldn't do it."

Simon nodded. "We could have left the phone in the forest, buried it somewhere. I could have thrown it in the river, but I threw the player instead."

"Let's be clear about one thing," Dad said. "That phone, those photographs. If you hadn't opened it when you did, then run with it . . . if they'd gotten ahold of those pictures . . . I'd never have gotten out of there." He looked into Mia's eyes, then Simon's. "You really did save me."

They had done it. They had saved Dad.

Finally, Dad had looked at Mom. "Kay?"

She frowned at each of them. "All of you." She shook her head. "I'll need some time." For some reason, that made them all laugh.

Mia had been right. Her family would never look the same to her again.

There was a clang from the kitchen.

"Oh, for goodness' sakes!" Mom's voice, exasperated.

Dad leaned his head against Mia's. "You want to see if your mother needs a hand in there, sweetie?"

"O-kay." She sighed and pulled away from him.

The kitchen counter looked like the shelf of a small grocery store. Half a dozen cans of beans. A package of meat and one of fish. Boxes and bags of pasta and rice. Tomatoes, peppers, and onions. A large wooden salad bowl full of lettuce.

"Mom, what's going on?"

"I can't decide what to serve." She was holding a saucepan in one hand, a frying pan in the other. "There's the pasta sauce I was thinking of making, but what if he prefers meat? Or I have this fresh cod I got this morning —"

"Mom. Stop. You're not feeding a volunteer army. It's just dinner. For five of us. Just choose one thing."

"But Daniel Moon —" Her voice cracked. Mia stepped closer and put her hand on her mother's arm. Mom was the ultimate campaign organizer. The Master Multitasker. Mia couldn't remember ever seeing her flustered like this.

"Mom? What's wrong?"

"It's just that . . . if it weren't for Daniel — staying in touch with me, being there to meet you in China, being part of the negotiations to get your father released — I just don't know what I would've done. The more I learn about what happened, how much he did, the more grateful I feel to him. No matter what I think of cooking, it's not enough."

She was right. What would have happened if Daniel hadn't been there in Dandong to answer the phone? If it weren't for Daniel, they probably wouldn't all be here, together. A family again.

Mia smiled at her mother. "Mom. Daniel will like whatever you serve. Your pasta sauce is great. Let's have that."

Mom blew out a breath. She set the pans back on the stove, turned to the counter, and started slicing up vegetables with scary efficiency. Back on track.

Mia put the fish in the fridge. Wow, they really did have enough to feed a volunteer army.

At first the whole food thing — regular meals, leftovers, grocery shopping, eating out, restaurant ads on TV — had been challenging for her and Simon. The number of choices, the huge servings, the waste. It felt overwhelming, and kind of obscene.

A month later, she was mostly used to it. But she still couldn't see food wasted without remembering the soldiers on the road or the photos of the starving people in the camp. Or even her own and Simon's few days of hunger, what they would have done for just one of the plates she saw being tossed out in the middle school cafeteria every day.

With everything put away, the pasta sauce simmering on the stove, Mia went up to her room to get ready. Daniel would be here soon. She felt a little fizzy with anticipation. All that time they'd spent together in China had turned him into kind of a favorite uncle. A young, handsome uncle that she might have a little crush on.

She also couldn't wait to hear any news he might bring. His last message had said that there might still be some kind of shake-up in the ministries, which could result in some minor changes. Better food distribution to the people, or less harsh treatment in the prisons.

"But real change isn't something that can be forced from the outside," Daniel told them. "That will have to come from the North Korean people."

Mia had thought of Mr. Lee, Miss Cho, and Mr. Kim.

The prison guard who took the photographs, whoever he was. Soon-ok. Mr. Shin and his mother. The men who'd let them escape.

That was the one thing she wanted that Daniel couldn't give her: information about all the people who'd helped them. What had happened to the guides after Mia and Simon ran away from the tour? Daniel said they'd probably never know.

Yet bit by bit, some of them were learning the truth about their country. They were the strength that might one day break down the prison walls. The people of North Korea.

My people, Mia thought.

She pulled on a clean shirt. Studied her reflection in her closet door mirror, turning to one side, then the other. She took the shirt off, tossed it on on her bed, reached for another. And another. Somewhere in here she had to have the right one.

She wanted to look . . . different. Maybe more sophisticated. More knowing. Like North Korea had changed her. Like she was more mature and interesting than . . .

Really, Mia?

She stopped in place and made a face at herself. She'd just seen Daniel last week. He wasn't going to notice what she was wearing. Just like she'd told Mom about the food. If she was going to let Daniel see how deeply her North Korean experience had affected her, it certainly wouldn't be by obsessing over her outfit. Anyway, Daniel already thought she was great, just the way she was.

She grabbed her most comfortable shirt, the soft red one that felt so good on her skin. Buttoning it up, she caught her own eyes in the mirror.

There she was again. There, back behind her eyelids, that lively something, looking out at her. She gazed at herself. *Hi, there.*

Mia had always known that to Dad she was . . . well, a light in his life. In this last month she had discovered, again and again, just how much her mother loved her, in her own way. And after everything they'd been through together, Mia knew she had her brother. For good.

But most of all, now she knew she could count on herself. If anything, that's what she wanted Daniel to see.

She gave herself a smile and turned to join her family downstairs.

IM KWANG-SOO

He had to stop for a moment or his lungs would burst. Sheer blind panic had propelled him straight up the steep slope, thighs and calves burning, but he couldn't take another step without a break. Kwang-soo grasped a pine and hauled himself around it, collapsing against the trunk as he gasped for air.

As soon as he could breathe, he peered back down the valley toward the camp far below. A convoy of trucks, tiny in the distance, crawled past the guards' barracks to the south, but there was no movement near the main gate, nor where he'd hidden the jeep, down an embankment and behind a crop of bushes. So far, it seemed, his treachery hadn't been detected. He needed to get as far away as possible before the alarm sounded.

He turned and forced himself upward, catching hold of branches to keep himself from slipping in the dusty, brush-covered soil. Hong had not been at their arranged meeting place, and Kwang-soo had acted instinctively, before he could think or plan. If Hong had been caught, it was only a matter of time before they came for him. The fear jolted him like an electric charge, kicking him into action from which there was no turning back.

He was nearly to the summit now; once he'd cleared it, he'd be out of sight of the camp. Still, if they let the dogs loose, he was finished. He'd seen the broken body of one girl the beasts had mauled — and the extra rations the handlers gave the dogs as a reward. At least a death like that, however painful, would be quick. If they discovered what he carried, he'd endure weeks or months of torture first.

Two last, labored steps and he crested the hill. He risked a final look back, scanning the length of the camp. It filled the narrow, branching cleft between steep wooded hills that cast deep shadows in the late afternoon light. Clusters of buildings spread out along the length of the valley for nearly twenty kilometers: the main gate, the guards' barracks, the detention center. He could just make out the first group of mud huts for mothers and children, the quarters for single prisoners, the execution grounds. Out of sight beyond the far hills were the fields, the mines, and more living quarters. He'd heard that all together, there were some fifty thousand prisoners.

A death camp. That was the truth of it, though he hadn't seen it that way when he'd first arrived. His training had deeply instilled the belief that the "re-settlers" brought here were insects, vermin, scum. They tainted the purity of the people. Whether their deaths came by overwork or accident, by beatings or starvation, by torture or execution, they deserved to be exterminated. They were enemies of the state, and all the bad things that were happening in the country at large — the shortages of food and power, the failure of missile launches or economic programs — were their fault.

Still no sign of any unusual movement. He turned and started making his way north along the ridge, recalling the moment everything had changed. Last spring, he'd been lined up with the other guards, ready to sort and herd a new batch of prisoners to their quarters. The trucks pulled to a stop in the dirt square. As people began clambering out, Kwang-soo had caught sight of a familiar face: Yoon-ah, his schoolmaster's daughter. Only sixteen, three years younger than he, she was a soft-spoken girl with a beautiful singing voice. She blinked in the bright light, then she reached back to lift out a smaller girl, perhaps six years old, who clung to her, sobbing. The next person to climb from the truck was the schoolmaster, followed by his wife.

The schoolmaster and his family were the most respected

citizens of Kwang-soo's town. He remembered the light in the schoolmaster's eyes as he talked of the glory of the socialist state they were building together. Everyone in their neighborhood knew about the food the schoolmaster or his wife had delivered to needy students during the terrible hunger of the Arduous March.

Kwang-soo had forced himself to concentrate on his habitual tasks, separating the families. The men would be transported to quarters near the mines, the women and children to the huts. None of them would ever see each other again.

"Ah-bbah!" the little girl had cried as her father was pulled away.

"Keep her quiet!" another guard bellowed, then reached out and whacked the side of Yoon-ah's head.

Kwang-soo had dropped his gaze, grateful that the group of men he was corralling didn't include the schoolmaster. He was terrified that he'd exposed himself when he had seen them. Had he gasped involuntarily? Had his cheeks reddened?

Later, Kwang-soo sought out Yoon-ah. He had to know: Why was she here? What possible crime had someone in her family committed?

Yoon-ah was bewildered. Someone had accused her father of criticizing the Grand Marshall. She knew it was a lie. Remembering the schoolmaster, Kwang-soo did too.

Over the next few weeks, he had watched Yoon-ah from a distance, helpless to protect her. It wasn't long before the guards took note of the pretty young woman. Soon the bloom in her cheeks faded, and dark shadows stained her face. She no longer sang at all.

Quietly, when none of the guards were watching, Kwang-soo began to ask other prisoners why they had been sent to the camp. One woman had crumpled a newspaper, unaware that a photograph of the Grand Marshall was on the other side. An old man's son had dropped a portrait of the Great Leader while cleaning it smashing the glass. The father of a girl his age had tried to cross the river to China to find food for his family. Many had no idea why they had been imprisoned. Most were guilty only by association, or too poor to pay the bribes that could have kept them out of prison. The more Kwang-soo learned, the more his heart sickened.

So when Officer Hong contacted him (how had he known?), he was ready. Yes, he would take the forbidden mobile phone and shoot photos out of a small hole in his shirt pocket. Yes, he would meet Hong again, hand the phone over, receive a new one. This trade had happened three times over the past six months. Hong did not say what he did with the images, and Kwang-soo did not ask. He only knew he must act, or lose something more precious to him than his own safety.

And now, the fourth time, Hong wasn't where he said he would be. If Kwang-soo was caught with the photographs, not only he but his parents, his grandfather, his younger brother, would all end up in a camp like the one behind him. When his superiors discovered he was gone, his family might still be taken. There was nothing he could do to prevent that.

In the dying light, he followed the ridge as it rose toward a higher peak. Ahead lay eighty kilometers of mountainous wilderness. He had no food, no water, no light, no weapon, no blanket, no map. Winter was coming on. He might die trying to reach the Chinese border or trying to cross. But he would surely die if he stayed.

He had heard rumors of others who had made it out. He wore a guard's uniform and a sturdy winter coat, not prison rags. He hadn't been starved. He was young and strong; if prisoners could eat grass and insects to survive, so could he. When he agreed to Hong's proposal, he'd already decided that the evidence he now carried — the truth — was worth risking his own life. Here was the test of his devotion.

As night fell, he pressed north.

AUTHOR'S NOTE

Writing this novel has been a ten-year journey of research, hard work, conversation, and reflection, especially on the subject of identity. I'm a white American whose own identity was profoundly shaped by moving from New Hampshire to South Korea in 1960, when I was seven years old. Korea, where my parents worked as medical missionaries, was our family's home base for twenty-one years. I speak fluent conversational Korean, spent my junior year of college at a Korean university, and have returned to Korea many times throughout my adulthood. Korea is "home" to me, even as my connection remains that of an outsider-insider. But prior to this book, my sphere of personal knowledge, experience, and interest in Korea had never included the North. Even when I was a child and teenager in South Korea, the country occupying the other half of the peninsula seemed unknowable, foreign, and menacing — a feeling exacerbated by the bellicose threats and posturing of the DPRK, and its 1968 assassination attempt on South Korean President Park Chung-hee.

Ten years ago, a chance interview question about reunification led to the idea for a novel about two American kids on the run in North Korea. I did some reading and daydreaming, but I felt uncertain about my connection to the material until I met Reverend Peter Yoon, a member of the Council on Korean Studies of Michigan State University. In 2007 he had traveled into the DPRK from China by train and had an hour and a half of video footage of the countryside between Sinuiju and Pyongyang. The images were spellbinding, and to my surprise, they were familiar. Rural North Korea in 2007 — wide plains filled with rice fields, farmers planting in flooded paddies, people pushing carts and riding bicycles, clunky concrete apartment buildings painted pink and blue — looked exactly like the South Korean countryside of the 1960s where I grew up. I realized the DPRK was not unknowable and foreign; despite its government, it was part of a land I knew and loved. Over the years of research and writing that followed, North Korea came into focus more and more as a place of enormous complexity and contradiction, and most of all a place full of real *people*.

Indeed, contrary to the popular image of a country shrouded in mystery about which we know almost nothing, I've found an extensive amount of information available about the DPRK. These books and films emerged as some of the most significant for me, especially in illuminating the variety of contemporary life experiences of North Korean people. I encourage readers to seek out primary sources, to learn from authentic North Korean voices speaking about their own experiences. (Resources appropriate for younger audiences are marked with an asterisk.)

- The Bradt Travel Guide, *North Korea** (2003, 2007, and 2014 editions) by Robert Willoughby, the "only major standalone tourist guide to North Korea." The guidebook Mia brings with her is based on the 2005 reprint of the 2003 edition.
- *Camp 14: Total Control Zone*, a filmed interview with Shin Dong-Hyuk, the only person known to have been raised

in and to have escaped from a no-release North Korean prison camp. Shin has since admitted that not all details of his account were accurate, in both the film and a book about his experiences — for instance, that he was not born in the camp but sent there with his family as a young child. But observers seem to agree that as his story is similar to accounts of other former adult inmates and guards, it still provides important and accurate information about the realities of prison camp life.

- *Dear Leader: My Escape from North Korea* (Atria, 2015) by Jang Jin-sung, a rare account from the elite perspective of a poet laureate to Kim Jong-il.
- *Every Falling Star** (Amulet Books, 2016) by Sungju Lee and Susan Elizabeth McClelland, a young adult memoir of a boy, born into a privileged family, who spent five years scrounging on the streets as a "flower swallow" before escaping to South Korea.
- *The Girl with Seven Names* (William Collins, 2015) by Hyeonseo Lee, a richly detailed memoir of growing up in a high-status, relatively affluent family and crossing the border into China as a willful teenager, an unwitting defector. (Ms. Lee, now an activist on behalf of North Korean defectors, has a popular 2013 TED talk*: https://www.ted.com/talks/hyeonseo_lee_my_escape_from_north_korea?language=en.)
- "My Daily Life in North Korea (MYSTERIOUS 7 DAY TRIP)"* (2016), a 14-minute video by "digital nomad" Jacob Laukaitis that takes the viewer along for a typical DPRK tour: https://www.youtube.com/watch?v=uMoSyk0rK9s.
- *North Korea Confidential* (Tuttle, 2015) by Daniel Tudor and James Pearson, the most up-to-date and comprehensive

account of the astonishing changes that North Korean society is currently undergoing.

- *Nothing to Envy: Ordinary Lives in North Korea* (Spiegel & Grau, 2009) by Barbara Demick, a rare picture of daily life in the northeast and the devastating impact of the 1990s famine, based on interviews with defectors.
- *A State of Mind** (2004), a documentary film that follows two young gymnasts in Pyongyang as they compete for the privilege of performing in the Mass Games.
- *Under the Same Sky: From Starvation in North Korea to Salvation in America* (HMHC, 2015), by Joseph Kim with Stephen Talty, a memoir of a North Korean childhood, from comfort to deprivation to street life, before escaping as a teenager. (See also his TED talk* at https://www.ted.com/talks/joseph_kim_the_family_i_lost_in_north_korea_and_the_family_i_gained?language=en.)
- *Without You, There Is No Us: Undercover Among the Sons of North Korea's Elite* by Suki Kim (Broadway Books, 2015), an account by a Korean American investigative reporter posing as an English teacher at a Pyongyang school run by foreign missionaries.

For details of North Korea tours, I consulted numerous online blogs and photo essays. NKNews.org (by subscription) offers a comprehensive source of news about the DPRK. In 2015, I traveled to Dandong, China, where I was thrilled to discover that my hotel room window faced the Yalu River with a view of the city of Sinuiju. I took a motorboat ride through the waters that separate the two countries, and traced Mia and Simon's steps up a section of the Tiger Mountain Great Wall, where I sat and gazed at "One-Step Crossing" and the North Korean countryside. Additionally, throughout the development of this book — and the thirty years of our life together — our beloved daughter, Yunhee, has shared her experience of being a transracially adopted Korean American.

I am also enormously indebted to those who provided expert and essential feedback on the final draft (a number of whom can't be named for fear of difficulties if they return to the DPRK): A, an international observer of North Korean affairs who travels frequently to the DPRK; D, a foreign resident of Pyongyang, for detailed information about city life; SJK, who taught English in Pyongyang, for a Korean American perspective on North Korea; David McCann, Korea Foundation Professor of Korean Literature, Harvard University, who has traveled to the DPRK four times and lectured there; and Seongmin Lee and J, both of whom were born and raised in North Korea and escaped as young adults. These readers, as well as an expert on Korean transracial adoption, corrected many mistakes and mis-impressions and challenged me to go deeper into the material. Any remaining errors of fact or interpretation are my own.

Drawing on all of these sources, I have attempted to present the realities of life in current-day North Korea as accurately as possible based on the present available information. (By the time this book is in print, some of what I have written may already be outdated.) But I have also made a few decisions in service of my story. For instance, the Arirang Mass Games have not been held since 2013, but I included a performance here, because the scale, organization, and presentation of the event is a uniquely and definitively North Korean phenomenon. It's possible to trace Mia and Simon's entire journey as I plotted it on Google Earth, but I did add the stairs down which they escape at Mangyongdae, and the park along the river in Sinuiju.

I met one of the most important influences on this book in 2010, at the invitation of my friend Yoo Myung Ja. She introduced me to Professor Kim Hyun Sik, formerly one of North Korea's foremost educators, and the personal Russian tutor to the teenaged Kim Jong-il. In 1991, while working in Moscow, Professor Kim was approached by a South Korean agent with the astonishing news that his sister, whom he hadn't seen since the Korean War and had long thought dead, was alive and waiting to meet him. A double agent reported their reunion to the DPRK, and Kim was forced to make the excruciating decision between returning home to face certain death, or defecting, knowing his entire family in North Korea would be killed. He spent a number of years in South Korea before moving to the US, where he served as a research professor at George Mason University. (You can read Professor Kim's account of his years in North Korea, the circumstances of his defection, and his life since in this article: http://www.plough.com/en/topics/life/forgiveness/forgiving-kim-jong-il.)

Throughout the hours of our conversation over several days, Professor Kim, a gentle, soft-spoken man, was often in tears recalling the struggles of his former countrymen. He was the first North Korean defector I'd ever met, and he told me I was the first white American with whom he'd had such a personal encounter. "They told me you were my enemy," he said. I shared my book idea with him and asked what he would hope to see a novel about his homeland accomplish. "To create empathy for the North Korean people," he said. In the course of writing *In the Shadow of the Sun*, this has become my hope too.

As I complete this book, my research has also led to questions about ways in which I, as an American, might bear some responsibility, based on the past and present actions of my government, for the separation of the Korean people and for current conditions in North Korea. I long to know more, and for the heartache and pain of the division to end. If you'd also like to know more and perhaps get involved, there are many organizations dedicated to making a difference in the lives of suffering North Koreans:

- Free North Korea Radio, staffed by North Korean defectors: http://www.fnkradio.com
- Liberty in North Korea (LiNK): http://www.libertyin northkorea.org/
- North Korea Freedom Coalition: http://www.nkfreedom .org/index.aspx; "Ways You Can Get Involved": http:// www.nkfreedom.org/Get-Involved/Ways-You-Can-Get -Involved.aspx
- United Nations International Children's Emergency Fund (UNICEF) DPRK Country Programme: http:// www.unicef.org/dprk/

ACKNOWLEDGMENTS

Creating a novel is like assembling an intricate mosaic, with fragments collected or gifted from many sources. This stone, that jewel, this shell, that bead — each piece is essential to building the patterns, bit by bit, that eventually form the whole. There are so many people and communities to whom I am deeply grateful for the assistance, information, inspiration, and support that made the creation of *In the Shadow of the Sun* possible. (These are the names that come to mind; thanks also to those I'll remember after this goes to print.)

This book is rooted in love for the people of Korea — *my* people — as a response to the friends, colleagues, and extended family members who welcomed my parents and their four children into their lives, their culture, and their hearts, over the twenty years that South Korea was our home, and far beyond.

Thank you to the book community of Maine, New England, and beyond: in particular, my buddies Rosie Benson, Joan Chamberlain, Deb Eaton, Kevin Hawkes, Jennifer Jacobson, Joan McCarthy, David Neufeld, Pat Spalding, Maria Testa, and other members of the Maine House of Peers retreats, where I began to learn how to write a novel, and especially the incomparable Emily Herman, whose "Writer's Toolbox" templates were foundational in structuring and shaping the narrative and whose early reading of the manuscript provided crucial feedback; the Society of Children's Book Writers and

Illustrators for its invaluable support throughout my career, and all the leaders of the NESCBWI conference workshops I attended; the founders of National Novel Writing Month and participants in NaNoWriMo 2008, which I "won" by completing my first draft of this manuscript (51,000-plus words); Mitali Perkins, who introduced me to my agent; the Maine Writers and Publishers Alliance; Peaks Island librarians Priscilla Webster and Rose Ann Walsh, who stoked my research with all those inter-library loan books; Francisco X. Stork, marvelous writer and teacher, and Bethany Hegedus, who hosted him at the Writing Barn; and my fabulous critique group partners, Liza Kleinman and Sarah Thomson.

Thank you to friends and neighbors, in particular Yvonne Torstensson, college buddy who became my B&B host (over 36 years) for NYC trips to visit publishers; envisioning partners Ronda Dale and Nancy 3. Hoffman; Steve Schuit for the moment-by-moment account of his DPRK tour; and the extraordinary community of Peaks Island, Maine.

Thank you to the Korean American community: in particular, visionary and booster extraordinaire Yoo Myung Ja; Reverend Peter Yoon, for his video of North Korea; soul mate Hyaekyung Jo and the Camp Sejong family; the dynamic trio, Dr. Agnes Ahn (where's our next adventure?), Sheila Jaung, and MinJeong Kim of the Korea Studies Program, University of Massachusetts-Lowell; Professor Kim Hyun Sik, for the profound inspiration of his life, his generosity and grace, and his wife, Kim Hyun Ja, who translated for him; and HJ Lee of Korean American Story and Sam Yoon and John Kim of the Council of Korean Americans, for their work and for invaluable assistance in locating the expert beta readers listed in the Author's Note.

Thank you as well to my American readers for their generosity and helpful feedback: Emily Herman, Yunhee O'Brien Keough, Perry O'Brien, Jean Sibley, Frances Taylor, and Tami Charles.

Thank you to my book-making team, about each of whom I could gush endlessly: my first and second agents, both of Andrea Brown Literary Agency — the wise and wonderful Laura Rennert, whose enthusiasm made me believe this could happen, and the brilliant and delightful Lara Perkins, whose editorial guidance gave me the support to make it happen; my publicist and adored friend, the inestimable Kirsten Cappy of Curious City; and the crew at Arthur A. Levine Books/Scholastic — Cheryl Klein, the editor of my dreams; her assistant, Weslie Turner; Carol Ly, book designer; and my publicist.

And thank you to my beloved immediate and extended family, in particular those who've been with me for every step of this ten-year journey: our daughter Yunhee and son Perry, who listened, read, helped me think, and provided so many kinds of assistance; my husband, O.B., my thesaurus, encyclopedia, plot and logic adviser, and crucial support system, always assuming I will succeed, at this and anything; my mother, Jean Butler Sibley, who is always interested in and supportive of everything I do and who first sparked in me the love of books; and in memory, my father, Dr. John R. Sibley, whose love, vision, and example will always inspire and guide me.

ABOUT THE AUTHOR

Anne Sibley O'Brien was raised bilingual and bicultural in Seoul, Daegu, and Geoje Island, South Korea, as the daughter of medical missionaries. She has written and/or illustrated thirty-five picture books and is a frequent speaker in classrooms across the country and in international schools around the world. *In the Shadow of the Sun* is her first novel. She lives on Peaks Island in Maine. She can be found on the web at her website, www.annesibleyobrien.com; her blogs, *Coloring Between the Lines*, at www.coloringbetweenthelines.com and www.intheshadowofthesunbook.com; and on Twitter at @AnneSbleyOBrien.

This book was edited by Cheryl Klein and designed by Carol Ly. The text was set in Janson Text LT Std. The book was printed and bound at R.R. Donnelley in Crawfordsville, Indiana. The production was supervised by Rachel Gluckstern, and manufacturing was supervised by Angelique Browne.